Mayne Reid

Stories About Animals

Mayne Reid

Stories About Animals

ISBN/EAN: 9783337237219

Printed in Europe, USA, Canada, Australia, Japan

Cover: Foto ©Andreas Hilbeck / pixelio.de

More available books at **www.hansebooks.com**

STORIES

ABOUT

ANIMALS.

BY

CAPT. MAYNE REID, AND OTHERS.

A NEW EDITION,
WITH A MEMOIR BY R. H. STODDARD.

NEW YORK:
THOMAS R. KNOX & CO.,
SUCCESSORS TO JAMES MILLER,
813 BROADWAY.
1885.

MEMOIR OF MAYNE REID.

No one who has written books for the young during the present century ever had so large a circle of readers as Captain Mayne Reid, or ever was so well fitted by circumstances to write the books by which he is chiefly known. His life, which was an adventurous one, was ripened with the experience of two Continents, and his temperament, which was an ardent one, reflected the traits of two races. Irish by birth, he was American in his sympathies with the people of the New World, whose acquaintance he made at an early period, among whom he lived for years, and whose battles he helped to win. He was probably more familiar with the Southern and Western portion of the United States forty years ago than any native-born American of that time. A curious interest attaches to the life of Captain Reid, but it is not of the kind that casual biographers dwell upon. If he had written it himself it would have charmed thousands of readers, who can now merely imagine what it might have been from the glimpses of it which they obtain in his writings. It was not passed in the fierce light of publicity, but in that simple, silent obscurity which is the lot of most men, and is their happiness, if they only knew it.

Briefly related, the life of Captain Reid was as follows: He was born in 1818, in the north of Ireland, the son of a Presbyterian clergyman, who was a type of the class which Goldsmith has described so freshly in the " Deserted Village," and was highly thought of for his labors among the poor of his neighborhood. An earnest, reverent man, to whom his calling was indeed a sacred one, he designed his son Mayne for the ministry, in the hope, no doubt, that he would be his successor. But nature had something to say about that, as well as his good father. He began to study for the ministry, but it was not long before he was drawn in another direction. Always a great reader, his favorite books were descriptions of travel in foreign lands, particularly those which dealt with the scenery, the people, and the resources of America. The spell which these exercised over his imagination, joined to a love of adventure which was inherent in his temperament, and inherited, perhaps with his race, determined his career. At the age of twenty he closed his theological tomes, and girding up his loins with a stout heart he sailed from the shores of the Old World for the New. Following the spirit in his feet he landed at New Orleans, which was probably a more promising field for a young man of his talents than any Northern city, and was speedily engaged in business. The nature of this business is not stated, further than it was that of a trader; but whatever it was it obliged this young Irishman to make long journeys into the interior of the country, which was almost a *terra incognita.* Sparsely settled, where settled at all, it was still clothed in primeval verdure—here in the endless reach of savannas, there in the depth of pathless woods, and far away to the North and the West in those monotonous ocean-like levels of land for which the speech of England has no name—the Prairies. Its population was nomadic, not to say barbaric, consisting of tribes of Indians whose hunting grounds from time immemorial the region was; hunters and trappers, who had turned their backs upon civilization for the free, wild life of nature; men of doubtful or dangerous antecedents, who had found it convenient to leave their country for their country's good; and scattered about hardy pioneer communities from Eastern States, advancing waves of the great sea of emigration which is still drawing the course of empire westward. Travelling in a country like this, and among people like these, Mayne Reid passed five years of his early manhood. He was at home wherever he went, and never more so than when among the Indians of the Red River territory, with whom he spent several months, learning their language, studying their customs, and enjoying the wild and beautiful scenery of their camping grounds. Indian for the time, he lived in their lodges, rode with them, hunted with them, and night after night sat by their blazing camp-fires listening to the warlike stories of the braves and the quaint legends of the medicine men. There was that in the blood of Mayne Reid which fitted him to lead this life at this time, and whether he knew it or not it educated his genius as no other life could have done. It familiarized him with a large extent of country in the South and West; it introduced him to men and manners which existed nowhere else; and it revealed to him the secrets of Indian life and character.

There was another side, however, to Mayne Reid than that we have touched upon, and this, at the end of five years, drew him back to the average life of his kind. We find him next in Philadelphia, where he began to contribute stories and sketches of travel to the newspapers and magazines. Philadelphia was then the most literate city in the United States, the one in which a clever writer was at once encouraged and rewarded. Frank and warm-hearted, he made many friends there among journalists and authors. One of these friends was Edgar Allan Poe, whom he often visited at his home in Spring Garden, and concerning whom years after, when he was dead, he wrote with loving tenderness.

The next episode in the career of Mayne Reid was not what one would expect from a man of letters, though it was just what might have been expected from a man of his temperament and antecedents. It grew out of the time, which was warlike, and it drove him into the army with which the United States speedily crushed the forces of the sister Republic—Mexico. He obtained a commission, and served throughout the war with great bravery and distinction. This stormy episode ended with a severe wound, which he received in storming the heights of Chapultepec—a terrible battle which practically ended the war.

A second episode of a similar character, but with a more fortunate conclusion, occurred about four years later. It grew out of another war, which, happily for us, was not on our borders, but in the heart of Europe, where the Hungarian race had risen in insurrection against the hated power of Austria. Their desperate valor in the face of tremendous odds excited the sympathy of the American people, and fired the heart of Captain Mayne Reid, who buckled on his sword once more, and sailed from New York with a body of volunteers to aid the Hungarians in their struggles for independence. They were too late, for hardly had they reached Paris before they learned that all was over: Görgey had surrendered at Arad, and Hungary was crushed. They were at once dismissed, and Captain Reid betook himself to London.

The life of the Mayne Reid in whom we are most interested—Mayne Reid, the author—began at this time,
when he was in his thirty-first year, and ended only on
the day of his death, October 21, 1883.   It covered one-
third of a century, and was, when compared with that
which had preceded it, uneventful, if not devoid of incident.   There is not much that needs be told—not much,
indeed, that can be told—in the life of a man of letters
like Captain Mayne Reid.   It is written in his books.
Mayne Reid was one of the best known authors of his
time—differing in this from many authors who are popular without being known—and in the walk of fiction which
he discovered for himself he is an acknowledged master.   His reputation did not depend upon the admiration
of the millions of young people who read his books, but
upon the judgment of mature critics, to whom his delinea-
tions of adventurous life were literature of no common
order.   His reputation as a story-teller was widely recognized on the Continent, where he was accepted as an
authority in regard to the customs of the pioneers and the
guerilla warfare of the Indian tribes, and was warmly
praised for his freshness, his novelty, and his hardy origi-
nality.   The people of France and Germany delighted in
this soldier-writer.   "There was not a word in his books
which a school-boy could not safely read aloud to his
mother and sisters."   So says a late English critic, to which
another adds, that if he has somewhat gone out of fashion
of late years, the more's the pity for the school-boy of the
period.   What Defoe is in Robinson Crusoe—realistic idyl
of island solitude—that, in his romantic stories of wilder-
ness life, is his great scholar, Captain Mayne Reid.

R. H. STODDARD.

4

CONTENTS.

Stories of Animals.

THE CAMELOPARD.

THERE is, perhaps, no living animal so graceful in form, more beautiful in color, and more stately in appearance than the giraffe. Measuring eighteen feet from the hoof of the fore leg to the crest of its crown, it stands, to use an American expression, " The tallest animal in creation." There is but one species of the giraffe, and from the elegance and stateliness of its shape, the pleasing variety of its colors, its first appearance in Europe excited considerable interest.

Although this animal was well known to the ancient Romans, and played no inconsiderable part in the gorgeous exhibitions of that luxurious people, yet, with the ultimate overthrow of the

13

Roman Empire, the camelopard finally disappeared from Europe, and for some centuries became a stranger to the civilized world. We do not find the giraffe again mentioned until the close of the fifteenth century, when it is reported Lorenzo de Medici exhibited one at Florence. The first of these animals seen in England was a gift from the Pasha of Egypt to George IV. It arrived in London in 1828, and died the following year.

On the 24th of May, 1836, four giraffes were exhibited in the Zoological Gardens in the Regent's Park, London. They were brought from the southwest of Kordofan, and cost to transport £2,386 3s. 1d., or over twelve thousand dollars.

From a cursory glance at the giraffe, its fore legs appear to be twice as long as the hind ones, but such is really not so. This difference of appearance is caused by the great depth of the shoulder compared with the hips. The giraffe has a very small head, supported on a neck nearly six feet in length, gently tapering towards the crown. His height, reckoning from the top of the head to his fore foot, is about equally divided between neck, shoulders, and legs; measuring from the summit of the hips to the hoofs of the hind feet it seldom exceeds seven feet. The head of the giraffe is furnished with a pair of excrescences of a porous bony texture, covered with short coarse bristles. These are usually called horns, though very unlike the horns of any other animal. They cannot be either for defence or offence, as they are too easily displaced to afford any resistance in case of collision ; nor can we conjecture any use for them. The eyes of the camelopard are worthy of all praise. They are very large, softer and more gentle than those of the far-famed gazelle, and are so placed that it can see in almost every direction without turning its head. All its senses are so very acute and it is so very timid, that it can only be approached by man when mounted on a fleet horse. The giraffe feeds on the leaves and blossoms of an umbrella-shaped tree, called mokhara by the Africans, and kameeldoorn (camelthorn) by the Dutch settlers of the cape.

As a grasper or feeler the tongue of the giraffe is used in the same way as the trunk of the elephant ; but its great height enables it to feed on the leaves of the mokhara far beyond the reach of the latter.

The skin of the camelopard is exceedingly thick, often as much as an inch and a half, and so hard that frequently twenty or thirty bullets are required to bring the creature to the ground. These wounds are always born in silence, for the animal is dumb. The coat of the beast becomes darker with age. The color of the female is lighter than the male, and she is also inferior in point of size.

The giraffe's only means of defence is in its legs, and it uses its heels for kicking to an extraordinary extent, more so than any other animal, not excepting the horse. The prominence of the eyes enable it to see behind, when directing its heels against an enemy, while the blow it gives will crush in the skull of a man, or give him some broken ribs. If unmolested, it is one of the most innocent of animals. Though sometimes it meets its death from animals far below itself in size and strength, as the following account will show.

A FIGHT BETWEEN A GIRAFFE AND A LEOPARD.

THE hunters were now intent upon but one object—that of procuring the giraffe.

By the side of the mimosa grove ran a small stream; on its bank they found traces of giraffes, at which they were quite elated.

Some of the tracks were of small dimensions, but certainly the marks of calves. Here was again a chance to satisfy the hunters' ambition.

The next day, on the borders of the kameeldoorn forest, a drove of giraffes were seen coming from the timber and making for the water.

The timid animals, unaware of their proximity

to man, walked on, until within two hundred paces of where the hunters stood, without seeing them.

They then turned quickly, and with a swift but awkward gait retreated across the plain and away from the forest. The next day passed without seeing anything more of the giraffes, so the next day the party started on the trail of those they had seen previously.

Fifteen miles farther to the west they found another mimosa forest with a small lagoon, whose banks bore hoof-marks of many giraffes.

These were evidently new, and belonged to the same herd they had seen the previous day.

The next day, being on the watch, their ears were assailed by the noise of breaking branches and the rushing of some large animals through the thicket. A few seconds only elapsed ere the forms of two full-grown giraffes were seen breaking from the thicket, and on the back of one of them clung a leopard. Blood was flowing down its breast and it was reeling wildly from side to side. Knowing the leopard to be a cowardly creature, and its capability for taking its prey so great that it rarely suffers from want of food, and never where there is an abundance of game, we knew that its attack on the giraffe must have been caused by some other motive than hunger. On reaching the open ground we noticed that the other giraffe quickly forsook its mate, which was now showing unmistakable proof of fatigue, from the loss of blood which flowed from its neck ; we could see the stately beast was about to topple over from the severe injuries it had received from its ferocious enemy.

We were now spectators of a scene such as probably had never before been witnessed—that of a leopard killing a giraffe. Circumstances had favored the beast of prey ; and the great animal was being killed by one not the tenth part of its own strength and size.

Two dogs that were with us, not heeding our voices, essayed to take part in the rencontre. Both ran yelping after the giraffe, trying to take hold of its heels. Raising one foot, the camelopard struck with unerring aim one of the dogs, dashing him several feet, where he lay sprawling in the last convulsions of expiring life. By making this effort, the reeling body of the giraffe lost its balance, and throwing its head violently to one side it fell heavily to the earth, crushing the leopard to death under it. What little life remained in the giraffe soon departed from it, along with the blood which the beast of prey had let out of its veins.

Standing over the bodies, we tried to arrive at some comprehension of the extraordinary scene we had just witnessed. We had heard of a lion having ridden on the back of a giraffe, but did not believe it.

Before us was evidence that a leopard had done
the same. Notwithstanding the thickness of the
hide that covered the neck of the giraffe, it had
been torn to shreds, that were hanging down over
its shoulders. The long claws and teeth of the
leopard had been buried in its flesh, arteries and
veins had been dragged from their beds and laid
open, ere the strength of the giraffe had forsaken it.

A LION HUNT.

AS soon as we had got to the north of the
Gareep, we fell in with an adventure worth
relating.

We had chosen for our camp the side of a lake
in the midst of a wide plain where there happened
to be both grass and water, though of an indifferent sort. The plain was open, with here and
there clumps of low bushes, and between these
stood at intervals the dome-shaped houses of the
white ant, of the *Termes mordax*—rising to the
height of several feet above the surface.

We had just outspanned and allowed our oxen
to wander upon the grass, when a voice exclaimed,
—" De leuw! de leuw!" and there sure enough
we espied a black-maned lion—right out on the

plain and beyond the place where the oxen were feeding.

There was a clump of "bosch" just behind the lion. Out of this he had sighted the oxen; and having advanced a few yards, he had lain down again among the grass, and now was watching the animals as a cat would a mouse.

Just as we noticed him, another was seen advancing with stealthy trot to the side of her companion. Her companion I say, because the second was a lioness, as the absence of a mane and the tiger-like form testified. She was very little inferior in size to the lion, and not a bit less fierce and dangerous in any encounter she might fall in with.

Having joined the lion, she squatted beside him; and both now sat upon their tails, like two immense cats, with full front towards the camp, eying the oxen with hungry looks. They most certainly contemplated supping either upon ox-beef or horse-flesh.

These were the first lions we had encountered upon the expedition. "Spoar" had been seen several times, and the terrible roar of the king of beasts had been heard around the night camp; but this was the first time he had made his appearance with his queen along with him, and of course his presence created no small excitement, amounting almost to a "panic," among us.

Our first fears were for our own skins; after a time, however, this feeling subsided: we knew the lions would not attack the camp, it being a thing they very rarely do. It was the animals they were after, and so long as these were present they would not touch their owners.

The lions lay quietly on the plain, though still in a menacing attitude. But they were a good way off—full five hundred yards—and were not likely to attack the oxen and horses so near to the camp. The huge wagons—strange sight to them—no doubt had the effect of restraining them for the present. They were evidently waiting for night or till the oxen strayed nearer to them.

It wanted yet an hour or two of sunset. The lions still sat squatted on the grass, closely watched by the hunters.

All at once the eyes of the latter became directed upon a new object. Slowly approaching over the distant plain came two strange animals, similar in form and nearly so in color and size. They were about the size of an ass, and not very unlike in color the buff variety. Their forms, however, were more graceful than that of the ass, though far from being light or slender. They were singularly marked on the head and face; the ground color was white, but they had four dark bands so disposed as to give the appearance as though they had on a headstall of black leather.

A reversed mane, a dark list down the back; and a long black bushy tail reaching to the ground were characters to be observed, but the most distinguished part of them was a splendid pair of horns, which were straight and slender, pointing backwards almost horizontally. They were regularly ringed till within a few inches of their tips, which were as sharp as steel spits—they were black as jet, and full three feet in length. The horns of the female were longer than those of the male, though she was the smaller of the two. At the first glance we all recognized the beautiful oryx, one of the loveliest animals of Africa, in fact of the world.

On seeing the "Gemsboks"—for such is the name by which the oryx is known in South Africa, our first thought was how to kill them, for we knew the delicacy of their flesh, which is not surpassed by that of any other antelope, and thought how far superior a stake of that would be to the jerked meat we had cooking, that we all felt willing to wait if we could only get some.

What was the best course to pursue? It would scarce be possible to stalk the gemsboks, they are so very wary. They rarely approach near any cover that might shelter an enemy; and when alarmed they strike off in a straight line for the open plain—their natural home.

They can only be captured by a swift horse and after a severe chase; even then sometimes they manage to escape, for in the first mile they run like the wind. We at once thought of our horses, but as quickly changed our minds, for the antelopes were coming straight for us, and would perhaps come within gunshot, and so save us the trouble of a chase.

This was agreeable, as we were hungry, and our horses tired after a hard day's work. We at first thought they were coming for the water, forgetting that the oryx is an animal *that never drinks*, so being quite independent of springs, streams, or lakes, they are one of those creatures Nature has formed to live in deserts; so it was evident they were not coming for the water; still they were certainly approaching the camp, to which they still kept steadily on, quite unconscious of danger.

It was not their fate to die by a leaden bullet, as the sequel will show.

As we lay watching the approach of the gemsboks we had forgotten the lions, but a movement on their part again drew our attention to them. Up to this time they had remained in an upright position, but now we observed them crouch flat down, as if to conceal themselves in the grass, and turn their heads in a new direction, towards the gemsboks. The lions had caught sight of the antelopes and contemplated an attack; but if the oryx kept on in the same direction they would pass far out of the reach of the lion, as he is but a poor runner compared with the antelope, and has to catch his prey by a few vigorous bounds. Unless, therefore, the lion could get within springing distance, he had a poor chance of securing his prey. They knew this. The lion was observed to crawl forward so as to get in the path of the oryx. Crawling along and hiding himself, he soon reached an ant-hill that stood right in the path by which they were advancing. But where was the lioness? Where had she gone? Not with the lion. On the contrary she had gone in the opposite direction. We saw she was progressing in the same way as the lion had done, evidently making for the rear of the antelopes.

The "strategy" of the lions was now perfectly plain. The lion was to place himself in the front while the lioness swept round to the rear and forced the prey to his grasp; or should they retreat or become frightened, then the lion could drive them to the lioness. Now we had grown so interested in the movement we could not help but watch them, though it was likely to rob us of our game.

The ambuscade was well planned, and in a few minutes its success was no longer doubtful. The gemsboks advanced steadily towards the ant-hill,

The lioness had arrived in the rear and was quietly following them. As the antelopes drew near the hill, the lion was observed to draw in his head under his shaggy mane. They could not have seen him nor he them, but he trusted to his ears to tell him their location. He waited till both were opposite and broadside to him at a distance of less than twenty paces. Then, his tail was seen to vibrate with one or two quick jerks, his head shot suddenly forth, his body spread out apparently to twice its natural size, and the next instant he rose like a bird in the air.

With one bound he cleared the space, alighting on the hind quarters of the gemsbok. A single blow of his powerful paw brought the antelope to the ground on its haunches, and another stretched its body lifeless on the plain.

Without looking after the other or caring about it, the lion seized its throat and commenced to suck its warm blood.

As the lion sprang upon her companion, the cow of course started with affright, and we expected to see her start off across the plain. To our astonishment she did nothing of the sort. Such is not the nature of the noble oryx : recovering from her fright, she wheeled round towards the enemy, and, lowering her head to the very ground, so that her horns projected horizontally, she rushed with all her strength upon the lion. The first

intimation he had of this attack was to feel a
pair of spears pierce right through his ribs.   For
some moments a confused struggling was observed
in which both lion and oryx seemed to take part;
but the attitudes of both appeared so odd, and
changed so rapidly, that we could not tell in what
way they fought.

The roar of the lion now ceased, and was succeeded by the shrill notes of the lioness, who,
bounding forward, mixed at once in the mêlée,
and with a single blow of her paw brought the
cow oryx to the ground and ended the strife.
The lion was dead; the sharp horns of the oryx
had done the work; but she was unable to withdraw
her horns, so would have perished with her victim,
had the lioness not ended the affray.   This is not
an uncommon occurrence on the plains.

MRS. STRUTT'S SEMINARY.

THE bells of Farmfield's Church rang merrily when young Mr. Strutt married his neighbour's daughter, Miss Waddle. The school-children had a holiday, and the labourers at all the farms in the village dined off roast beef and plum-pudding. Young Mr. Strutt had passed the College of Surgeons, and set up in practice in London, in a new and fashionable neighbourhood at the West End; that is, he had hired two rooms in a respectable looking house, and bargained to have his name on a great brass plate on the door. But neither his wedding nor his brass plate brought him any patients; and after a two years' trial, Mr. Strutt retired from the profession in disgust.

It luckily happened that Mrs. Strutt's papa, Mr. Waddle, determined that his daughter should receive a *superior* education, had sent her to a very distinguished seminary, where young ladies were taught the most wonderful accomplishments by the very first masters; but where, unfortunately, they did not include the art of making apple-dumplings.

As Mrs. Strutt had no children of her own, she now determined to devote her acquirements to the benefit of the children of other people. So Mr and Mrs. Strutt opened an "Academy for Young Ladies and Gentlemen" at Kentish Town; and, as good fortune would have it, they were soon intrust ed with the care of half-a-dozen "boarders," who brought their own forks and spoons, and were the children of very genteel parents, at least so Mrs. Strutt told her visitors.

One thing must be said, that both master and mistress were very kind and attentive to their young charges; and if they did not teach them much, it was simply because they did not know how.

One fine summer's afternoon they all went together for a ramble in the Highgate Fields. The elder Master Hawke took his drum, and the younger had Mrs. Strutt's parasol; Miss Duckling's two brothers had a kite and a boat; and Charley Light-hair a whirligig. They flew the kite high up till they could hardly see it, and sent card-messengers of every colour up to it: they swam their boat in the pond; and when it sailed beyond their reach, Mr. Strutt pulled it back with his walking cane: they ran across the meadows, and tried to see who could get over the stiles first; and then when they were hot and tired, they all sat under the shade of the great elm-trees, and Mr. Strutt told them the following anecdote:—

"Many years ago, as I was passing through the country town where I lived, my attention was drawn to a great crowd of people assembled round some apparently very amusing objects. Led by curiosity, I mixed in with them; and what did I behold but a fellow whom I had long known,

named Bruin, teaching a monkey to perform all
kinds of tricks? The animal stood on his head,
and, with his hind feet, threw sticks up into the
air; then he leaped on Mr. Bruin's head, and
balanced himself on one hand, and jumped over
the heads of the spectators; among whom, I re·
member, were my neighbours, Mrs. Kangaroo and
her daughter; my shoemaker, old Pidgeon, and
his little girl; Shark the lawyer; Mrs. Whinchat
the milliner; a fellow named Ratt, who had been
twenty times taken up for thieving; and the poul-
terer's son, Bill Goose. I wish you had been with
them to have seen how Bruin made Jocko the
monkey dance, and how all these folks laughed.
They capered about finely to get out of his way;
but at last Jocko jumped from his master's head
on to Mrs. Whinchat's back, tore off her bonnet,
and in two seconds put it on the head of little Miss
Kangaroo. Oh, how the crowd shouted! Bruin
tried to beat the animal, but he laughed too much
to be able to catch him; and Jocko, pleased at his
own performance, jumped on to Ratt's back, and
the rascal ran half way down the street before the
monkey would dismount. Bruin ran after them,
and so great was the crowd that pursued, that he
was glad to hide both himself and Jocko in an
inn-yard."

The young ones all laughed famously at this
story; and then, as it was near tea-time, they set
off home, where they had, for a treat, hot toast for
tea, and a game at forfeits afterwards.

A HEAVY COMBAT.

THE white rhinoceros came out of the thicket, and without halting, headed up the valley to a small lake, his object being to reach the water. This lake was nearly circular in shape, and about one hundred yards in diameter; on its upper side its shore was high, and in one or two places rocky. On the west or outer side of the lake, the land lay lower, and the water at one or two points lipped up nearly to the level of the plain, the bank being paddled all over with tracks of animals that had been to drink.

It was for the lower end of the lake the rhinoceros was making—his old drinking place, a little to one side of where the waste stream of the lake ran out. It was a sort of cove, with bright sandy beach. By entering this cove the tallest animal might get deep water and good bottom, so that they could drink without stooping. The rhinoceros was evidently aware of this, for in a few moments he was knee-deep in the water, and swallowing copious draughts; soon he plunged his snout, horn and all, into the water, tossed it about, finally lying down in it, wallowing like a hog.

Our first thought was how to circumvent the mighty beast and destroy him, as there was not any provisions in camp, and we had heard the food was good. We had not any horses fit to mount, and to attack him on foot would be idle and dangerous, as he would very likely either impale or trample us to death under his huge feet: so we determined to try and get near him, fire from an ambush, and by a lucky shot kill him by striking him in a vital spot.

We had determined to make the attempt, and had got to our feet for that purpose, when a sudden fit seemed to have attacked our black servant, who kept muttering, "Da klow! da klow!" We looked in the direction in which he pointed; there, sure enough, were signs of the elephant. Its rounded back was easily distinguished over the low bushes, and its broad hanging ears were moving as it marched. We all saw at a glance he was coming toward the lake, and in the same track the rhinoceros had taken.

This at once disconcerted our plans, the elephant at once taking the place of the other in our minds. Before we could arrange anything, the elephant had got to the edge of the lake. Here he halted, pointed his proboscis in different directions, stood quite still and seemed to listen. There

was nothing to disturb him: even the rhinoceros
for the moment was quiet.

After standing a minute or so, the hugh creature moved forward again, and entered the gorge
already described. He seemed an immense mass,
being an old bull, his long yellow tusks projecting
more than two yards from his jaws.

Up to this time, the rhinoceros had not had the
slightest intimation of the elephant's approach,
for the tread of the latter, big as he is, is as silent
as a cat's. It is true that a loud rumbling noise,
like distant thunder, proceeded from his inside as
he moved along; but the rhinoceros was in too
high a caper, just then, to have heard or noticed
any sound that was not very distinct.

The hugh body of the elephant coming suddenly into "his sunshine," and flinging its dark
shadow over the lake, was distinct enough, and
caused the rhinoceros to get to his feet with an
agility truly surprising for a creature of his build.

At the same time a noise something between a
grunt and a whistle escaped him, as the water was
ejected from his nostrils. The elephant also
uttered his salute, and halted as soon as he saw the
rhinoceros. There is no doubt both were surprised, as they stood eyeing each other for some
seconds in astonishment.

Symptoms of anger soon began to show themselves, as the elephant could not get to the water

comfortably unless the rhinoceros left the cove, and the rhinoceros could not well get out so long as the elephant filled the gorge; he might have swum away to some other point, but that evidently did not suit him, as he fears neither man nor beast. Hence the old rhinoceros had no intention of yielding ground to the elephant. It remained to be seen how the point was to be decided. Affairs had become so interesting that we all stood gazing with fixed eyes upon the two great bulls, for the rhinoceros was a bull, and one of the largest of his species.

For several minutes they stood eyeing each other, the elephant well knowing the power of his antagonist. Perhaps, ere now, he had had a touch of the rhinoceros's tusk.

His patience, however, became exhausted, his dignity was insulted, and his rule disputed; he wished to have his bath, and would put up with the insults of the rhinoceros no longer.

With a bellow that made the rocks ring again, he charged forward, placed his tusks firmly under the shoulder of his adversary, gave a lift, and turned the rhinoceros over in the water. For a moment the latter plunged, blowed and snorted, his head half under water; but in a second he was on his feet, and charging in turn. We could see that he aimed right at his antagonist's ribs with his horn, and that the latter did all he could

to keep his head towards him ; again the elephant
threw him, and again he rose and charged madly
upon his huge foe, and so both fought, until the
water around them was white with foam. The contest so far had been carried on in the water, until
the elephant, seeming to think his adversary had
the advantage there, backed himself into the gorge,
and stood waiting with his head towards the
lake.

In this position, the sides of the gorge did not
protect him as he fancied. They were too low,
and his broad flanks rose far above them ; they
only kept him from turning round, and so interfered with his movements.

As the elephant took up his position, the rhinoceros clambered out on the bank, and then
wheeling suddenly, with head to the ground, he
rushed on his antagonist, striking him right among
the ribs with his long horn. The loud scream of
the elephant, with the quick motion of his trunk
and tail, told plainly he had received a severe
wound. Instead of standing any longer in the
gorge, he rushed into the lake, and did not stop
until he was knee-deep ; drawing the water up
into his trunk, he discharged large volumes over
his body and into the wound he had received.

He then ran out of the lake, and charged about
in search of the rhinoceros, who could not be
found, for as soon as he had delivered his blow,

he had galloped off, and disappeared among the brushes.

The elephant, after looking about for his enemy, retired to the lake and repeated the operation of bathing his back and wound, his tail continually in motion, and uttering low screams, he lifted his huge limbs and then plunged them back until foam covered the water. Suddenly he ceased to churn with his feet, and no longer raised water in his trunk; and now we saw the water was red with his blood. For several minutes he kept the same position, but his tail no longer switched, and his attitude was drooping. He now made a motion as though he was coming out of the water, when he was seen to rock and stagger, and then roll over into the waters of the lake.

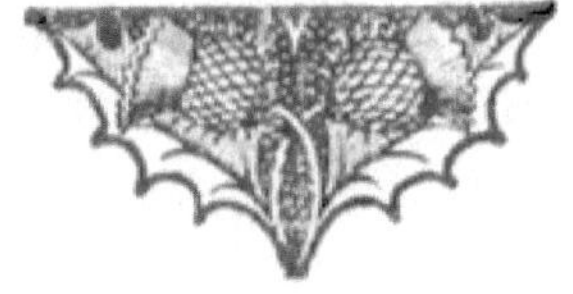

THE

ADVENTURES OF A BEAR,

AND A GREAT BEAR TOO.

BY ALFRED ELWES.

AT HOME.

YES, it is an "at home" to which I am going to introduce you; but not the at-home that many of you—I hope *all* of you—have learnt to love, but the at-home of a bear. No carpeted rooms, no warm curtains, no glowing fireside, no pictures, no sofas, no tables, no chairs; no music, no books; no agreeable, cosy chat; no anything half so pleasant: but soft moss or snow, spreading trees, skies with ever-changing, tinted clouds, some fun, some rough romps, a good deal of growling, and now and then a fight. With these points of difference, you may believe the *at-home* of a bear is not quite so agreeable a matter as the at-home of a young gentleman or lady; yet I have no doubt Master Bruin is much more at his ease in it than he would find himself if he were compelled to conform to the usages of human society, and behave as a gentleman ought to do.

But there is a quality that is quite as necessary to adorn one home as the other, without which the most delightful mansion and the warmest cavern can never be happy, and with which the simplest cottage and the meanest den may be truly blest; and that one quality is, good temper. Of what avail are comforts, or even luxuries, when there is no seasoning of good temper to enjoy them with? How many deficiencies can there not be over-looked, when good temper is present to cover them with a veil? Perhaps you have not yet learnt what a valuable treasure this good temper is; when you have read the history of my bear, you will be better able to form an opinion.

I cannot tell you when this bear was born, nor am I quite sure where; bears are born in so many parts of the world now, that it becomes very diffi-cult to determine what country heard their first growl, and they never think to preserve a memo-randum of the circumstance. Let it suffice that our bear was born, that he had a mamma and papa, and some brothers and sisters; that he lived in a cavern surrounded by trees and bushes; that he was always a big lump of a bear, invariably wore a brown coat, and was often out of temper, or rather, was always *in* temper, only that temper was a very bad one.

No doubt his parents would have been very willing to cure this terrible defect, if they had known how; but the fact is, they seemed always too much absorbed in their own thoughts to attend much to their family. Old Mr. Bruin would sit in his corner by the hour together sucking his paw; and his partner, Mrs. Bruin, would sit in her corner sucking her paw; whilst the little ones, or big ones, for they were growing up fast, would make themselves into balls and roll about the ground, or bite one another's ears by way of a joke, or climb up the neighbouring trees to admire the prospect, and then slip down again, to the imminent destruction of their clothes; not that a rent or two would have grieved their mother very much, for she was a great deal too old, and too ignorant besides, to think of mending them. In all these sports Master Bruin, the eldest, was ever the foremost; but as certain as he joined in the romps, so surely were uproar and fighting the consequence. The reason was clear enough; his temper was so disagreeable, that although he was quite ready to play off his jokes on others, he could never bear to receive them in return; and being, besides, very fierce and strong, he came at length to be considered as the most unbearable bear that the forest had known for many generations, and in his own family was looked on as quite a bug-bear.

Now I privately think, that if a good oaken stick had been applied to his shoulders, or any other sensitive part of his body, whenever he displayed these fits of spleen, the exercise would have had a very beneficial effect on his disposi-

tion; but his father, on such occasions, only uttered his opinion in so low a growl that it was
impossible to make out what he said, and then
sucked his paw more vigorously than ever; and
his mother was much too tender-hearted to think
of mending his manners in so rude a way: so
Master Bruin grew apace, until his brothers and
sisters were wicked enough to wish he might some
day go out for a walk and forget to come home
again, or that he might be persuaded by a kind
friend to emigrate, without going through the
ceremony of taking leave of his family.

It began to be conjectured that some such event
had occurred when, for three whole days, he never
made his appearance. The respectable family of
the Bruins were puzzled, but calm, notwithstanding, at this unusual absence; it evidently made
them thoughtful, though it was impossible to guess
what they thought about: if one could form an
idea from the attitudes of the different members,
each of whom sat in a corner sucking his right
paw and his left paw alternately—it was a family
habit, you must know—I should say their thoughts
were too deep for expression; but before their
meditations were converted from uncertainty into
mourning, the object of them made his appearance
at the entrance of the cavern, with his coat torn,
limping in his gait, and with an ugly wound in his
head, looking altogether as disconsolate a brute as
you can well conceive. He did not condescend to
say where he had been, nor what he had been
doing; perhaps no one made the inquiry: but it

was very evident he had been doing no good, and
had got his reward accordingly. If, however, this
great bear's ill temper was remarkable before,
judge what it must have been with such a sore
head !

The experience of mankind has led to the opinion,
that there are few more disagreeable beings in creation than ill-nurtured bears,—bears that have been
ill-licked—those great, fierce, sullen, cross-grained,
and ill-tempered beasts, that are, unhappily, to be
found in every part of this various world ; but
when all these unhandsome qualities are found in
one individual of the species, and that one happens
to have a sore head into the bargain, it is easy to
believe the *at home* which he honours or dishonours
with his presence can neither be very quiet nor particularly comfortable.

Habit makes many things supportable which at
first would seem beyond our powers of endurance.
Mr. and Mrs. B., and, indeed, all the other B.'s,
male and female, had got so used to the tyranny
of this ill-tempered animal, that they put up with
his moroseness almost without a growl ; but there
is a limit to sufferance, beyond which neither men
nor bears can travel, and that boundary was at last
attained with the B.'s. As what I am now about
to relate is, however, rather an important fact in
my biography, I must inform you how the matter
occurred, and what were the circumstances which
led to it.

You are, perhaps, aware that bears, being of
rather an indolent disposition, are not accustomed

to hoard up a store of provision for their wants in winter, but prefer—in their own country, at least—sleeping through the short dreary days and long bitter nights, and thus avoid the necessity of taking food for some weeks, although they grow very thin during their lengthened slumbers. I forget what this time is called in bears' language, but we give it the name of hybernation. Now it happened that Mrs. Bruin had taken it into her head to lay by this winter a nice little stock, which she very carefully buried at a short distance from the mouth of the cavern, when she felt the usual drowsiness of the season coming on, and having covered the spot with a heap of dead leaves that she might know it again when she woke up, she crawled into bed, and turning her back to her old partner, who was already in a comfortable state of forgetfulness, went fast asleep.

The whole family rather overslept themselves, for the sun was quite brilliant when they awoke, and it was very evident that they had been dozing away for some months. The ill-tempered bear was the first on his legs, and kicking his two nearest brothers as he got up, just to hint to them that he was awake again, he opened his mouth to its whole extent—and a very great extent it was, too—and stretching his limbs one after another, and giving himself a hearty shake instead of washing, shaving, and combing, he scuffled to the entrance of the cavern and sniffed at the fresh air. He sniffed and sniffed, and the more he sniffed, the more certainly did his nose whisper that there was some-

6*

thing else besides fresh air which he was inhaling. The smell of the fresh air, too, or the *something else*, caused him a tremendous appetite, which was every moment becoming greater; and then it entered his bearish brain that where there was a smell there must be something to occasion it. Whereupon, following that great nose of his—and he could not have had a better guide—he scuffled out of the cavern and down the path, till he reached a little mound of earth and leaves, where, the odour being strongest, he squatted down. With his great paws he soon demolished the entrance to his mamma's larder, and lost no time in pulling out some of the dainties it contained, which, without more ado, he set about devouring. Meanwhile his brothers, who had been aroused by the affectionate conduct of the eldest, were by this time also wide awake, and had quite as good appetites as Bruin himself; and though on ordinary occasions they stood in great awe of that most ill-tempered brute, it must be admitted that this was an *extra*-ordinary occasion, and they acted accordingly. Just fancy being months without anything to eat, and having appetites fierce enough to devour one another.

So they rushed to the spot where Bruin was making so excellent a meal, and without any other apology than a short grunt or two, they seized upon some of the hidden treasures, and with little ceremony crammed them into their hungry jaws. Bruin was thunderstruck! Never before had they ever presumed to dip their paws into his dish, and now they were actually before his face, converting the most delicate morsels to their own use, and, as it were, taking the food out of his very mouth! After an internal struggle of a few seconds, during which it seemed doubtful whether his emotions or his greediness in filling his jaws so full would choke him, he uttered a savage growl, and, with one stroke of his huge paw, felled his younger brother to the ground. Then turning to the second, he flew at him like a fury, and seemed resolved to make him share a similar fate; but the other, who was not wanting in courage, and who was strengthened by the idea that there was something still in the larder worth fighting for, and which he would certainly lose if he ran away, warded off his blows, and, by careful management, now dodging, now striking, kept his brother at bay, and avoided coming to such close quarters as to subject himself to Bruin's hug; for he knew, if he once felt that embrace, there was not much chance of his having any appetite left with which to complete his half-finished breakfast.

The noise of the combat had now, however, roused the family. Mrs. B. was the first to make her appearance, and she was soon followed by the rest. Explanations ensued, although the facts of the case were sufficiently clear, and Bruin's character was well known. Old Ursus Major drew himself up, and, for once in his life, assumed a dignified demeanour. The ill-tempered bear stood abashed before his parents, although he moved his head to and fro in an obstinate manner, as though rejecting all interference.

It is a pity I cannot relate to you what was said upon this occasion, for Old Bruin is reported to have made a very eloquent discourse on the horrible effects of ill-temper and greediness; and good advice is worth having, whether uttered by a bear or any other animal. Suffice it, that after lecturing his son on the enormity of his offences,—which probably he was himself partly the cause of, through not punishing many of his previous errors,—he bid him quit for ever his paternal roof, and seek his fortune elsewhere; cautioning him at the same time, that if he ever expected to get through the world with credit to his name, and even comfort to his person, he must be honest, good-tempered, and forbearing.

Bruin took this advice in most ungracious part; and without exchanging a word with any of the family, although it was evident his poor old mother longed to hug him in her arms, he growled out some unintelligible words, and set forth upon his travels.

-------•●•-------

UPON HIS TRAVELS.

THERE is no denying that when Bruin had got clear of the old familiar path, and lost sight of the dwelling where he had hitherto spent his days, he felt most particularly uncomfortable; and if he had had the power of recalling the past, he would, in his present state of feeling, no doubt have done so. For the first time in his life, the sense of his ill-temper struck him in all its ugliness; and as he sat down on a huge tree which was lying across his road, he looked such a picture of disconsolateness, that it was evident he would have felt great relief if he could have shed some tears. Alas, how much does Bruin's condition remind us of little scenes among ourselves! We give way to our bad tempers and our selfishness; we make ourselves disagreeable, and our friends unhappy; we quarrel, if we do not actually fight; and when we meet the reward of our waywardness, and find ourselves abandoned by those who would have loved us had we acted differently, we then moan over our fate, and bitterly regret what we might have avoided. Alas, poor human nature! alas, poor bear!

I am truly sorry to observe that no act of repentance followed Bruin's sense of desolation. His first feeling of sorrow over, he felt indignant that he should have been so treated; but, more than that, as he was still hungry, he felt regret at being denied a closer search into his old mother's larder.

Whilst engaged in his various reflections he happened to cast his eyes up to a neighbouring hollow tree, where, at some height from the ground, a number of bees were flying in and out a great hole, with all the bustle and buzzing usual to those busy people. Now, it is well known that bears are mightily fond of honey, and will run great risks in order to obtain this dainty, and Bruin was very far from being an exception to his tribe. He was too ignorant to reflect that it was a great deal too

early in the season to hope for any store, but, con·
sulting only his own inclinations, he lost no time
in climbing up the tree; and when he had reached
the spot where the now angry bees were hurrying
to and fro more vigourously than ever, he thrust
his great paw into a hole with the hope of drawing
forth a famous booty. But the indignant insects
now came out in a swarm, and attacked him with
the utmost fury; three of them settled on his nose,
and pricked him most unmercifully; a dozen or
two planted themselves on a great patch behind,
where his trowsers were worn thin; and a whole
troop fastened on to the sore place in his head—for
it was not quite healed up—and so stung him, that,
roaring with pain and rage, he threw himself rather
than descended from the tree, and went flying
through the wood to get rid of his determined little
enemies: they stuck fast, however, to their points
of attack, nor did Bruin get clear of his tormentors
till he dashed himself into a pool of water and
buried his head for a moment or two under the
surface.

It was with some degree of trepidation that he
raised his nose above water and peeped about him;
the bees were all gone, so he crawled out of the
mud, and after an angry shake or two, for his coat
was quite wet, he resumed his journey.

Bruin now travelled on till noon; and what with
hunger and his long walk, you may believe his
temper was not improved. A rustling noise on the
left, accompanied every now and then with a short,
contented kind of grunt, attracted his attention,

and looking through some brambles, he descried in an open space a very large boar, with two most formidable tusks protruding from his jaws, busily engaged in rooting up the ground, from which he had extracted a curious variety of roots and other edibles. the sight of which made Bruin's mouth water. For the first time in his life he felt the necessity of civility; for though he had never made any personal acquaintance with the tribe to which the animal before him belonged, there were many tales current in his family of their ferocity when provoked; and the few reasoning powers he possessed were sufficient to assure him, that not even his rough paws or burly strength would secure him from those glistening tusks if directed angrily against him. So Bruin resolved to try and be civil; and with this determination walked into the stranger's domain, and accosted him in as polite a way as his rude nature would permit him to assume.

The animal, who was known in his neighbourhood as Wylde Boare, Esquire, on account of the extent of his property, received Bruin's advances with great caution, for he was naturally of a suspicious temper, his bright reddish eyes twinkling in a very unpleasant manner; perceiving, however, that his unexpected visitor was but a mere youngster, and that he looked very hungry and tired, he grunted out a surly sort of welcome, and, jerking his snout in the direction of the heap of provisions, bade him squat down and make a meal. Bruin did not wait for a second invitation, but, stretching

out his huge legs, picked up the fresh vegetables,
which he thrust into his capacious jaws with every
appearance of relish.

When his repast came to an end—and this did
not happen till there was an end of the food—he
wiped his mouth with the back of his arm, and
looked at the boar; and the boar, who had said
nothing during the disappearance of the fruits of
his morning's work, but had contented himself with
uttering a grunt or two, looked at Bruin. At
length he observed,—

"Hurgh, you have a famous appetite!"

"Ah," answered the bear, "and so would you,
if you had not eaten anything for the last few
weeks!"

After a pause:—

"Hurgh, hurgh!" said Mr. Boare, in a guttural
voice; "I never tried; but a big fellow like you
ought to be able to get through a deal of work!"

"Perhaps so," observed the surly bear; "but I
don't intend to make the experiment."

After another pause:—

"Hurgh, an idle fellow, I'm afraid!" said Mr.
Boare, half aside; "and not quite so civil as before
his breakfast." Then he exclaimed aloud, "I suppose you will make no objection to help me dig up
some more food, seeing that you have made away
with my dinner, hurgh?"

"Who do you take me for?" said the ungrateful
beast, springing to his legs, and eyeing his entertainer with one of his furious looks.

"Who do I take you for, hurgh, you graceless

cub?" exclaimed Mr. Boare, in a rage, for he was
rather hasty in his manner, and his red eyes twin-
kled, and his back began to get up in a way which
showed his agitation; "who do I take you for?
Why, I did take you for one who would be at least
thankful for food given you when almost starving:
but I now perceive you are only an ugly lump of
a bear.   Out of my sight this instant, or, from want
of my own dinner, which you have devoured, I
shall, perchance, make a meal of you!—hurgh,
hurgh!"

As he said these words the bristles on his back
started up so furiously, and his tusks glistened so
horridly in a little ray of sunlight, which was peeping in to see what was the matter, that Master
Bruin felt thoroughly frightened, and made a precipitate retreat, turning round at every few steps
to observe whether he were followed, and if it would
be necessary to take refuge in one of the trees; but
Wylde Boare, Esq. only grunted out his favourite
expression, which, in this case, was mixed with a
great deal of contempt, and recommenced digging
for his dinner as if nothing had occurred to disturb his usual contented state of mind.

Bruin now travelled on till he reached a stream,
which came bounding through this part of the
wood at a very rapid pace, and making a terrible
fuss because sundry large stones in the middle of
its course rather impeded its progress.   The noise
it made, and the anger it showed, seemed to please
our sulky bear mightily, so he sat down on the
bank with his toes in the water to enjoy the spec

7

tacle. The scene was a very striking one, and was fitted to charm the most indifferent eye; and Bruin, bear as he was, could not help being attracted by it. Whatever his meditations, however, it was not destined that he should pursue them long without interruption; for his quick ear soon detected the sharp, quick bark of several dogs—a sound that was carried along by a breeze which swept by him at intervals. He raised his head with his huge nose in the air to sniff out any possible danger, and did not seem at all pleased with the result of his observations; for he drew first one foot and then the other out of the water, and raised himself to his full height. As he did so, a more than usual commotion in the stream drew his attention, when he perceived the round head of a large otter appear above the surface, whilst two bright eyes gave a hasty look all round. On observing Bruin, the head immediately disappeared, and at the same moment a whole pack of terriers, in hot haste, came sweeping round a bank hard by, but stopped short on finding themselves in presence of such a formidable creature.

Bruin perceived that he had made an impression, and his usual insolence returned; for he had at first been startled, and he attributed the pause of the terriers to fear, when, in fact, it was only the result of surprise. If he had been a little better physiognomist, he would have observed a certain air of determination about the little fellows, which sufficiently showed that it was prudence or a sense of duty which stayed them, and not a lack of courage: they had been sent out to procure an otter, and they were now deliberating among themselves whether it would be wise to spend their time in quarrelling with a bear.

After a short consultation, one who appeared to have the guidance of the pack uttered a decided little bark, and turning a little aside, endeavoured to pass between Bruin and the stream, but sufficiently near to show that he was not afraid to come into contact with him, followed by his companions. This evidently contemptuous mode of treating him, aroused all our ill-tempered hero's bad humour; so, without considering the consequences of the action, he raised his big paw and knocked the leader down. The sturdy little fellows wanted no further provocation; as if influenced by a single will, they turned upon him, and attacked him in front, flank, and rear, with an impetuosity which was at first irresistible, because unexpected. Finding that those behind him were his greatest and most successful tormentors, he very prudently sat himself down, crushing one or two of them in his descent; then springing to his legs, and as he did so catching several more in his arms, he hugged them till they had no more breath in their bodies, when he dropped them and took up a fresh supply. One of the pack, however, more alert than his fellows, sprang up and seized him by the nose, making his teeth meet in that prominent feature, and caused Bruin such intense pain, that, forgetting all his strategy, he tried to beat down his determined little foe with his paws, and ran off howling

in a most terrific manner, pursued by the remain-
der of the pack, who bit at his hind legs, tore his
already ragged coat till it hung in ribbons; and
when Bruin, who, having at length got rid of the
bold little fellow that had fastened to his nose,
climbed up a tree, they stood yelping at the foot
of it, till evening had completely set in, when they
slowly retired.

And what were our ill-natured hero's thoughts,
as he sat upon an elevated branch, and gently rubbed his wounded snout? Why, unfortunately for
his own happiness, he laid the blame of his mishap
on any one or any thing, rather than the right being or circumstance. It was the otter's fault, or
the dogs' fault—those dogs were always so quarrelsome; or it was his father's fault in driving him
away from home: in fact, every one was in error
rather than himself and his own disagreeable disposition. And here we may observe, that they are
such characters as Bruin who bring disrepute on a
whole tribe; for we are too apt to form our opinions
of a nation by the few individuals we may happen
to fall in with, although, probably, no conclusions
can be falser. Let us, therefore, be careful ere we
form our judgments, and let us not believe that all
Bruin's kindred and compatriots were sulky and
ill-tempered because he himself was such a disagreeable lump of a bear.

TOWN LIFE.

BRUIN woke up next morning with so uncomfortable a feeling of soreness from the rough treatment he had received, that it was with some difficulty he was enabled to move his heavy limbs; and he found sitting so unpleasant a posture, that he lay stretched across two or three branches for several hours, and in a very ill-humour, indeed, watched the activity displayed beneath and around him. Now a stealthy fox, upon some foraging expedition, would come creeping along, his foot fall scarcely heard on the withered leaves and dead branches; now a timid mouse would leap nimbly by, and, at the least signal of danger, would disappear as if by enchantment; then a frolicsome squirrel, vaulting as fearlessly from bough to bough as if he were not fifty feet from the ground, would arouse him for a minute from his sulky mood, and light up his fierce eye with an expression of interest which it was very clear had no higher source than a hope that the little tumbler might fall down and break his neck, for daring to be in such a good humour. But the birds, above all, excited his anger; for seeing them flying about gaily in the sun, which tinged the tops of the trees so gloriously, Bruin actually growled with indignation—a sound which nearly caused that accident to Master Squirrel that our ungracious hero had desired for him, so terribly was he frightened.

7*

A few days thus spent sufficiently recovered him
to render him capable of moving, when he descended
from his temporary hospital, and, with the aid of a
thick staff, which he had provided himself for the
purpose, set off once more, supplying his wants in
the way of food with such edibles as fell in his
way, a bear not being remarkably particular concerning its quality or kind. One only thought
now possessed him,—that of quitting the wooded
ground where his life had hitherto been passed, and
reaching one of those spots where, as he had heard
his parents relate, animals of various kinds congregate together, and live in habitations raised by
their own ingenuity ; in fact, a city.

"At least," he thought, "if what I have heard
of such places be true, and that merit of every kind
is certain there to meet its reward, and be properly
appreciated, I shall stand a better chance than my
neighbours." With this reflection, he shuffled on
a little quicker; and the reader, who has been thus
allowed a private view of his motives, will observe
that modesty was not among Bruin's list of vir-
tues.

After a day's march, with sundry restings by the
way—for he was not in good travelling order—he
reached the outskirts of the wood; and when he
got beyond it, he stood still to mark the prospect,
which was, in sooth, a very charming one, and the
more striking to him as being so entirely novel.
As he stood on a rising ground, the scene lay
beneath ; and the sun, which was nearing the ho-
rizon, darted his level beams through a gentle mist

that was beginning to rise from the valley, and made a wondrous golden haze, shedding beauty over every object within its influence. A silvery brook ran from some distant hills, and, after numerous windings, spread into a broad pond; then narrowing again, with an abrupt fall or two, which made its pace the faster, it ran noiselessly through some green meadows, where cattle and horses were grazing, then made a bend into the wood, where it was lost to view. Bruin's quick eye scarcely, however, watched its course, for his whole attention was rivetted on what to him was of more interest,— the city to which his weary steps were directed. It stood upon the margin of the rivulet, just before its waters expanded into the little lake, and seemed to occupy a considerable extent of ground. It was neither handsomely nor regularly built, yet it had an imposing effect as a whole, and in Bruin's eyes seemed to need nothing in the way of architecture. Its inhabitants, I may observe in passing, were principally descendants of canine tribes, with a few pussies, who, for some worldly advantage, had overcome their prejudices to such society; and a flock or two of birds: as the latter, however, were of a volatile disposition, and were constantly on the move, they resided principally in the higher portions of the city, so that they might come and go without interfering with the steadier habits of the animal population. Several horses and black cattle resided in the environs, but, with the exception of a donkey or two, rarely entered the town, for they found few inducements in the noisy streets to compensate them for the charm and tranquillity of a rural life.

After contemplating the scene for some time, Bruin slowly descended the hill, his confidence in his own powers somewhat weakened now he was in sight of the spot where they were to be called into action ; one reason for this slight depression of his spirits arising, probably, from his ignorance of the dwellers in the great city, for the intelligence just communicated to the reader was at that time totally unknown to him. The strange appearance, also, of every creature he now met, contributed to abash him ; for every one who had any pretensions to respectability wore over the coats with which nature had provided them, clothes of a cut that looked wonderful in the eyes of the untutored Bruin. His own aspect was, meanwhile, not less odd in the opinion of the more civilised animals. His untrimmed hair and beard, his ragged coat, his queer gait, and the unrestrained gape of wonder with which he stared around him, were sufficient to excite the attention of the most indifferent, and it was with a tolerably large train at his heels that he reached the entrance to the principal street. Here crowds of well-dressed dogs, both male and female (the latter always well attended), were walking about or idling the time away ; town-bred puppies, with insolent stare, were lounging at every turn, their delicate paws proving how little they were used to labour. On one side Bruin observed a gracefully-proportioned white cat, veiled, gliding demurely along, whilst a strong tabby, her nurse, purred behind, with three little kittens in her arms, mewing to their heart's content; and on the other several huge mastiffs, stalking gravely in a row, like policemen in our London streets going to their beats, the animals to which they have been compared being bound on a similar errand.

These various sights proved to Bruin that there must be a different agency at work to that which existed in his native forest. He was wise enough to perceive that mere animal force was not likely to succeed here, or hold the same position as it did in the land where he was born and had spent his earlier years. The appearances of wealth on one hand, the evidences of a soldier-like discipline and order on the other, convinced him that this was no place to vent his ill-humour by an exhibition of brute strength, for that it was sure to meet more than its match; whilst the uncertainty of the punishment which would attend such outbreak, provided it were indulged in, made him resolve, at least, to put a curb upon his public conduct. This was the first great step in Bruin's education; a step, alas! merely taught him by his fears. Had it sprung from higher sources, there would have been a chance of its doing permanent good; but what solid benefit can be reckoned on or attained which arises from such a motive?

The attention that the rough stranger from a distant country met with from the civilized population of Caneville (for that, or something ike it was the name of the city), was beginning to be rather irksome to him. Every lady-dog, as she passed him, seemed anxious to allow him plenty of room; the three kittens in arms, at sight of him set up a chorus of cries, which their nurse tried in vain to appease; a mastiff, who was on guard on the opposite side of the way, seemed very much inclined to interfere for the preservation of public peace; whilst a couple of puppies, touched off in the extreme of the then prevailing fashion at Caneville, turned up their noses and their tails in a way which seemed to render it perfectly marvellous how they kept upon their legs. All this was sufficiently irritating, even to the most good-natured of beings, and Bruin found it especially hard to bear; he was assisted, however, in his prudential resolution to abstain from any outward exhibition of wrath by a sound which was as new to his ear as it was exciting to his feelings. It came from the upper end of the street, where a crowd had assembled; and as every one in his neighbourhood seemed to think the amusement it promised would be of a more interesting kind than baiting a bear, and had hastened in the direction whence it proceeded, Bruin thought he could not do better than follow their example.

On reaching the spot, his great height enabled him to get a view of what was going on; and as he pressed forward, the animals with which he came in contact gladly made way at his approach, so that in a few seconds he stood in the front row of a large circle, the centre of which was occupied by a fat, overgrown pig, with an astonishingly long snout, and a couple of rings through it by way of ornament; two equally long ears, that had evidently been submitted to some curious operation, for they were slit in various places, and hung down from his head like uncombed locks of hair; and a pair of very sharp little eyes, which seemed to have the unpleasant power of piercing right through you, if in their incessant wanderings they chanced to catch a look from your own. It was very evident that this animal, who was quite a *savant*, or, as we should say, a learned pig, enjoyed a high reputation in the community of Caneville, where he had been setttled some time; and whenever, as now, he chose to make an outdoor exhibition of himself and his powers, he was certain of a very full audience.

Behind him stood a punchy little bull-dog, with an inflamed countenance, evidently caused by too close application to a mouth-organ, arranged in such a way as to be at a convenient distance from his capacious muzzle; and before him was a drum, an article on which Bruin looked with a curious and most ludicrous expression of physiognomy. As he was now in the foremost van, he gradually edged near and nearer to the object of his attraction, whilst the learned beast was making preparations for a grand display; and just as Bruin had reached the place where the drummer had taken his stand, Herr Schwein (so was he called) gave orders for a flourish of music by way of opening the performance. But how describe the effect which the sound produced on our bear? At the first stroke of the stick on the drum, he leaped from the ground as if he had been shot; then giving utterance to a

prolonged howl, he began dancing about in a way
which would have been irresistibly funny, if the
audience had not been too frightened to stop and
witness it.   As it happened, a general panic seized
the multitude, and off went good part of the population of Caneville, howling, screaming, and yelping to their various homes, where they, of course,
each gave a different version of the story.   The
learned pig alone, and his faithful Tom, who would
not run away for anybody, were the only creatures
who stood their ground; the former, because he
had travelled much and was acquainted with the
peculiarities of bears; and the latter, partly for the
reason just given, and in part because he was so
fixed to the drum that to go away without it was
impossible; and to go away with it, without previous packing, would have been equally difficult,
so he stood his ground and watched the proceedings.

On the ceasing of the music and dispersing of
the crowd our hero also stood still, as much surprised as any of the former spectators at the effect
he had produced; and then feeling still more sen
sibly the effects of his fatigues, he sat down panting and exhausted.   The pig, who had been quietly
watching him, and had evidently been revolving
some interesting thoughts in his contemplative
brain, shortly after rose, and gathering up the
things which were to have figured in his evening's
performance, and assisting to pack the drum comfortably on Tom's back, beckoned to the bear, and
waddled gently off in an opposite direction of the

city to that where Bruin had entered. **Our in-**
teresting brute hesitated a moment; but being
nudged by Tom, who uttered at the same time a
word or two of encouragement, which, to render
intelligible, may be translated by "Come along,
stupid!" he mechanically followed this fast young
dog, and they all reached the pig's habitation just
as evening was falling.

After the bear had been regaled with a most
hearty supper—for pigs, it may be remarked by
the way, are famous caterers—his learned host un-
folded to him his plans. He explained the nature
of his own avocations; how that he had supported himself, and saved a nice little store be
sides, through telling the fortunes and relating
the age of the lady-dogs and doglets of Caneville;
and how he performed sundry conjuring tricks,
which, though easy enough when found out, had
earned for him an astonishing reputation among
the simple animals of the city, who never *had*
penetrated the secret. He explained, besides, that
there were many more he could perform if his
figure were more slim and his movements as active
as they had been some years ago, before time, by
increasing his rotundity, had lessened the ease of
his motions; but that if Bruin would undertake to
learn them, his fortune was as good as made: for
he, Herr Schwein, would not only teach him all
he knew, but would reward him with half the pro-
fits derived from his performance, when he should
have mastered his studies. This proposal so
jumped with Bruin's humour, that he consented

without further solicitation, and it was agreed that his engagement should commence from the following day.

With the morning's sun did our hero's lessons begin; and as Nature had not added stupidity to his various weaknesses, he made really rapid progress. But poor Piggy found it dreadfully hard work, and more than once repented his bargain; for though reflection and circumstances had made him a philosopher, and travelling had taught him experience, it required all his philosophy and his utmost skill to support the weight of Bruin's unhandsome temper and prevent an utter breach between them. Pride, however, and a natural wish to reap the harvest which he had sown at the cost of so much pains and labour, induced him to persevere, and the day at length arrived when Bruin was to make his next appearance in public. Since the first evening of his arrival he had kept strictly within his employer's grounds, and had familiarised his mind with the mouth-organ and the drum. But now the sun had risen that was to shine on him again abroad; he felt considerably elated; the idea of sporting a handsome pair of silk drawers, and a medal with a ribbon round his neck, and a silver anklet, contributing not a little to produce the feeling.

The pig, who knew the value of notoriety in such cases, had, from early morning, kept Tom parading the streets with a large placard over his shoulders, announcing

THE ARRIVAL

OF A

DISTINGUISHED FOREIGNER!

ENGAGED BY HERR SCHWEIN AT A RUINOUS EXPENSE!!

FOR A LIMITED NUMBER OF REPRESENTATIONS,

TO PERFORM

HIS EXTRAORDINARY AND INTENSELY INTERESTING FEATS

BEFORE THE

HIGHLY-DISCRIMINATING PUBLIC

OF CANEVILLE!!!

The highly-discriminating being thus prepared, assembled in the great square, the place chosen for the exhibition, long before the appointed hour. The ladies were arranged in the foremost rank, with a politeness that was perfectly edifying, whilst knots of fashionable dogs and cats got as near as possible to the reigning favourites; curs of inferior degree occupied the outermost ranks, and a bird or two got gallery places above the heads of the animal spectators. It was when expectation was raised to that pitch which usually finds vent in the most discordant cries, that Bruin, carrying a bag, followed by Tom with the drum, made his appearance,—a sight which caused universal approbation. Some praised his evident strength, others admired his dress, and some again criticised his figure; but when he drew out from his bag a quantity of singular objects, and Tom struck up an extraordinary extempore air with variations on the pipes, accompanied by sundry vicious blows on the drum, public curiosity was strained to the utmost.

When the music ceased, Bruin imperatively waved the spectators back, and the performance began. He handled a pair of knives in a way which made the beholders tremble; for those implements were swallowed and appeared again at the tips of his paws or the end of his nose, without doing him any injury, and they were forced into his arms and drawn furiously across his throat without causing the slightest wound; and then they were tucked into his waistband, and after sundry contortions and leaps, and affected attitudes, they were pulled from out his capacious jaws, where they had stuck fast, to the wonder and delight of the spectators. Then he took up three balls of polished brass, which seemed too heavy for any fashionable puppy present to lift, and commenced a wonderful series of exploits with them. Now they leaped a great height into the air, one after another, with a rapidity which made the crowd's eyes water; then they ran over his shoulders, and down his back, and between his legs, and over his shoulders again in a continuous stream; and then they went bumping over every projecting part of his body, leaping here, jumping there, now on the top of his head, now on the tip of his nose, and never falling to the ground, and always going this game with such wondrous swiftness, as though there were thirty balls instead of three. But the feat which pleased them most, and which may be called the crowning effort of the display, was when Bruin balanced a short stick on his forehead with a pewter plate on the top of it,

which, by some mysterious agency, was made to
spin round and round, and dazzle the optics of the
crowd as it glittered in the sun.   At this marvellous sight there was a burst of admiration !   Tom
blew at his pipes and hammered at his drum with
the utmost energy. Two well-dressed young dogs,
who had been paying particular, attention to a tall
young lady with a long sentimental nose, over
which a veil dropped gracefully (she was evidently
one of the aristocratic greyhound family), gaped
with wonder as they stared at the whirling pewter;
the young lady herself looked on with a gaze where
surprise and admiration were singularly mingled;
and the curs, who are less accustomed to restrain
their feelings, gave vent to them in vigorous howls.
The success was, indeed, complete ; and when Tom
went round with the plate, a rich harvest amply re-
paid the pains which had been bestowed on the re-
hearsals.

———•———

PROSPERITY.

HERR SCHWEIN, that very learned pig, who
had stationed himself in an unobserved corner
of the throng, in order that he might witness the be-
haviour of his pupil, was delighted, though not
astonished, at his success, and gave vent to his
feelings in as marked a manner as a philosopher
and an animal of his peculiar temperament could
be expected to betray. He even went so far as to

8*

beg Bruin to embrace him—an experiment he was not likely to desire repeated, for that malicious beast gave him so severe a squeeze, as to cause him an indigestion for several days after. Piggy's calculations, and the joy which he built on them, would not have been of so solid a kind, if he had known a little more of Bruin's disposition; but, though an animal of experience and knowledge of the world, he was in this case too blinded by his pride to form his usually correct judgment. He only considered what the bear owed to him in the way of gratitude for clothing, feeding, and civilising; he grunted with satisfaction as he revolved in his thoughts the goodly treasure which Bruin might be the means of his acquiring; for, philosopher and animal of the world as he was, he had not been able to divest himself of two grand vices,—gluttony and avarice. The former belonged to his tribe, the latter to himself; and though at first sight they would seem in contradiction with each other, he managed somehow to permit, in his own proper person, that both should have equal sway; and the older he grew, the larger and firmer-rooted did these two passions become. He was getting also so unwieldy, that indolence was, to a certain extent, forced upon him; and this was another powerful consideration which induced him to look on the accession of Bruin as a real benefit.

Unhappy, however, the lot of that animal who should repose any degree of confidence in good to be derived from such a temper and disposition! As day by day developed some new feature which helped to betray a character singularly anamiable and unattractive, so day by day did Herr Schwein's habitation resound with growls and grunts of anger, where formerly reigned the completest calm. Bruin's performances also lacking novelty, began to pall upon the public taste; and though Tom trudged about with his placards more vigorously than ever, and wore the soles of his poor paws thin with the exercise, the novelty was dying out, and the fashionable puppies began to be witty in their whispered remarks upon the person of the bearer. The bear had got a great deal too lazy to learn any fresh exploits; and the pig, indeed, was almost too much out of spirits to teach them. Besides this, Bruin had acquired habits of rather an expensive kind, to indulge which required a good deal of money; and, as Herr Schwein suspected that his due half of the now diminished receipts was withheld from him, quarrels not unnaturally ensued.

These various annoyances produced a great change in poor Piggy, who, perhaps, felt more deeply the overthrow of his pet projects, than the actual loss his bargain had entailed on him; though the loss itself was not trifling, for Bruin's enormous appetite, which he indulged to a frightful extent, went considerably beyond the income that his diminished exertions produced, and there was a chance, as matters stood, that this resource would soon fail altogether. It is not surprising, then, if the Herr should contemplate breaking off his engagement, and terminating at once the difficulties which seemed to threaten him, by turning the great bear adrift upon the world. But a stronger power than a pig's was about to settle the question, a power to which all animals are equally amenable: and thus was it brought into action.

It was evening; Bruin and Tom, the former in excessively ill-humour, the latter much as usual, though sulky, returned home, where the Herr awaited them with impatience. It did not require a very great amount of sagacity to learn that they had been unsuccessful, for disappointment was plainly visible on the features of both. From Bruin nothing could be obtained in the way of information, for he had thrown himself on the ground, and stuffed his wide jaws with some delicacies Piggy had reserved for his own supper, so it was to Tom his master's eyes were directed for an explanation. Now that valuable servant's *fort*, never lay in making an eloquent discourse, or even in describing the most ordinary facts in a plain and intelligible manner; and in this instance, as his feelings interfered with the relation of facts, a tolerably large stock of patience, and some cleverness to boot, were needed to understand the account.

This was, after cross-examination, what Herr Schwein managed to comprehend. They had gone to the market-place as usual, and, to their delight, found it crowded, immediately jumping to the conclusion that the public mind of Caneville was not so utterly degraded as they had begun to fancy it. The innocent conjecture was soon, however, disabused; for on their drawing nearer they observed that faithless population gathered about

"Another Distinguished Foreigner," with a remarkably long beard and a fierce pair of horns, who proclaimed himself a magician from beyond the land where the sun rose, and rejoiced in the name of Doctor Capricornus, A.V.G.T., and M.U. H.S., which the great learning of Herr Schwein interpreted by A Very Great Traveller, or Thief, and Member of the Universal Herbage or Humbug Society. Now, the feats displayed by this new candidate for public favour, were of the stupidest order (remember, this is not the statement of a disinterested party), consisting merely in pointing out any pebble on the ground that any one of the crowd should have previously fixed on, and mounting to the top of a little ladder and balancing himself on the tips of his horns at the upper round; yet it was enough to excite the enthusiasm of the lookers-on: nor could all the cries of Bruin, bidding them come and see what true genius really was; nor all the dulcet notes of Tom, though he blew at his pipes till he was black in the face, and thrashed his drum till he beat in its crown, procure them a single spectator. Thoroughly disgusted, they quitted the spot and returned home, Bruin getting into a dispute with one of the City police by the way for comporting himself bearishly towards a richly-dressed and genteel-looking cat, who was quietly serenading his mistress, seated at a balcony.

As Tom finished his relation, a slight squeak issued from the pig's throat, but from its profoundest depths, as if it came from the bottom of his

heart. Once or twice, indeed, he turned his snout
to the place where the bear, who had finished his
employer's supper, lay at his full length asleep, as
though he intended to arouse him; but his philosophy or his physical weakness made him change
his resolution, and, making a motion to Tom to
lend him some assistance, he tottered off with difficulty to bed, where he cast himself down as if he
were tired of the world and its struggles. At least
his manner so far affected Tom that he could not
prevail on himself to quit his master's side; but
after watching him with interest for a full hour,
and observing him in a deep sleep, he stretched
his body upon some clean straw, instead of seeking
his own crib, and was soon likewise in a state of
forgetfulness.

It must have been about midnight that Tom was
aroused by a suppressed grunting; he started up,
and, by the aid of the moon, beheld Herr Schwein
lying on his back, and convulsively kicking his
legs in the air. He ran to his head and tried to
raise him up, but his weight was more than he
could manage, so he called out in his loudest voice
for the assistance of Bruin. That ungracious beast,
however, though waked by the noise, felt no inclination to have his repose disturbed; so bid him hold
his peace, and let honest folks go to sleep. Tom
was a thoroughly faithful creature at heart, though
a rough and untutored one. The want of feeling
displayed by the bear, and his ingratitude in thus
allowing his master to struggle without even lending him a paw, aroused all the indignation of his

honest nature; so, flying at Master Bruin, he caught hold of the tip of his ear and bit it till the great beast roared with pain, and, effectually roused, followed his adversary about the place in order to punish him for his insolence. In his awkward evolutions he caught one of his legs in a heap of straw, and fell full sprawl over poor Herr Schwein. A small grunt, like a sigh with a bad cold, escaped the learned Pig: it was his last! for, when Bruin raised himself up, he found his late employer perfectly motionless; nor did all his efforts, such as pulling his snout, and shaking his trotters, and twisting his tail, succeed in producing the slightest impression. The bear was puzzled. He squatted down beside his old master, and, sucking his right paw, whilst he scratched his pate with his left, gazed long at the prostrate body. Meanwhile Tom drew nigh, and guessing at the truth from his companion's attitude and the pig's breathless quiet, raised his nose to the roof of the dwelling and uttered a long and dismal howl of sorrow. Again and again, at brief intervals, did the faithful servant thus deplore his master's fate, till Bruin, angered by the noise, threw the broken drum at the unconscious mourner, with such effect, indeed, that the shattered extremity alighted on his crown, and for the time completely buried him, his voice sounding singularly sepulchral from the depths of the hollow instrument. It effectually stopped the current of his grief by creating a flood of irritation, which only respect for the dead prevented his giving vent to, for he would otherwise have little

heeded either the strength or ferocity of his antagonist.

Bruin, who had betrayed no feeling of any kind
at the sight of his late benefactor thus converted
into pork, now returned to his own bed, and was
soon again in a comfortable snore; but the faithful
Tom still sat by the body of his master, and patiently watched there till daylight.

The sun rose, and many neighbours, apprised of
the event, made their appearance; some urged by
curiosity to see how a dead pig looked, some stim-
ulated by avarice, hoping there might be a trifle
or two to pick up, and a few from a higher motive
—the wish, namely, to show respect for the memory
of the deceased, by assisting, if necessary, his sur-
vivors. Herr Schwein, however, had come amongst
them alone, nor was it thought that he had kith or
kin; for no mention of any amiable *frau*, or sow,
no syllable of any interesting piglet, had ever issued
from his learned jaws. He died as he had lived,
among strangers; and, alas! all the learning he
had acquired was destined to perish with him: for,
with one exception, Herr Schwein had never committed any of his thoughts or experiences to writing. I have said, with *one* exception; for the occasion is worth noting, as it was on a matter interesting, indeed, to every epicure in the universe. The
subject which then engaged his pen bore the following title:—"*Signs by which the most unobservant
may detect in the soils of the world the existence of
Truffles; together with an Essay on the most effectual
mode of cultivating them.*" And it may well be con-

jectured, from the great learning and fitness of the writer to deal with such a subject, how much new light must have been thrown upon it. Unfortunately for the tribes of gourmands, and poor Piggy's fame, this valuable paper was never destined to electrify the world; for, cast into the street by Bruin among other articles, considered, alas! of no value, it was picked up by some ignorant puppy passing by, who, seeing it written in German character, and not understanding a word of it, tore up the priceless document to make lights for his cigars.

Two mastiffs, who had been informed of the death, kept watch meanwhile without the house; and when night again came on they were joined by a couple of ugly curs, whose business it was to convey the body to its last resting-place without the city; for the dogs, with great good sense, had an intense dislike to bury the dead among the living. The mortal remains of Herr Schwein being placed upon a kind of sledge, were drawn slowly down to the little lake, followed by Tom, as chief and only mourner, for Bruin was so devoid of feeling as to refuse even this last tribute to the memory of one who had been his best friend; and when the funeral procession reached the water, the body was gently let down into the current, which bore it gradually away. Poor Tom sent after it a prolonged and melancholy howl, the last sad adieu of a simple but faithful heart; and then turning his steps, which were mechanically leading him towards his late home, in quite an opposite direction, he set off upon a lonely pilgrimage, resolv-

9

ing in his own mind that many a scene should be
traversed ere he again gazed on his native city of
Caneville.

Meanwhile Bruin, who felt not the least alarm
at Tom's continued absence, found himself suddenly in a position of the highest prosperity. As no
one was there to claim the property of the deceased,
he took possession of it as his right. Every corner
was ransacked, every hiding-place examined, and
a large store of costumes, and things of every kind,
gathered in the course of the late Herr's wanderings in different lands, were dragged from their
obscurity.

His present habitation did not, however, suit his
change of fortune: he must have a house in the
most fashionable quarter of the town. When this
was obtained, not satisfied with the simple name
his fathers had honestly borne for so many generations, he resolved to dub himself a nobleman,
which he could the more easily do in a place where
his connexions were unknown, so styled himself
Count von Bruin forthwith. The wardrobe of his
late learned employer furnished him with a suit of
astonishingly fine clothes, which fitted him to a
nicety; so on every fine morning, dressed therein,
with hat cocked upon his crown, his paws grasping
a cane, and placed under his coat-tails, so as to show
off all the glory of his waistcoat, frill, and splendid
jewellery, he marched into the streets. He made
so imposing a figure in his new dress, and assumed
such an air of pomposity, that it was no wonder
the uninitiated should have been deceived, and

have taken him for a lion of the very first nobility;
nor can we be surprised that a poor cur, almost in
a state of nudity, should, in the most abject manner, supplicate a trifle from "His Lordship;" that
an ignorant cat, in passing, should take off his cap
and make a profound bow; or a kitten, just behind, cross its paws as though it stood in the presence of a superior. There was one, however, who
penetrated through all his disguise; one who had
watched him with interest when he made his *debut*
in the public square and drew down such abundant admiration, and who, by some feeling for
which she could not account, had followed his
varying fortunes till she saw him thus rich, superbly dressed, and strutting down the street, as
though Caneville were too small to hold him,—
and that one was the Hon. Miss Greyhound.

———•◆•———

REVERSES.

SOLITARY as were Bruin's habits by nature, he
had felt, since his residence in a town, a change
stealing gradually over him, and the necessity of
companionship becoming every day more sensibly
experienced. In his late position, he had had the
constant companionship of Tom and the learned
society of his master, which, indeed, he was but
little capable of appreciating, besides the acquaintance of some inferior animals whom he had man-

aged to fall in with during his idle hours; though
that these must have been of the very lowest class,
the reader, who is aware of the character of that
great beast, will readily suppose. Tom was, however, now gone; poor Schwein, too, had departed;
and Bruin's fine clothes and altered condition entirely precluded at present a return to his former
associates. Society, he felt, he must have, and
upon his choice now depended his future fortunes.
It was whilst this necessity was pressing on his
brain that one morning, when lolling in all the indolence of ignorance allied to wealth, he was surprised at the appearance of a diminutive spaniel,
admitted by his porter, who, dressed in a rich scar-
let livery, bore a letter in his belt, which he presented with a certain fawning grace to our hero,
and hastily departed. This was the first epistle
that worthy had ever held in his own paws, so it
may well be judged he was but little prepared to
investigate its contents. He turned it over and
over, and then put it to his nose, for the scent
which it emitted was pleasant to his sense of smell;
but still this gave him no hint at its meaning.
Never before had he felt the annoyance which a
want of education inevitably causes; but now that
it did strike him, instead of arousing his energies
to cure so serious a defect,—a cure, too, which he
could under present circumstances so easily accomplish,—it only moved his anger to think that the
little scrap of paper which he held in his paw, and
which he could without the slightest effort crush
into nothingness, withheld its secrets from him,

whilst every mincing puppy in the streets could command its every word. Ah, Master Bruin ! Master Bruin ! you are not the first to make the discovery that knowledge is superior to brute force. Angry or not, he wished to know the meaning of the note; and summoning to his presence one who had managed to procure the chief place in his household, cunning Fox as he was, he commanded that worthy to read its contents aloud. Fox obeyed, not at all displeased that he should be selected for this duty, as he foresaw, from the so-called Count's ignorance, that he would be able at a future period to turn his intimate knowledge of his master's secrets to good account. He, therefore, read as follows :—

"You may believe I must be actuated by a strong feeling in your favour, when I thus forget what is due to my sex and rank, and overcome all the prejudices which canine society builds up as a barrier to intercourse with foreigners. I confess it; the feeling is a strong one: but I rely on your honour to save me from the ill effects my imprudence might otherwise lay me open to. If you are willing to know farther, and are the animal I take you for, you will be in waiting to-morrow evening after sunset, at the extremity of the mews in the cat's quarter of the city."

This missive, written in bold but feminine characters, was without a signature; and when Fox had retired, with a cunning leer upon his sharp features, and Bruin was left alone to medi-

9*

tate upon the singularity of the adventure, that great beast lost himself in conjectures as to the writer, and figured to his imagination a creature very different, no doubt, to the being actually in question. His impatience, however, to get over the interval of time which must elapse ere his curiosity could be gratified, was sensibly felt by every inmate of the mansion. Nothing seemed to go right; the soup was tasteless, the viands were overdone, and the vegetables raw. Never was there so fastidious a bear; the cook more than once contemplated some rash act; the poor little turnspits crept into corners with their tails between their legs, fully expecting to be sacrificed in some moment of wrath; whilst the various house-servants, pussies of doubtful reputation, seemed to creep about the place as though they were every moment in dread of being accused of purloining certain savoury made-dishes, reserved especially for cook's private friends. Fox, too, the steward and factotum of the establishment, appeared not to possess his usual sleek and quiet ease, but, as the evening drew near, got restless and fidgetty, though he tried to be calm, and even more jocose than usual. He had been absent half the morning, no one knew for what purpose; not that he ever condescended to divulge the causes of his movements, but there was a slyer look in his eyes, and a sharper appearance about his clever, pointed nose, than ordinarily animated those features.

The hour drew nigh. The sun was going down when the Count von Bruin, most superbly dressed, sallied forth from his dwelling. His demeanour was observed and criticised by every domestic in his household, who, crowding to the windows, watched that great bear go forth,—as he fancied, to conquer. Fox allowed him to turn the corner; then, enveloped in a cloak which completely hid his figure he let himself out and glided after his master.

Bruin, meanwhile, strutted on till he reached the quarter of the city inhabited by the descendants of the feline race; and as he had never before been in that part of the town, he was at first utterly confounded by the discordant cries. Instead, too, of the order prevailing in the canine portions, the inhabitants seemed to take delight in the wildest gymnastic demonstrations, and certainly seemed to prefer the house-tops to any other lounging-place. Kittens, in horrible abundance, were frisking about in every direction, and the scene was altogether of a character which seemed to justify the wisdom of the magnates of Caneville in obliging this singular people to dwell in a distinct part of the town; a rule which, with a few exceptions, was strictly carried out.

On reaching the mews, a place so called at the outskirts of the city in this direction, and sufficiently removed from the noisy streets as to make the spot a very solitary one, Bruin perceived he was alone at the rendezvous; so, to while away the time, he strutted to and fro, and meditated, in his usual style, on his own self-importance. He was aroused from his reverie by a slight bark, or cough; and raising his head, he perceived in the dim light a tall and graceful figure deeply veiled.

He hastily advanced, his rough nature for the first time touched at this proof of confidence, and his vanity suddenly rising to a dangerous height, and taking the delicate white paw, which drooped gracefully from a mantle, within his own, he unclosed his jaws to make some tender speech. But before he had time to commit himself by his ignorance, the young lady uttered an aristocratic squeak, and darted away with the utmost swiftness, and Bruin at the same instant found himself seized by a strong grip from behind. He turned round with a violence which threw his assailant a dozen paces off, into a pool of stagnant water, his own coat being slit right up the back by the movement; but he was at once attacked by half-a-dozen others, who seemed bent on his destruction. Bruin's great strength, however, served him in good stead; with his back against an old wall, he received the assaults of his adversaries with all his wonted ferocity: so that after ten minutes' fighting they drew off, leaving two of their number motionless on the ground, and a third struggling in vain to escape from the unsavoury hole where the whisk of Bruin's coat-tails had cast him. To this spot Bruin now proceeded: and sitting himself down on the edge, told the struggling dog he would help him out if he would divulge the meaning of this unexpected attack on him. The half-drowned cur, having supplicated the bear in vain to let him out before he commenced his narration, in accents sadly interrupted by his throat getting at intervals choked with dirty water, explained that himself and the others of his assailants were the attendants of one of the most noble families in Caneville; and that their master, learning from some member of Count von Bruin's household that he (the Count) intended meeting the eldest daughter at this spot to-night, had commanded a body of his servitors to be in readiness to fall upon him, and if possible take him prisoner, for presuming to raise or lower his eyes to a damsel of such standing.

Scarcely had Bruin heard this communication to an end, than, despite his promise and the poor dog's cries, he caught up a huge clod of earth and dropped it upon the devoted head of the struggling animal beneath. There was a great splash; a bubble or two came to the surface of the horrid pool, and the brutal deed was consummated. Yet at the same moment Bruin regretted he had been so precipitate, for he had not learnt *which* member of his household had played the spy. As he slowly left the place, he revolved this subject in his mind, but could come to no satisfactory conclusion; for though Fox appeared the most likely to be guilty, that worthy animal had made himself so useful to his master, that he could not well manage without him. He resolved, nevertheless, to wath him closely, and with this prudent resolve he reached his own door.

Very different was his appearance now to that which it presented on his issuing from the mansion. His coat torn to ribbons, his hat without a crown, his majestic frill rumpled and bloody, and his waistcoat without a single button left wherewith to restrain the exuberance of his linen. All his domestics were eager in their inquiries and offers of service; and Fox was so overpowering in his expressions of regret, that all suspicion vanished from Bruin's brain at once; and he attributed his informant's tale to some malicious calumny, invented to save his life and conceal the true cause of the attack upon him.

Our hero, finding that the paths of gallantry were filled with so much unpleasantness, resolved, like a prudent animal, to avoid them carefully in future; but as his desire for an introduction to society continued, he availed himself of the offer of his steward, who promised to procure him introductions to youth of the best families. The class with which Fox managed to bring him into connexion was the most worthless in Caneville, consisting of fast young dogs, who had a singular knack of reversing the order of nature, and going to bed when other animals were getting up, and thinking of rising when the discreet part of the world deemed it time to retire to rest. They had formed themselves into a sort of club, which they called the "Hard and Fast;" and, indeed, no terms could better express the habits of the members; for they gamed hard, drank hard, and talked hard, and lived so uncommonly *fast*, that it was not surprising that, though quite young, they should have many of the infirmities of age. To these worthies Bruin was an acquisition; for he was rich, ignorant, and gullible, whilst they were poor, grasping and unscrupulous. At the very first interview, all parties were equally delighted with each other; the ease of his new companion's manners was perfectly charming to Bruin, who considered it as a proof of their breeding, and every following day strengthened the connexion. Riotous parties of pleasure were constantly projected, for which their friend Von Bruin paid; banquets of the most expensive kind were always spread upon his table, at which his "dear fellows of the club" assisted—themselves; and, indeed, so closely were the bonds of union drawn, that after some time many of them could not bear to separate from their esteemed Count; and, therefore, took up their residence with him altogether.

If disorder were running such a race in company with the chief of the establishment, it may be conjectured that but little prudence or economy was displayed by the domestics. Extravagance of every kind ran riot amongst them as wildly as with their master, and they scrupled not at all sorts of petty pilfering, where there were none to censure or restrain. Fox, it is true, had the right, and possessed the influence requisite to do so; but, for some evil design of his own, possibly that his private pecadilloes might escape unnoticed, he seemed tacitly to submit to such a state of things, and in some instances actually encouraged it. And what could be the only result of such a life of dissipation, unchecked by a single effort of discretion? Why, nothing but the most irretrievable ruin; and ruined the bear was after three months' trial. And

when, following a banquet of several days' duration, the clouded intellects of the beast were made
sensible of the fact; when he found his table
cleared for the last time both of servants and
guests; when he traversed the various apartments
of his mansion, and observed all stripped, destroyed,
and echoing only to the sounds of his own foot-
steps; when, in fine, he discovered that he was
again alone in the world, without any portion of
that wealth which he had so sadly abused, and
with many new and vicious tastes which he had no
longer the means to gratify; bitter, indeed, were
his lamentations, shocking his fits of anger.   These
over, and they lasted long, long days, he seriously
examined the state of his affairs.   With the exception of the clothes upon his back, and a little change
in his pocket, he possessed absolutely nothing, so
effectually had his kind friends and faithful servants stripped him of his means : it was, therefore,
with no enviable feelings he left the house, his
house no longer, to seek a shelter for his head, and
a crust to appease his hunger.

He carefully avoided all his former resorts, and
directed his steps to those parts of the town where
poverty and vice were accustomed to assemble,
strong in their numbers and their misery.   Among
them he now strove to bury his griefs and acquire
consolation; but, alas, it was at the cost of every
hope of virtue which might yet lurk in his nature!
Characters like Bruin's, that are ever more apt to
imitate the evil than the good which is around
them can only acquire some fresh stain from every

contact with the wicked; and thus our bear sunk lower and lower in the scale of beasts, till many even of his new associates at last shrunk from him.

Some months after Bruin's being turned out of his splendid home there was a great fair held, just without the town of Caneville; and, as is usual in such cases, the lowest orders of the population assembled there. The Hon. Miss Greyhound, who had been a prey to feelings of a very mixed nature since her interrupted interview with Bruin, had joined a party of fashionables in an unusually long walk, and on their return to the city by a different route they came upon the fair. They stopped on a rising ground at some little distance to view the sports; then observing a group with a tall ungainly figure in the centre, a little to the right, they drew nearer to observe the proceedings. The great beast in the centre had his back to them, so they could not observe his features; but they saw that his clothes were ragged, his whole appearance very dirty, and his hat a particularly bad one. A dozen of heavy sticks were at his feet, and a couple were under his arm; whilst at some twenty paces distant two wands, with an ornament or trinket at the top of each, were stuck upright in a straw bag, ready to be thrown at by any adventurous puss or puppy who had a coin at his disposal. A couple of cats were lovingly walking at some distance, another was climbing a large tree which overhung the place, and a fourth was lazily seated high above; whilst in the neighbourhood of the animal who was presiding over the scene, were several dogs and a

10

cat or two waiting for their turn. The tall beast now altered his position, and the strongly marked features of a bear became plainly visible to the party; at the same time he caught sight of the fashionable group, and, with a fierce expression in his eye, surlily invited the well-dressed males to take their chance at "Three throws a penny."

A gentle howl from Miss G. was the only reply as the party hastily retreated; for she recognized in the dirty, degraded beast, who was presiding over this vulgar sport, the object she had once looked on with affection, the once wealthy Count von Bruin.

<hr>

PROGRESS.

THE fair of Caneville was like fairs in most other parts of the world, and contained the usual elements of fun and wickedness, toys and dirt, sweets and other messes. As all these various ingredients looked best at night, when the broad sun was withdrawn and an artificial light very feebly supplied its place, it was towards evening that the fair began to fill, and doubtful characters to ply their various vocations. It was matter of remark that there was much more quarrelling and ill-humour in the fair this particular year, than there had been for several previous periods; and it was also observed that a tall and powerful bear—no other than our hero Bruin—was ever in the midst of it, either as an instigator or a principal. Th s circumstance made the authorities more than usually alert, and caused Master Bruin to be closely watched.

It was at the close of the last day, after many scenes of evil which it is not necessary to describe, that a serious disturbance arose in the part of the field where Bruin had his stand. Blows soon followed angry words; the contending parties flew at each other with great ferocity; growl followed growl, and bite succeeded bite, so that a good deal of blood was shed—ill blood; so, perhaps, better out than in;—and as Bruin's sticks were conveniently at hand as weapons of offence, they were soon seized upon, and used so indiscriminately, that almost every throw told. Many were stretched on the ground, and one of the mastiff-police was thought to be killed. This was a serious offence, indeed, and those who knew the penalty attending such a calamity instantly took to flight. They were as instantly pursued; and when about to be captured, with one voice denounced Bruin as the culprit; though, in fact, it was not he who had struck the blow, and they knew it: but such was his known ferocity and ill-temper, that to shield themselves they were ready to give up the wrong beast, whom no one loved, and whom every one would have suspected as the author of the calamity. So the bear, in spite of his protestations of innocence, and in spite too of a most furious resistance, in the course of which he got more than one savage bite from some small animal he had injured, he was dragged off to prison.

The place used for this purpose was a portion of a ruined castle, standing in the centre of the town, on the banks of the rivulet before spoken of; the ruin itself being of great antiquity, and having been evidently erected by a very different class of beings to that which formed the present population of Caneville. Several compartments were adapted for the purpose, all more or less secure; but the square stone chamber into which Bruin was thrust, was the strongest of them all. The door opening outwards was closed on him, and secured by a heavy mass of rock, which the united efforts of several of the police rolled against it; and having thus deposited the prisoner in safety, a couple mounted guard at the entrance, in case by any chance the great strength of the bear should succeed in removing the fastening. Bruin seemed, however, in no humour to make the experiment. Sore and worn out, he crawled into a corner and was soon fast asleep, resuming in his dream some of his old avocations. He woke at daylight, and immediately rose to examine his prison. The door he sniffed at, but passed by; the window was at so great a height from the floor that he could not reach it upon tiptoe, but he remarked that a very delicious puff of fresh air came down an aperture originally used as a chimney. He moved hastily towards it, and many feet above observed the blue sky, and the large branch of a tree waving over the aperture. Had Messieurs the Police been aware of Bruin's climbing propensities, they would scarcely have left this point unguarded; as it was, the bear

proceeded immediately to take advantage of it.
With a spring he caught hold of an opening formed
by a missing stone, and drawing his body up to his
paw, he stuck his foot into the hole and pressed his
broad back against the opposite side; a projecting
brick gave him a second hold, and then the difficulty was over, for the chimney narrowing, he
managed to get up by the simple pressure of his
knees and back, and the use of his broad and mus-
cular paws. A few seconds sufficed for him to
reach the top, on which he sat with his heels dang-
ling in the air, to enjoy the prospect and take
breath, while he deliberated on his farther pro
ceedings.

Meanwhile an inquiry had been entered upon
by the authorities of Caneville concerning the riot,
in which one of the police was alleged to have
been killed, but as the object of the inquiry limped
into the assembly during the sitting, it was not
considered worth while to hear evidence as to the
authors of his death; and as he, moreover, distinctly stated that the beast who struck the blow
was not a bear, it was ordered that the bear who
was in custody on the charge should be liberated
forthwith. Great was the surprise of his guards,
however, on proceeding to his prison, to find that
he had anticipated the verdict and had taken the
liberty of setting himself free; in what way was
pretty clear, as, on looking up the chimney, they
were no less amused than astonished to see him
just in the act of swinging himself on to the projecting branch of the tree and disappear from their

10*

view. They ran round into the court to mark the
end of Bruin's manœuvres, but he had been too
quick for them; not knowing of his being again a
free bear, and apprehensive of being pursued, he
had descended the tree with the utmost velocity,
climbed over a ruined wall, and dropping, not
lightly, into the stream, with a few bold strokes
reached the opposite shore, where he immediately
climbed a leafy oak, with the intention of waiting
till the hue and cry was over.

He kept his position very quietly all day, rather
surprised that no commotion should be visible in
and about the prison, of which he commanded a
good view; and as evening was falling he resolved
to descend, and, recrossing the stream higher up,
seek refuge in some one of his late haunts. Just
as he was about putting this resolution into effect
he heard voices beneath the tree, and lay quite
still to listen. But what was his astonishment, as
they drew nearer, to perceive that one of the two
foxes from whom the sounds proceeded, was his
former steward and factotum! His interest in their
movements was of course increased, and he listened,
with his ears and eyes bent down, to catch their
every syllable and look. The stranger Fox, it appeared, was about crossing the brook to the city,
and the other one had accompanied him thus far,
but refused to enter the town. On this, the following words reached Bruin's ear:—

Stranger.—I have noticed more than once,
cousin, that you avoid the town and yet I have

known you declare that no one but a cow could live in the country.

Fox.—True enough, my dear fellow; but since I left *his* service, you know, I don't care to run the risk of meeting him.

Stranger.—Ha! ha! I see. You are rather apprehensive he should seize you by the throat, and exclaim, "*My* money or *your* life!"

Fox.—Hush! hush! who knows what ears may be listening? Enough that I have a comfortable competency, and don't choose to run the risk of losing it.

Stranger.—Well, well, cousin, I say no more; but remember, your grandfather and mine never left his home for fear of meeting with a wolf who owed him a grudge, and was found dead in his bed, having been murdered by the very wolf after all. Come! you needn't look so down about it, old fellow; nothing half so bad, I hope, will come to you.—Ta! ta!

So saying, the stranger fox took leave of his cousin, and was soon on the opposite shore.

Fox waited till he saw him land, and then slowly turned to retrace his steps.

Scarcely, however, had he taken half-a-dozen paces, than a rushing noise smote his ears; and before he could raise his head a heavy body struck him between the shoulders, with a violence which dashed him flat on to the ground. He neither moved nor uttered a cry; his neck was broken. With a savage howl, Bruin—for it is easy to guess that it was he—put his heavy paw upon the other's

chest; but finding all still, he examined his clothes
whence he took all the valuables. He paused in
his work to chide his own precipitancy; for had he
followed the Fox he might, perhaps, have learnt
his dwelling and regained great part of his property.
It was too late now; so, giving a savage kick on
the face of the unfortunate animal, he heaped it
over with leaves, and pursued his original intention of regaining the city, and before night was
once more beneath the roof of a late associate.

He remained for several days perfectly quiet and
inactive; but finding no search was instituted for
him, he, little by little, resumed his old habits, and,
as many knew to their cost, his old overbearing
temper.

Among the tastes prevailing to an immense extent in the community of Caneville, a great love
for those dainties which we call oysters had always been remarkable. It occurred to Bruin, as
he had now some trifling capital, that he would
invest a portion in such articles as made up the
fixtures and stock-in-trade of an oyster-merchant:
the former expression is, however, a misnomer, for
the stall and tubs included under the term fixtures
would be more properly described as moveables.
This was soon effected; and Bruin having chosen
a semi-respectable thoroughfare, where he would
have a chance of a customer or two from the upper, and would not be too far removed from the
lower class of Caneville society, he planted his
stall, arranged his tubs, spruced up his own person
with the addition of a most formidable collar and

a most doubtfully clean apron, and vociferated his
"Penny a lot, pups! penny a lot!" in a way
which greatly edified the bystanders. The bystanders were, however, soon induced to become
purchasers, for very few of them could resist oysters,
if they had the wherewithal to purchase them; and
Bruin's natives were so fine and fresh, and he had
so clever a knack of opening them, that it was
really worth the money to see him do that, and
many actually went there for the purpose: so that
it really seemed he had at last hit upon a business
for which he was entirely suited, which met also
the public views, and that a short time would enable him, with prudence, to save provision for his
old age.

But, alas, the perversity of bears! No sooner
did anything like a smile from Fortune's face alight
upon him, than he seemed resolved by his uncom-
promising temper, to turn it to a frown! As long
as the business was new to him, he took pleasure
in performing the duties belonging to it in a proper
manner; a little roughly, it may be, but still—
properly. Directly it grew familiar, he became
careless; and he had a most wilful habit of aggra-
vating his customers, which could not, of course,
continue without seriously injuring his trade. For
instance, when some pert young puppy would come
forward, and civilly enough request his "one or
two penn'orth of natives," Bruin would first insist
on having the money paid down, and would then
tantalise his customer by offering him the opened
oyster and hastily withdrawing it just as the impa-

tient jaws were about to close on the desired morsel,
and so on to the end, to the vast irritation of many
an irascible little animal.

And a day came when this same spirit caused
the upset of his trade, and set a veto upon his "selling the natives," at least in Caneville, for the future.
A fox and a young terrier had both paid their
money, and were eagerly waiting for their oysters,
disturbing by their clamour a grave old dog who
was licking the shell of his last penn'orth, when a
domestic from a wealthy family, arrayed in a su-
perb livery cloak, came up to order a lot for his
master. The usual game—if it can be called so,
when all the fun was on one side, was being played
—three distinct efforts had been made by Terrier
to get his second instalment, when, in the struggle
which ensued, the vinegar-bottle was knocked over,
the cork came out, and the perfidious liquid, highly
adulterated with vitriol (for, to their shame be it
spoken, the dogs of distillers did not hesitate to
endanger the lives of the inhabitants by such practices), poured in full volume over the rich livery-
cloak of the servant, which was completely spoiled.
The master, who was as powerful as he was avari-
cious, made a formal complaint against Bruin and
his stall as a nuisance; and as it was impossible
even in Caneville to obtain perfect justice, the report, without other inquiry, was taken as correct,
and Bruin, boiling with rage, had the mortification
of seeing his tubs smashed, his stall destroyed, and
his " natives" scattered all abroad without being
able to strike a blow in their defence.

DOWN HILL.

BRUIN, that great animal, was seated on a bank overhanging the river, which, being shallow at this spot, brawled loudly over its pebbly bed, some parts of which were dry. It was at such a distance from the city, that all the noises common to its streets were united into one buzz or hum, and the whole scene was well adapted to suggest meditations upon private matters, or the affairs of the world in general. Yet Bruin did not seem influenced by any such reflections: if one might venture a guess from the appearance of his physiognomy, one would say that nothing in particular occupied his brains; true, his looks were black, and his head was cast down, his eyes, as usual, were cunning and ferocious, but then they were always so, and consequently presented no index of what was passing within.

Suddenly his features brightened, his face assumed an expression of interest, and he put his paw gently behind him to secure a stone, whilst his gaze was intently fixed on a dry spot of the bed below. Following the direction of his look, one might have perceived an uncommonly fat frog pulling with all his strength at the leg of another one whose body was hidden behind a heap of pebbles, and certainly the sight was one to amuse a wiser head than a bear's. The standing-place of the paunchy little animal being very green and slippery, and the leg which he so tightly clasped belonging to a fellow creature of no ordinary robustness, the struggle was diversified every few seconds by the fat fellow toppling on to his nose or back, or being dragged behind the heap, and then suddenly reappearing, still holding with passionless determination to that devoted leg, and tumbling about without uttering a syllable. It was when the greater part of his body was exposed to view in a position more comical than dignified, so great were his exertions, that Bruin's stone, cast with unerring aim, descended upon the unfortunate frog. It hit him upon the softest and most projecting part of his back, and had the effect of raising him instantly into a perpendicular position, when looking round and observing the huge beast above about to repeat the application, he clapped his broad hand over the wounded place, and limped hastily away ; nor could all the enticements of the bear, conveyed, it is true, in very unflattering language, induce him to expose his person to the chances of a second throw.

Bruin's attention was shortly after aroused anew, by observing a wretched old dog tottering under the weight of a large bundle, strapped upon his back, which he was conveying to the city. He came within a few feet of the bear, whom he knew slightly, and casting down his load, which he seemed to have brought from a distance, wiped his face with his ragged tail. Bruin was the first to speak.

Bruin (with a grunt).—Hard at work as usual, eh ! Flip?

Flip.—Yes, Master Bruin, these are hard times; no bone to pick without it, you know.

Bruin (with a very emphatic grunt).—That depends; some have lots of bones, and fine clothes, and warm beds, without doing anything harder for them than picking the one, putting on the other, and sleeping on the third;—but never mind that; what have you got there in your bundle, old fellow?

Flip.—Why, songs, Master Bruin; and you, who are fond of music, might make mints of money by selling 'em, if you'd only choose to do it.

Bruin (pricking up his ears).—Ah, Master Flip! and in what way?

Flip.—Why, here are all the new songs that have been sung for the last ten seasons by the Caterwaullic Society at their new Hall, and a lot more besides, printed in half-a-dozen columns three times as long as my tail, and all for a penny. Why, the very names of them are worth double the money. I'm going to take this package to old Powtry the bookseller, and, if you're in want of a job, I'll recommend you to him as one of the venders.

The proposal in Bruin's state of finance was not to be despised, for since his forced retirement from business, he had found his stomach and his pockets, by a very natural sympathy, suffering from precisely the same complaint—a degree of emptiness, namely—which there seemed no chance of finding a remedy for; but he had sundry doubts as to his capabilities for the new employment he was about seeking, particularly as he was aware his reputation was more notorious than favourable. To his surprise, however, though his person was well known to the individual Powtry, not the slightest objection seemed to be made on the score of anything. The terms of his agreement, alas! not remarkably liberal, were arranged; Bruin spent a couple of days in conning over his task, and forgetting to thank the poor dog who had procured him his situation, he once more entered the busy streets of Caneville to add his bass voice to the other cries of that populous city. His appearance, as he made his way into the centre of the most active thoroughfare, holding in one paw his lists of songs—longer than most of the inhabitants—whilst his other was thrust into his trowsers' pocket; the impudent leer upon his face, as he surveyed his audience, and the careless set of his clothes, which, big as he was, seemed a size too capacious for him,—immediately attracted a crowd. A butcher's dog, who had been ordered to make all speed to No. 10 in this same street with a leg of mutton in his basket, stayed to gape and listen, although he was standing opposite No. 9. A young pup from a neighbouring alley ran out at the sound of his voice to learn the news. A spaniel, with long curly hair and medicine-basket on his arm, could not resist the temptation of just stopping to hear, though three servants of one of his master's patients were scouring the streets in search of him; nor could an eminent vocalist of the feline tribe, la Signorina Pussetta Scracciolini, pass by without lending an ear to the wonderful list of melodies,

There was another figure, too, who slackened her pace as she was passing the group, and by an irresistible impulse seemed compelled to draw near and listen; she was richly dressed in mantle and hood, which, thrown gracefully back, displayed a head and neck of aristocratic proportions; she seemed ill, however, and weak, for her delicate paws were resting on a stick, as though such aid were requisite, whilst her short breathing seemed to hint that her sorrows were bringing her nearer to her doom. She must have been once possessed of considerable beauty, and even now there was enough remaining to distinguish the Hon. Miss Greyhound.

Thus surrounded, Bruin vociferated with all the power of his lungs,—

"O...O...O...O...O...Y...........A! Never were such times! Here you are! only look! Double your own length of songs for one penny! Enough paper to make yourselves a coat to wrap yourselves in melody! Only one penny! Five hundred of the choicest songs of the Caterwaulic and Puppeeyan Amalgamated Harmonic Societies; and upwards of five hundred more of the most popular ditties of Caneville, and all for one penny!!"

And then he croaked forth the following doggrel (the most acceptable poetry, by the way, of the city), in which the titles of the songs were dragged in, without any regard to order, to make up a rhyme:

"Here's ' What's a Clock!'
And 'Like a rock
He stood upon his dignity;'

> With ' Pups alive,'
> And ' We are Five,'   .
>   And dozens more.   Who'll buy! who'll buy!
> Here's 'Puss was out,'
> And 'Piggy's snout
>   Was longer far than I can tell ;'
> With 'Merry Dogs,'
> And 'Yellow Frogs'
>   In scores, I'm ready here to sell.
> Here's 'Burning sighs,'
> And 'Ah! those eyes!'
>   And 'Songs for kittens newly born ;'
> With 'Stay, oh, stay!'
> And 'Don't say nay,'
>   And some no worse for being worn.
> Here's 'Love's an ass!'
> And 'Pass the glass,'
>   And 'Jocky is the dog for me ;'
> Here's 'Did you ever!'
> 'No, I never!'
>   And 'I hope it yet may be,'
>   And all for one penny!"

And thus he went dòwn the street disposing of his wares with wonderful rapidity, and producing sundry forced accompaniments to his own wretched song by treading on the toes of all the pups who were attracted by curiosity to his vicinity.

A second and a third supply was exhausted before the canine and feline public of Caneville got tired of purchasing their own measure of song; whether a fourth would have been successful there was no chance of discovering, for Old Powtry looked in vain for Bruin with the proceeds of the last lot. Day after day passed by and still he was absent, until it was deemed necessary to have a search after him. For some time he eluded all inquiries, as he well knew his fate if his hiding-place were discovered; for having appropriated the money of his master to his own use, he was fully aware that his person would have to pay the penalty of his transgression. He skulked about the lowest purlieus of the city, among curs of the most degraded character, as dirty and negligent in body as they were debased in mind, until, in hourly fear of being betrayed, he felt that the worst certainty would be preferable to such a state of suspense and alarm, so resolved to deliver himself up and brave the worst. He was again cast into prison: for that he was prepared; but he was not prepared for the wretched place of confinement to which he was now condemned. On being first thrust into it, he could not behold all its horror; but when his eyes got accustomed to the semi-darkness, he found himself in a dismal cell under ground, half full of water from the overflowing of the river, and teeming with numerous crawling, slimy things. A little hole, half choked with earth and stones, let in all the place possessed of light and air; and as the only air which could ever visit the place had to pass over a bed of stagnant mud ere it reached the spot, it possessed but few refreshing properties.

Bruin, who had in his despair given himself quietly up to the authorities, thinking probably that by the very act he might procure some mitigation of his sentence, now that he perceived his doom, gave way to one of those fearful bursts of rage which no experience had succeeded in teaching him to curb. He howled till the dirt sticking

about the vaulted ceiling, and the earth choking **up**
the air-hole, dropped piecemeal to the ground, and
every insect that had ears covered them up the
best way it could to prevent its becoming instan-
taneously deafened by the horrid sound; then
tearing round and round and round the confined
space of his cell, till there seemed to him fifty windows instead of one, and the single door appeared
suddenly placed in every part of the miserable
vault,—he struck his head against the rugged wall
of his prison, and toppled over senseless on to the
ground.

AT REST.

IT is not easy to say how long Bruin remained
insensible, but it must have been some time;
for when he recovered himself, there was a feeling
of weakness about him as though he had been
fasting long. His head, too, felt sadly dizzy as he
rose from his cold bed and pushed his nose against
the hole of a window to procure a little air. From
this he withdrew to pace his narrow cell; and as
the turning round increased his giddiness, on reaching the opposite wall he retraced his steps backwards, and so continued for a full hour, gently
moving his head meanwhile to the right and left,
as was his wont. Then getting into the driest
corner, he threw himself of a heap on the ground,
and mechanically resuming the **old** family practice
of sucking his paw, tried to bring his mind to bear

upon his situation. But this was a matter of no little difficulty, for the late events of his life had tended very considerably to weaken an intellect that was never remarkable for strength; and so he sat, and relapsed into a dozy state, where forgetfulness, for the most part, presided. At times, it is true, he would wake up, and the old fire lighting in his eyes, he would dash his paw on the ground as he observed the prison-walls close around him; but the feeling was momentary, and it was evident that the indulgence of his evil passions had so far clouded his reason, that a few weeks' solitary confinement would deprive him of all power of reflection for ever.

Evening had come again, though it was dark night in Bruin's cell, and had been so for hours; when suddenly he heard, or fancied he heard, his name uttered in a loud whisper. A fear he had never before experienced, an apprehension of he knew not what, stole over him; and it was not till the voice, a little louder, exclaimed,—

"Bruin! Bruin, I say!" that he dared venture a reply; when, after an effort, he said,—

"Who calls?"

"A friend," was the ready answer.

"A friend!" exclaimed Bruin, savagely; "then you can't be seeking *me*, for I have got no friends."

"Come, come, Bruin," said the voice again, "don't be testy; it's I, the Captain, and you know I never played you false."

Bruin now, indeed, recognized the voice as that of, perhaps, the most desperate dog in Cane-

ville. He was a bloodhound of large size and formi
dable strength, and such ferocity and daring, that
few cared to come into contact with him, lest by some
chance they should be involved in a quarrel which
could only have a disastrous termination. Public
report fixed more than one deep crime upon this
canine desperado; but still, somehow, he escaped
the power of the law. Bruin felt flattered at his
attention, and inquired what had brought him there.

"Why," replied the Captain, "this is the third
time I have been here already; but though I have
called out your name so loudly that I expected to
alarm the guard, I have got no answer till to-night.
I shouldn't have come back again, for I thought
you were dead."

"So I have been nearly, Captain," answered
Bruin; "but I am not quite gone yet, you hear.
Now you *have* found me alive, though, what is it
you want; and how can I, shut up here, be of any
interest to you?"

"Listen to me, Bruin," said the Captain, as he
squeezed his nose into the tiny window, and dropped his voice to a low whisper; "if you were out,
and at liberty, would you feel inclined to join me
and one or two others in a job we intend to come
off to-night?"

Bruin hastened to reply, but the Captain interrupted him, saying,—

"Don't be in a hurry to make a promise, until
you know what it is; for, shut up here as you are,
you can't betray the secret if you would, so I don't
mind revealing it. Four of us mean to break into

old Lord Greyhound's house to-night, where we hear there's money enough to enrich us for our lives; but as we're likely to have some hard work and stout resistance, and think we are not strong enough yet for the business, we should like you to join us, if you choose to do so.

Bruin reflected a moment, where reflection was ruin. Had he at once and scornfully rejected the horrible temptation, there would still have been hope for him; but, besides the prospect of liberty, though he did not yet know how that was to be effected, there was the chance of enriching himself once again; and, above all, there was a prospect of revenge against the dog who had once sought his life, because he had been selected as an object of preference by his daughter. His meditations, therefore, were at once brought to an end, by his resolution to accept the proposal; but before he did so, the caution he had acquired by associating with such beasts as the Captain made him say,—

"Let us understand each other clearly. You said just now, 'if I were out and at liberty;' have you, then, the power to set me free?"

"Provided you will be of the party, and agree to our terms," answered the Captain.

"And how if I refuse?" pursued Bruin.

"Why," replied the Captain, quickly and ferociously, "you'll stop there till you starve."

"I accept your offer," said Bruin, after the slightest possible pause; "and I would have done so without the alternative, for private reasons of my own· so let me out, old fellow, as fast as you like."

"And you give your word?" said the Captain.

"The word of a bear," replied Bruin.

The other exclaimed,—

"All right! I shall see you again in half an hour."

Never did half hour seem so long. As minute after minute flew by, there broke upon Bruin's misty brain a notion that, perhaps, this was only a trick of the Captain's to get him to declare his willingness to join any desperate deed in order to ruin him; but then, again, he could discover no reason for such enmity, and could see no advantage accruing to that individual by such a course. At the very idea, however, of such betrayal, his teeth gnashed together, his eyes glared in that darkness like two live coals, and he involuntarily crossed his huge paws over his chest as though hugging some imaginary enemy. But he recovered his self-possession on hearing a grating noise at the other side of the cell, which gradually became louder, until at last a gust of air, which revived his spirits, came whistling round the vault, and told that his path was open. The Captain, too, was in an instant by his side to confirm it. He passed through an aperture, caused by an open iron door, preceded by his companion, who had, however, first cautiously reclosed and fastened up the secret entrance; and as they traversed a damp and dark tunnel, the Captain explained the mystery, by saying this place had been known to him some time, though it was unsuspected by the authorities; and that the exterior entrance was so covered up by brambles, that no one ignorant of

the spot could ever imagine what lay behind, or
would care to explore the threatening passage, if
by any chance they discovered it.

As Bruin was exhausted for want of food, and it
still wanted some hours of the time appointed for
their undertaking, they proceeded to one of the old
resorts and regaled most heartily, the sense of
liberty after his confinement raising the bear's
spirits to the highest pitch. At length the time
agreed on arrived, and the party, prepared for their
desperate and wicked undertaking, set out.

It has been mentioned in a previous part of this
history, that Lord Greyhound was one of the principal grandees in Caneville, both as regarded fortune and family, and that he lived in a palace be-
fitting his condition. A crowd of domestics belonged to his household, but the Captain was
aware that their cribs were remote, and that but
little in the shape of resistance was to be feared
from them, should they be aroused. Still great
caution was requisite, for if they did not bite they
could bark, and that would be equally as fatal to
their success on this occasion. The only difficulty
to be got over was the vigilance of a porter who
slept below, whose fidelity to his master had been
tried on more than one occasion, although what
made such attachment singular in this instance
was the fact that the said porter was one of the
feline tribe,—a cat, in fact, of large dimensions,
and peculiarly savage nature. Bruin, however,
took upon himself the task of quieting this servant
and keeping watch below, whilst the others should

ransack the mansion, a place of rendezvous being appointed where they were to meet in case of alarm.

To avoid suspicion they proceeded alone to the scene of their intended crime, and, favoured by darkness, they reached it unchallenged. Having gently tried the fastenings in one or two places, they resolved to make the attempt at a small door at the back, which seemed the most weakly guarded. Bruin pushed it first quietly with his huge shoulder, and finding it gradually yielding, without farther ado he placed his knee against the lower panel, and, with less noise than might have been expected, sent the door flying from its fastenings. He was the first to enter, though the others were close behind; but he had not taken two steps within the house than he saw, as he thought, two balls of fire on the floor before him,—it was his last look of worldly things,—for at the same moment the porter Cat, for it was he, sprang at the huge giant like a fury, and dug his long and pointed talons into Bruin's eyes. With a howl so dreadful, so awful in its intense agony and rage, that it seemed to spring from a supernatural source, the affrighted beast rolled over and over in his pain, crushing the Cat to death in his struggles; then feeling, even amidst his suffering, the necessity of safety, he rose to his feet, and ran on, on, on, he knew not whither, till he felt himself in the midst of water and heard the rushing which it made. So instantaneous had been the whole transaction that the truth was never rightly known. The family— nay, the neighbourhood—aroused by the horrid noise rushed to the spot, to find the faithful porter dead, with every bone shattered; the door was open, but no creature was there to tell the tale. One alone suspected it—one to whom that cry of agony was the death-blow; for, two days after the event, the Hon. Miss Greyhound slept with her fathers, the victim of a misplaced and unworthy attachment.

And Bruin, where was he? Alas! poor beast! Three days after this event he was discovered by the authorities, half dead with pain, and led back to prison, which he had left with so little ceremony. His senses, however, were so bewildered by his situation, that he could neither explain how he had escaped from his dungeon, nor the cause of his present deplorable condition; perhaps, too, he deemed it more prudent to be silent on both these matters. His judges, nevertheless, taking into consideration his now helpless state, and rightly thinking his powers of mischief were much abated by the loss of his eyes, pardoned his previous offence, and thrust him alone and helpless on the world.

For many a long year did the ill-fated animal drag on his wearisome existence, living on the charity—the scanty charity—of Caneville. Deprived of sight, no longer able to acquire a livelihood by his labour, weary, and full of remorse, he daily took his round through the public streets, soliciting a penny for the "poor blind." A dog, induced for a weekly trifle and the prospect of an extra bone or two thrown to him sometimes by the compassionate as they went their melancholy way,

12

led him in his wanderings. At first, however, either from ignorance or carelessness, or a currish malice, he would often guide his helpless master into positions of difficulty and danger, from which he could scarce have extricated himself but for the assistance of some benevolent passers-by; though his situation in such cases—be it said to the shame of the inferior population of Caneville—too often excited derision and laughter, instead of aid and consolation. Once, indeed, he was seriously hurt by the wilful inattention of his guide; for, tottering along as usual one fine morning with his staff in one hand, the string attached to the dog's collar in the other, and his head with the sightless eyes raised sadly in the air, while he uttered his plaintive cry of "Have pity on the poor blind!" the last word was suddenly converted from a doleful whine to a howl of pain as his body came in contact with a post which stood right across his path. Time, which cures all things, brought at last an effectual remedy to his sufferings, and that remedy was death! Ere that great foe or friend relieved poor Bruin, he had learnt to be repentant of his former life, and was often known to reprove in others any tendency to those faults of temper or disposition which had been his own ruin. If he could have recovered the use of his eyes and have mingled once more with the business of life, it is a question whether he would have acted up to the precepts which he now inculcated; but as the experiment was never tried, nor could be, it is but charitable to think the best.

Months after he had departed this sinful world, a sturdy traveller, with a particularly wide mouth and short address, entered the city of Caneville. He stated that he was a native of the place, and had been wandering far away in other lands. He made various inquiries concerning former inhabitants of the town, and among others asked for Bruin. His life, much as I have recounted it, was told to him, and long did the stranger ruminate over the details. Many portions of it were, indeed, known to him, for the traveller was no other than our old acquaintance Tom; but all was interesting.

When he had heard it to the end, he uttered these only words, which might, indeed, serve for moral and poor Bruin's epitaph:—

"Ah! he was a Great Bear!"

A TALK ABOUT TIGERS.

I NEED not describe a tiger. You have seen one, or the picture of one. He is the great *striped* cat. The large *spotted* ones are not tigers. They are either jaguars, or panthers, or leopards, or ounces, or cheetahs, or servals. But there is no danger of your mistaking the tiger for any other animal. He is the largest of the feline tribe —the lion alone excepted—and individual tigers have been measured as large as the biggest lion. The shaggy mane that covers the neck and shoulders of an old male lion gives him the appearance of being of greater dimensions than he really is. Skin him and he would not be larger than an old he-tiger also divested of his hide.

Like the lion, the tiger varies but little in form or color. Nature does not sport with these powerful beasts. It is only upon the meaner animals she plays off her eccentricities. The tiger may be seen with the ground color of a lighter or deeper yellow, and the stripes or bars more or less black; but the same general appearance is preserved, and the species can always be recognized at a glance.

The range or habitat of the tiger is more limited than that of the lion. The latter exists throughout the whole of Africa, as well as the southern half of Asia; whereas the tiger is found only in the southeastern countries of Asia, and some of the larger islands of the Indian Archipelago. Westwardly, his range does not extend to this side of the Indus river, and how far north in Asia is uncertain. Some naturalists assert that there are tigers in Asia as far north as the Obi River. This would prove the tiger to be not altogether a tropical animal, as he is generally regarde It is certain that tigers once did inhabit the countries around the Caspian Sea. There lay Hyrcania; and several Roman writers speak of the Hyrcanian tigers. They could not have meant any of the spotted cats,—ounce, panther, or leopard,—for the Romans knew the difference between these and the striped or true tiger. If, then, the tiger was an inhabitant of those trans-Himalayan regions in the days of Augustus, it is possible it still exists there, as we have proofs of its existence in Mongolia and northern China at the present day.

Were we to believe some travelers, we should have the tiger, not only in Africa, but in America. The jaguar is the tiger (*tigre*) of the Spanish Americans; and the panther, leopard, and cheetah, have all done duty as " tigers " in the writings of old travelers in Africa.

The true home of this fierce creature is the hot jungle-covered country that exists in extended tracts in Hindostan, Siam, Malaya, and parts of China. There the tiger roams undisputed lord of the thicket and forest; and although the lion is also found in these countries, he is comparatively a rare animal, and, from being but seldom met with, is less talked about or feared.

We, who live far away from the haunts of these great carnivora, can hardly realize the terror which is inspired by them in the countries they infest.

In many places human life is not safe; and men go out upon a journey, with the same dread of meeting a tiger, that we would have for an encounter with a mad dog. This dread is by no means founded upon mere fancies or fabricated stories. Every village has its true tales of tiger attacks and encounters, and every settlement has its list of killed or maimed. You can scarce credit such a relation, but it is a well-known fact that whole districts of fertile country have from time to time been abandoned by their inhabitants out of pure fear of the tigers and panthers which infested them! Indeed, similar cases of depopulation have occurred in South America, caused by a far less formidable wild beast—the jaguar.

In some parts of India the natives scarce attempt resistance to the attack of the tiger. Indeed, the superstition of his victims aids the fierce monster in their destruction. They regard him as being gifted with supernatural power, and sent by their gods to destroy; and under this conviction yield themselves up, without making the slightest resistance.

In other parts, where races exist possessed of more energy of character, the tiger is hunted eagerly, and various modes of killing or capturing him are practiced in different districts.

Sometimes a bow is set with poisoned arrows, and a cord attached to the string. A bait is then placed on the ground, and arranged in such a way that the tiger on approaching it, presses against the cord, sets the bow-string free, and is pierced by the arrow—the poison of which eventually causes his death.

A spring-gun is set off by a similar contrivance, and the tiger shoots himself.

The log-trap or "dead fall"—often employed by American backwoodsmen for capturing the black bear—is also in use in India for trapping the tiger. This consists of a heavy log or beam so adjusted upon the top of another one by a prop or "trigger," as to fall and crush whatever animal may touch the trigger. A bait is also used for this species of trap.

Hunting the tiger upon elephants is a royal sport in India, and is often followed by the Indian rajahs, and sometimes by British sportsmen and officers of the English army. This sport is, of course, very exciting; but there is nothing of a *ruse* practised in it. The hunters go armed with rifles and spears; and attended by a large number of natives, who beat the jungle and drive the game within reach of the sportsmen. Many lives are sacrificed in this dangerous sport; but those who suffer are usually the poor peasants employed as beaters; and an Indian rajah holds the lives of a score or two of his subjects as lightly as that of a tiger itself.

It is said the Chinese catch the tiger in a box-trap, which they bait simply with a looking-glass. The tiger, on approaching the looking-glass, perceives his own shadow, and mistaking it for a rival, rushes forward to the trap, frees the trigger, and is caught. It may be that the Chinese practice such a method. That part is likely enough; but it is not likely that they take many tigers this way.

Perhaps you may be of opinion that the plan which Ossaroo was about to follow was quite as absurd as that of the Chinese. It certainly did sound very absurd to his companions, when he first told them that it was his intention *to catch the tiger by birdlime !*

A TIGER TAKEN BY BIRDLIME.

THE plan of the shikarree was put to the test sooner than any of them expected. They did not look for the tiger to return before sunset, and they had resolved to pass the night among the branches of the banyan in order to be out of the way of danger. The tiger might take it into his head to stroll into their camp; and although, under ordinary circumstances, these fierce brutes have a dread of fire, there are some of them that do not regard it, and instances have occurred of tigers making their attack upon men who were seated close to a blazing pile! Ossaroo knew of several such cases, and had, therefore, given his advice, that all of them should pass the night in the tree. It was true the tiger could easily scale the banyan if the notion occurred to him; but unless they made some noise to attract his attention, he would not be likely to discover their whereabouts. They had taken the precaution to erect a platform of bamboos among the branches, so as to serve them for a resting-place.

After all, they were not under the necessity of

resorting to this elevated roost,—at least for the purpose of passing the night there. But they occupied it for a while; and during that while they were witnesses to a scene that for singularity, and comicality as well, was equal to anything that any of them had ever beheld.

It wanted about half an hour of sunset, and they were all seated around the camp fire, when a singular noise reached their ears. It was not unlike the " whirr " made by a thrashing-machine--which any one must have heard who has traveled through an agricultural district. Unlike this, however, the sound was not prolonged, but broke out at intervals, continued for a few seconds, and then was silent again.

Ossaroo was the only one of the party who, on hearing this sound, exhibited any feelings of alarm. The others were simply curious. It was an unusual sound. They wondered what was producing it—nothing more.

They quite shared the alarm of the shikarree, when the latter informed them that what they heard was neither more nor less than the "purr " of a tiger !

Ossaroo communicated this information in an ominous whisper, at the same instant crouching forward towards the main trunk of the banyan, and beckoning to the others to follow him.

Without a word they obeyed the sign, and all

three climbed, one after the other, up the trunk, and silently seated themselves among the branches.

By looking through the outer screen of leaves, and a little downward, they could see the quarters of venison hanging from the limb, and also the whole surface of the ground where the glittering leaves were spread.

Whether the haunch which the tiger had stolen on the preceding night had not been sufficient for his supper, and he had grown hungry again before his usual feeding-time, is uncertain. But certain it is that Ossaroo, who understood well the habits of this striped robber, did not expect him to return so soon. He looked for him after darkness should set in. But the loud "purr-r-r" that at intervals came booming through the jungle, and each time sounding more distinctly, showed that the great cat was upon the ground.

All at once they espied him coming out of the bushes, and on the other side of the rivulet—his broad whitish throat and breast shining in contrast with the dark green foliage. He was crouching just after the manner of a house-cat when making her approach to some unwary bird—his huge paws spread before him, and his long back hollowed down—a hideous and fearful object to behold. His eyes appeared to flash fire, as he bent them upon the tempting joints hanging high up on the branch of the tree.

After reconnoitering a little, he gathered up his long back into a curve, vaulted into the air, and cleared the rivulet from bank to bank. Then, without further pause, he trotted nimbly forward, and stopped directly under the hanging joints.

Ossaroo had purposely raised the meat above its former elevation, and the lowest ends of the joints were full twelve feet from the ground. Although the tiger can bound to a very great distance in a horizontal direction, he is not so well fitted for springing vertically upwards, and therefore the tempting morsels were just beyond his reach. He seemed to be somewhat nonplussed at this—for upon his last visit he had found things rather different—but after regarding the joints for a moment or two, and uttering a loud snuff of discontent, he flattened his paws against the ground, and sprang high into the air.

The attempt was a failure. He came back to the earth without having touched the meat, and expressed his dissatisfaction by an angry growl.

In another moment, he made a second spring upwards. This time, he struck one of the quarters with his paw, and sent it swinging backwards and forwards, though it had been secured too well to the branch to be in any danger of falling.

All at once, the attention of the great brute became directed to a circumstance which seemed to puzzle him not a little. He noticed that there

was something adhering to his paws. He raised
one of them from the ground, and saw that two
or three leaves were sticking to it. What could
be the matter with the leaves, to cling to his soles
in that manner? They appeared to be wet, but
what of that? He had never known wet leaves
stick to his feet any more than dry ones. Perhaps
it was this had hindered him from springing up
as high as he had intended! At all events, he did
not feel quite comfortable, and he should have
the leaves off before he attempted to leap again.
He gave his paw a slight shake, but the leaves
would not go. He shook it more violently, still
the leaves adhered! He could not make it out.
There was some gummy substance upon them,
such as he had never met with before in all his
travels. He had rambled over many a bed of fig-
leaves in his day, but had never set foot upon such
sticky leaves as these.

Another hard shake of the paw produced no
better effect. Still stuck fast the leaves, as if they
had been pitch plasters; one covering the whole
surface of his foot, and others adhering to its
edges. Several had even fastened themselves on
his ankles. What the deuce did it all mean?

As shaking the paw was of no use, he next
attempted to get rid of them by the only other
means known to him; that was by rubbing
them off against his cheeks and snout. He raised

the paw to his ears, and drew it along the side of
his head. He succeeded in getting most of them
off his foot in this way, but to his chagrin, they now
adhered to his head, ears, and jaws, where they felt
still more uncomfortable and annoying. These
he resolved to detach, by using his paw upon
them; but, instead of doing so, he only added to
their number, for, on raising his foot, he found
that a fresh batch of the sticky leaves had fastened upon it. He now tried the other foot, with
no better effect. It, too, was covered with gummy
leaves, that only became detached to fasten upon
his jaws, and stick there, in spite of all his efforts
to tear them off. Even some of them had got
over his eyes, and already half-blinded him!
But one way remained to get rid of the leaves
that had so fastened upon his head. Every time
he applied his paws, it only made things worse.
But there was still a way to get them off—so thought
he—by rubbing his head along the ground.

No sooner thought of than done. He pressed
his jaws down to the earth, and using his hind
legs to push himself along, he rubbed hard to rid
himself of the annoyance. He then turned over,
and tried the same method with the other side;
but, after continuing at this for some moments,
he discovered he was only making matters worse;
in fact, he found that both his eyes were now completely "bunged up," and that he was perfectly

blind! He felt, moreover, that his whole head, as well as his body, was now covered, even to the tip of his tail.

By this time he had lost all patience. He thought no longer of the venison. He thought only of freeing himself from the detestable plight in which he was placed. He sprang and bounded over the ground; now rubbing his head along the surface; now scraping it with his huge paws, and ever and anon dashing himself agains the stems of the trees that grew around. All this while, his growling, and howling, and screaming, filled the woods with the most hideous noises.

Up to this crisis, our travelers had watched his every movement, all of them bursting with laughter; to which, however, they dared not give utterance, lest they might spoil the sport. At length, Ossaroo knew that the time was come for something more serious than laughter; and descending from the tree with his long spear, he beckoned the others to follow with their guns.

The shikarree could have approached and thrust the tiger, without much danger; but, to make sure, the double-barrel, already loaded with ball, was fired at him along with Caspar's rifle, and one of the bullets striking him between the ribs, put an end to his struggles by laying him out upon the grass dead as a herring.

Upon examining him, they found that the fig-leaves so covered his eyes, as to render him completely blind. What prevented him from scratching them off with his huge claws was, that these were so wrapped up in the leafy envelope as to render them perfectly useless, and no longer dangerous, had any one engaged with him in close combat.

I have already said that there are many parts of India where the people live in great fear of the tigers—as well as lions, wild elephants, panthers, and rhinoceroses. These people have no knowledge of proper fire-arms. Some, indeed, carry the clumsy matchlock, which, of course, is of little or no service in hunting: and their bows, even with poisoned arrows, are but poor weapons when used in an encounter with these strong savage beasts.

Often a whole village is kept in a state of terror for weeks or months by a single tiger, who may have made his lair in the neighborhood, and whose presence is known by his repeated forays upon the cows, buffaloes, or other domesticated animals of the villagers. It is only after this state of things has continued for a length of time, and much loss has been sustained, that these poor people, goaded to desperation, at length assemble together, and risk an encounter with the tawny tyrant. In such encounters, human lives are frequently sacrificed, and generally some one of the party receives a blow or scratch from the tiger's paw which maims or lames him for the rest of his days.

But there is still a worse case than even this. Not unfrequently the tiger, instead of preying upon their cattle, carries off one of the natives themselves; and where this occurs, the savage monster, if not pursued and killed, is certain to repeat the offense. It is strange, and true as strange, that a tiger having once fed upon human flesh, appears ever after to be fonder of it than of any other food, and will make the most daring attempts to procure it. Such tigers are not uncommon in India, where they are known among the natives by the dreaded name of *man-eaters!*

It is not a little curious that the Caffres and other natives of South Africa, apply the same term to individuals of the lion species, known to be imbued with a similar appetite.

It is difficult to conceive a more horrible monster than a lion or tiger of such tastes; and in India, when the presence of such an one is discovered, the whole neighborhood lives in dread. Often when a British post is near, the natives make application to the officers to assist them in destroying the terrible creature—well knowing that our countrymen, with their superior courage, with their elephants and fine rifles, are more than a match for the jungle tyrant. When no such help is at hand, the shikarrees, or native hunters, usually assemble, and either take the tiger by stratagem, or risk their lives in a bold encounter. In many a tiger-hunt had Ossaroo distinguished himself, both by stratagem and prowess, and there was no mode of trapping or killing a tiger that was not known to him.

He was now called upon to give an exhibition of his craft, which, in point of ingenuity, was almost equal to the stratagem of the limed fig-leaves.

ABOUT TIGERS.

THE path which our travelers were following led them into one of the native villages of the Teräi, which lay in a sequestered part of the forest. The inhabitants of this village received them with acclamations of joy. Their approach had been reported before they reached the place, and a deputation of the villagers met them on the way, hailing them with joyful exclamations and gestures of welcome.

Karl and Casper, ignorant of the native language, and, of course, not comprehending what was said, were for some time at a loss to understand the meaning of these demonstrations. Ossaroo was appealed to to furnish an explanation.

"A man-eater," he said.

"A man-eater!"

"Yes, Sahib; a man-eater in the jungle."

This was not sufficiently explicit. What did Ossaroo mean? A man-eater in the jungle? What sort of creature was that? Neither Karl nor Casper had ever heard of such a thing before. They questioned Ossaroo.

The latter explained to them what was a man-eater. It was a tiger, so-called, as you already know, on account of its preying upon human beings. This one had already killed and carried off a man, a woman, and two children, besides large numbers of domestic animals. For more than three months it had infested the village, and kept the inhabitants in a state of constant alarm. Indeed, several families had deserted the place solely through fear of this terrible tiger; and those that remained were in the habit, as soon as night came on, of shutting themselves up within their houses, without daring to stir out again till morning. In the instance of one of the children, even this precaution had not served, for the fierce tiger had broken through the frail wall of bamboos, and carried the child off before the eyes of its afflicted parents!

Several times the timid but incensed villagers had assembled and endeavored to destroy this terrible enemy. They had found him each time in his lair; but, on account of their poor weapons and slight skill as hunters, he had always been enabled to escape from them. Indeed, on such occasions the tiger was sure to come off victorious, for it was in one of these hunts that the man had fallen a sacrifice. Others of the villagers had been wounded in the different conflicts with this pest of the jungle. With such a neighbor at their doors, no wonder they had been living in a state of disquietude and terror.

But why their joy at the approach of our travelers?

This was proudly explained by Ossaroo, who, of course, had reason to be proud of the circumstance.

It appeared that the fame of the shikarree, as a great tiger-hunter, had preceded him, and his name was known even in the Teräi. The villagers had heard that he was approaching, accompanied by two Feringhees (so Europeans are called by the natives of India), and they hoped, by the aid of the noted shikarree and the Feringhee Sahibs, to get rid of the dreaded marauder.

Ossaroo, thus appealed to, at once gave his promise to aid them. Of course the botanist made no objection, and Caspar was delighted with the idea. They were to remain all night at the village, since nothing could be done before night. They might have got up a grand battue to beat the jungle and attack the tiger in his lair, but what would have come of that? Perhaps the loss of more lives. None of the villagers cared to risk themselves in such a hunt, and that was not the way that Ossaroo killed his tigers.

Karl and Caspar expected to see their companion once more try his stratagem of the birdlime and the leaves.

Ossaroo had other resources besides the birdlime and the battue, and he at once set to work to prepare his plan. He had an ample stock of attendants, as the villagers worked eagerly, and ran hither and thither obedient to his nod. In front of the village there was a piece of open ground. This was the scene of operations.

Ossaroo first commanded four large posts to be brought, and set in the ground in a quadrangle of about eight feet in length and width. These posts when sunk firmly in their place stood full eight feet in height, and each had a fork at the top. On these forks four strong beams were placed horizontally, and then firmly lashed with rawhide thongs. Deep trenches were next dug from post to post, and in these were planted rows of strong bamboos four inches apart from each other—the bamboos themselves being about four inches in thickness. The earth was then filled in, and trodden firmly, so as to render the uprights immovable. A tier of similar bamboos was next laid horizontally upon the top, the ends of which, interlocking with those that stood upright, held the latter in their places. Both were securely lashed to the frame timbers—that had been notched for the purpose—and to one another, and then the structure was complete. It resembled an immense cage with smooth yellow rods, each four inches in diameter. The door alone was wanting, but it was not desirable to have a door.

Although it was intended for a "trap cage," the "bird" for which it had been constructed was not to be admitted to the inside.

Ossaroo now called upon the villagers to provide him with a goat that had lately had kids, and whose young were still living. This was easily procured. Still another article he required, but both it and the goat had been "bespoke" at an earlier hour of the day, and were waiting his orders. This last was the skin of a buffalo, such a one as we have already seen used by these people in crossing their rivers.

When all these things had been got ready it was near night, and no time was lost in waiting. With the help of the villagers, Ossaroo was speedily arrayed in the skin of the buffalo, his arms and limbs taking the place of animal's legs, with the head and horns drawn over him like a hood, so that his eyes were opposite the holes in the skin.

Thus metamorphosed, Ossaroo entered the bamboo cage, taking the goat along with him. The stake, that had been kept out for the purpose of admitting them within the enclosure, was now set into its place as firmly as the others; and this done, the villagers, with Karl and Caspar, retired to their houses, and left the shikarree and his goat to themselves.

A stranger passing the spot would have had no other thoughts than that the cage-like enclosure contained a buffalo and a goat. On closer examination it might have been perceived that this buffalo held, grasped firmly in its fore-hoofs, a strong bamboo spear; and that was all that appeared odd about it—for it was lying down like any other buffalo, with the goat standing beside it.

The sun had set, and night was now on. The villagers had put out their lights, and, shut up within their houses, were waiting in breathless expectation. Ossaroo on his part, was equally anxious—not from the fear of any danger, for he had secured himself against that. He was only anxious for the approach of the man-eater, in order that he might have the opportunity to exhibit the triumph of his hunter-skill.

He was not likely to be disappointed. The villagers had assured him that the fierce brute was in the habit of paying them a nightly visit, and prowling around the place for hours together. It was only when he had succeeded in carrying off some of their cattle that he would be absent for days—no doubt his hunger being for the time satiated; but as he had not lately made a capture, they looked for a visit from him that very night.

If the tiger should come near the village, Ossaroo had no fear that he could attract him to the spot. He had laid his decoy too well to fail in this. The goat, deprived of her young, kept up an incessant bleating, and the kids answered her

from one of the houses of the village. As the
hunter knew from experience that the tiger has a
particular relish for goat-venison, he had no fear
but that the voice of the animal would attract him
to the spot, provided he came near enough to hear
it.   In this the villagers assured him he would not
be disappointed.

He *was not disappointed;* neither was he kept
long in suspense. He had not been more than
half an hour in his buffalo disguise, before a loud
growling on the edge of the forest announced the
approach of the dreaded man-eater, and caused the
goat to spring wildly about in the inclosure, uttering at intervals the most piercing cries.

This was just what Ossaroo wanted. The tiger,
hearing the voice of the goat, needed no further
invitation; but in a few moments was seen trotting boldly up to the spot. There was no crouching on the part of the terrible brute. He had
been too long master there to fear anything he
might encounter, and he stood in need of a supper. The goat that he had heard would be just
the dish he should relish; and he had determined
on laying his claws upon her without more ado.
In another moment he stood within ten feet of
the cage!

The odd-looking structure puzzled him, and he
halted to survey it. Fortunately there was a
moon, and the light not only enabled the tiger to

see what the cage contained, but it also gave Ossaroo an opportunity of watching all his movements.

"Of course," thought the tiger, "it's an inclosure some of these simple villagers have put up to keep that goat and buffalo from straying off into the woods; likely enough, too, to keep me from getting at them. Well, they appear to have been very particular about the building of it. We shall see if they have made the walls strong enough."

With these reflections he drew near, and rearing upward caught one of the bamboos in his huge paw, and shook it with violence. The cane, strong as a bar of iron, refused to yield even to the strength of a tiger; and, on finding this, the fierce brute ran rapidly round the inclosure, trying it at various places, and searching for an entrance.

There was no entrance, however; and on perceiving that there was none, the tiger endeavored to get at the goat by inserting his paws between the bamboos. The goat, however, ran frightened and screaming to the opposite side, and so kept out of the way. It would have served the tiger equally well to have laid his claws upon the buffalo, but this animal very prudently remained near the center of the inclosure, and did not appear to be so badly scared withal. No doubt the coolness of the buffalo somewhat astonished the tiger, but in his endeavors to capture the goat, he did not stop to show his surprise, but ran round and round, now dashing forcibly against the bamboos, and now reaching his paws between them as far as his fore-legs would stretch.

All at once the buffalo was seen to rush toward him, and the tiger was in great hopes of being able to reach the latter with his claws, when, to his astonishment, he felt some hard instrument strike sharply against his snout, and rattle upon his teeth, while the fire flew from his eyes at the concussion. Of course it was the *horn* of the buffalo that had done this; and now, renderd furious by the pain, the tiger forgot all about the goat, and turned his attention toward revenging himself upon the animal who had wounded him. Several times he launched himself savagely against the bamboos, but the canes resisted all his strength. Just then it occurred to him that he might effect an entrance by the top, and with one bound he sprang upon the roof of the inclosure. This was just what the buffalo wished, and the broad white belly of his assailant, stretched along the open framework of bamboos, was now a fair mark for that terrible horn. Like a gleam of lightning it entered between his ribs; the red blood spouted forth, the huge man-eater screamed fiercely as he felt the deadly stab, and then, struggling for a few minutes, his enormous body lay stretched across tke rack, silent—motionless—dead !

A signal whistle from Ossaroo soon brought the villagers upon the spot. The shikarree and the goat were set free. The carcass of the man-eater was dragged into the middle of the village amidst shouts of triumph, and the rest of the night was devoted to feasting and rejoicing. The "freedom of the city" was offered to Ossaroo and his companions, and every hospitality lavished upon them that the grateful inhabitants knew how to bestow.

ADVENTURES OF A DOG,

AND A GOOD DOG TOO.

BY ALFRED ELWES.

* * *

PREFACE.

I LOVE dogs. Who does not? It is a natural feeling to love those who love us; and dogs were always fond of me. Thousands can say the same; and I shall therefore find plenty of sympathy while unfolding my dog's tale.

This attachment of mine to the canine family in general, and their affection towards myself, have induced me, like the Vizier in the "Arabian Nights," of happy memory, to devote some time to the study of their language. Its idiom is not so difficult as many would suppose. There is a simplicity about it that often shames the dialects of man; which have been so altered and refined, that we discover people often saying one thing when

137

they mean exactly the reverse. Nothing of the sort
is visible in the great canine tongue. Whether the
tone in which it is uttered be gruff or polished,
sharp or insinuating, it is at least sincere. Mankind
would often be puzzled how to use it.

Like many others, its meaning is assisted by gestures of the body, and, above all, by the expression
of the eye. If ever language had its seat in that
organ, as phrenologists pretend, it lies in the eye
of the dog. Yet, a good portion finds its way to
his tail. The motion of that eloquent member is
full of meaning. There is a slow wag of anger;
the gentle wag of contentment; the brisker wag of
joy: and what can be more mutely expressive than
the limp states of sorrow, humility, and fear.

If the tongue of the dog present such distinctive
traits, the qualities of the animal himself are not
less striking. Although the dispositions of dogs
are as various as their forms—although education,
connexions, the society they keep, have all their
influence—to the credit of their name be it said, a
dog never sullies his mouth with an untruth. His
emotions of pleasure are genuine; never forced.
His grief is not the semblance of woe, but comes
from the heart. His devotion is unmixed with
other feelings. It is single, unselfish, profound.
Prosperity affects it not; adversity cannot make it
swerve. Ingratitude, that saddest of human vices,
is unknown to the dog. He does not forget past
favours, but, when attached by benefits received,
his love endures through life. But I shall have
never done with reciting the praises of this noble

animal; the subject is inexhaustible. My purpose
now has narrower limits.

From the archives of the city of Caneville, I
lately drew the materials of a Bear's Biography.
From the same source I now derive my " Adven
tures of a Dog." My task has been less that of a
composer than a translator, for a feline editress, a
Miss Minette Gattina, had already performed her
part. This latter animal appears, however, to have
been so learned a cat—one may say so deep a puss
—that she had furnished more notes than there was
original matter. Another peculiarity which distinguished her labours was the obscurity of her
style; I call it a peculiarity, and not a defect, because I am not quite certain whether the difficulty
of getting at her meaning lay in her mode of ex-
pressing herself or my deficiency in the delicacies
of her language. I think myself a tolerable linguist,
yet have too great a respect for puss to say that
any fault is attributable to her.

This same feeling has, naturally, made me careful in rendering those portions which were exclu-
sively her own. I have preferred letting her say
little to allowing her to express anything she did
not intend Her notes, which, doubtless, drew
many a purr of approval from her own breast, and
many a wag of approbation from the tails of her
choice acquaintance, I have preferred leaving out
altogether; and I have so curtailed the labours of her
paw, and the workings of her brain, as to condense
into half-a-dozen pages her little volume of intro·
duction The autobiography itself, most luckily,

required no alteration. It is the work of a simple mind, detailing the events of a simple but not uneventful life. Whether I have succeeded in conveying to my readers' intelligence the impression which this Dog's Adventures made on mine, they alone can decide.

ADVENTURES OF A DOG,

--- • ---

INTRODUCTION.

BY MISS MINETTE GATTINA.

IT may seem peculiar to any but an inhabitant
of this renowned city of Caneville, that one of
our nation should venture on the task of bringing
to the notice of the world the memoir I have under-
taken to edit. But, besides that in this favoured
place animals of all kinds learn to dwell in tolerable
harmony together, the subject of this biography
had so endeared himself to all classes and to every
tribe by his kindness of heart, noble devotion, and
other dog-like qualities, that there was not a cat,
in spite of the supposed natural antipathy existing
between the great feline and canine races, who
would not have set up her back and fought to the
last gasp in defence of this dear old fellow.

Many a time has he saved me from the rough
treatment of rude and ill-conducted curs, when I
have been returning from a concert, or tripping
quietly home after a pleasant chat with a friend.
Often and often, when a kitten, has he carried me

on his back through the streets, in order that I might not wet my velvet slippers on a rainy day: and once, ah! well do I remember it, he did me even greater service; for a wicked Tom of our race, who had often annoyed me with his attentions, had actually formed a plan of carrying me off to some foreign land, and would have succeeded too, if dear Doggy had not got scent of the affair, and pounced on that treacherous Tom just as he was on the point of executing his odious project.

I can speak of these things *now* without the slightest fear of being accused of vanity. If I say my eyes were beautifully round and green, they are so no longer. If I boast of the former lightness of my step, it drags, alas! but too heavily now. If I dwell on the sweetness of my voice and melody of my purr at one period, little can be said in their favour at the present day, and I feel, therefore, less scruple in dilating on the elegance of my figure, and the taste of my *toilette*, as, when speaking of them, I seem to be referring to another individual Puss, with whom the actual snuffy old Tabby has little or no connection.

But, it will be said, these last matters have not much to do with the object I have in hand. I must not attempt to palm off on my readers any adventures of my own under the shadow of a dog. I must rather allow my Cat'spaw to perform the office for which it has become noted, namely, that of aiding in the recovery of what its owner is not intended to participate. I must endeavour to place before the world of Caneville, to be thence trans mitted to the less civilized portions of the globe, those incidents in our Dog's life which he has been too modest to relate himself, in order that after-generations may fully appreciate all the goodness of his character. To *greatness*, he had no pretension, although few animals are aware how close is the relation between these two qualities.

I think I see the dear old Dog now, as it has been often my privilege to behold him, seated in his large arm-chair, his hair quite silvered with age, shading his thoughtful, yet kindly face, his pipe in his paw, his faithful old friend by his side, and surrounded by a group of attentive listeners of both sexes, who seemed to hang upon every word of wisdom as it dropped from his mouth; all these spring to my mind when I recal his image, and if I were a painter I think I should have no difficulty in presenting to my readers this pleasant "family party." The very room in which these meetings were held comes as strongly to my recollection as the various young and old dogs who were wont to assemble there. Plainly furnished, it yet boasted some articles of luxury; works of statuary and painting, presented to old Job by those who admired his goodness, or had been the objects of his devotion.

One of these, a statuette representing a fast little dog upon a tasteful pedestal, used often to excite my curiosity, the more because Job showed no inclination to gratify it. I managed, however, at last to get at the incident which made Job the possessor of this comical little figure, and as the circumstance worthily illustrates his character, I will relate it as the anecdote was told to me.

It was once a fashion in Caneville, encouraged by puppies of the superior classes, to indulge in habits of so strange a nature as to meet on stated occasions for the express purpose of trying their skill and strength in set combats; and although the most frightful consequences often ensued, these assemblies were still held until put down by the sharp tooth of the law. The results which ensued were not merely dangerous to life, but created such a quarrelsome disposition, that many of these dogs were never happy but when fighting; and the force granted them by nature for self-defence was too often used most wantonly to the annoyance of their neighbours. It one day happened that Job was sitting quietly on a steep bank of the river where it runs into the wood at some distance from the city, at one moment watching the birds as they skimmed over the water, at another following the movements of a large fish, just distinguishable from the height, as it rose at the flies that dropped upon the stream; when three dogs, among the most celebrated fighters of the time, passed by that way. Two of them were of the common class, about the size and weight of Job; the other was a young puppy of good family, whose tastes had unfortunately led him into such low society. Seeing the mild expression of Job's face, and confident in their own prowess, they resolved to amuse themselves at his expense, and to this end drew near to him. Unobserved by their intended victim, with a rapid motion they endeavoured to push him head foremost into the river, Master Puppy having dexterously seized hold of his tail to make the somersault more complete. Job, although thus unexpectedly set upon from behind, was enabled, by the exertion of great strength, to defeat the object of his assailants. In the struggle which ensued, his adversaries discovered that, in spite of their boasted skill, they had more than found their match. One of them got rolled over into the stream, out of which he managed to crawl with considerable difficulty half a mile lower down; the second took to his heels, with his coat torn, and his person otherwise disordered; and the fashionable Pup, to his great horror, found himself seized in the formidable jaws of the unoffending but now angry dog. Imagine how much his terror was increased when Job, carrying him, as I would a mouse, to the edge of the precipitous bank, held him sheer over the roaring river. The poor fellow could not swim, and he had a perfect antipathy to the water, and he felt himself at that moment on the point of being consigned to certain death without a chance of safety. But he did not know the noble heart of the animal he had offended. Job let him feel for a few dreadful seconds the danger to which he had been so thoughtlessly and in joke about to consign himself, and then placed him in safety on the bank, with the admonition to reflect for the future on the probable result of his diversions before he indulged in them, and to consider whether, although amusing to himself, such games

might not be fatal to the animals on whom they
were played off. The shivering puppy was too
much alarmed at the time to attend either to the
magnanimity of his antagonist or to the wisdom of
his advice, but they were evidently not lost upon
him. Many can bear testimony to the change
which that hour wrought in his character; and
some weeks after the event, Job received that
statue of his little adversary, which had so often
struck me, executed by a native artist, with a long
letter in verse, a beautiful specimen of doggrel;
indeed, gifts both equally creditable to the sculptor
and the writer, and most honourable to the animal
in whose favour they had been executed.

My task will scarce be thought complete without
a few words concerning the personal appearance of
my old friend; although, perhaps, few things could
be more difficult for me to describe. Dogs and
cats are apt to admire such very different forms of
beauty, that the former often call beautiful what
we think just the reverse. He was tall, strong,
and rather stout, with a large bushy tail, which
waved with every emotion of his mind, for he
rarely disguised his feelings. His features were
considered regular, though large, his eyes being
particularly bright and full, and the upper part of
his head was broad and high.

But none who knew Job ever thought of his being handsome or otherwise. You seemed to love
him for something more than you could see, something which had little to do with the face, or body,
or tail, and yet appeared in them all, and shone

clearly out of his eyes; I mean the spirit of goodness, which made him so remarkable, and was so
much a part of Job, that I do believe a lock of his
hair worn near one's own heart would help to make
it beat more kindly to one's fellow creatures. This
idea may be considered too fanciful, too cat-like,
but I believe it notwithstanding.

Such was the Dog whose autobiography I have
great pleasure in presenting to the world. Many
may object to the unpolished style in which his
memoirs are clothed, but all who knew him will
easily pardon every want of elegance in his language; and those who had not the honour of his
acquaintance, will learn to appreciate his character
from the plain spirit of truth which breathes in
every line he wrote. I again affirm that I need
make no apology for attaching my name to that of
one so worthy the esteem of his co-dogs, ay, and
co-cats too; for in spite of the differences which
have so often raised up a barrier between the members of his race and ours, not even the noblest
among us could be degraded by raising a " mew"
to the honour of such a thoroughly honest dog.

EARLY DAYS.

I WAS not born in this city of Caneville, but was
brought here at so young an age, that I have no
recollection of any other place. I do not remember

either my father or my mother. An old doggess,[*]
who was the only creature I can recall to mind
when I was a pup, took care of me. At least she
said she did. But from what I recollect, I had to
take most care of myself. It was from her I learnt
what I know about my parents. She has told me
that my father was a foreign dog of high rank,
from a country many, many miles away, called
Newfoundland, and that my mother was a member
of the Mastiff family. But how I came to be under the care of herself, and how it happened, if my
parents were such superior animals, that I should
be forced to be so poor and dirty, I cannot tell. I
have sometimes ventured to ask her, but as she
always replied with a snarl or a bite, I soon got
tired of putting any questions to her. I do not
think she was a very good temper; but I should
not like to say so positively, because I was still
young when she died, and perhaps the blows she
gave me, and the bites she inflicted, were only intended for my good; though I did not think so at
the time.

As we were very poor, we were forced to live in
a wretched kennel in the dampest part of the town
among dogs no better off than ourselves. The
place we occupied overhung the water, and one
day when the old doggess was punishing me for
something I had done, the corner in which I was
crouched being very rotten, gave way, and I fell
plump into the river. I had never been in the

* I have preferred adopting this word in speaking of female
dogs as it comes nearer to the original, zaïyen.

water before, and I was very frightened, for the stream was so rapid, that it carried me off and past the kennels I knew, in an instant. I opened my mouth to call out for help, but as I was almost choked with the water that got into it, I shut it again, and made an effort to reach the land. To my surprise, I found, that by moving my paws and legs, I not only got my head well above the water, but was able to guide myself to the bank, on to which I at length dragged myself, very tired and out of breath, but quite recovered from my fear. I ran over the grass towards the town, as fast as I could, stopping now and then to shake my coat, which was not so wet, however, as you would suppose, but before I had got half way home I met the doggess, hopping along, with her tongue out of her mouth, panting for breath, she having run all the way from the kennel, out of which I had popped so suddenly, along the bank, with the hope of picking me up somewhere. She knew, she said, that I should never be drowned. But how she *could* know that was more than I could then imagine.

When we met, after I had escaped so great a danger, I flew to her paws, in the hope of getting a tender lick ; but as soon as she recovered breath, she caught hold of one of my ears with her teeth, and bit it till I howled with pain, and then set off running with me at a pace which I found it difficult to keep up with. I remember at the time thinking it was not very kind of her, but I have since reflected that perhaps she only did it to brighten me up and prevent me taking cold.
13*

This was my first adventure, and a.so my firsa acquaintance with the water. From that day I often ventured into the river, and in the end became so good a swimmer, that there were few dogs in Caneville who could surpass me in strength and dexterity afloat.

Many moons came and passed away, and I was getting a big dog. My appetite grew with my size, and as there was little to eat at home, I was forced to wander through the streets to look after stray bones; but I was not the only animal employed thus hunting for a livelihood, and the bits scattered about the streets being very few and small, some of us, as may be imagined, got scanty dinners. There was such quarrelling and fighting also for the possession of every morsel, that if you were not willing to let go any piece you had seized upon, you were certain to have half-a-dozen curs upon your back to force you to do so, and the poor weakly dog, whose only hope of a meal lay in what he might pick up, ran a sad chance of being starved.

One of the fiercest fights I have ever been engaged in occurred upon one of these occasions. I had had no breakfast, and it was already past the hour when the rich dogs of Caneville were used to dine. Hungry and disconsolate, I was trotting slowly past a large house, when a side-door opened, and a servant jerked a piece of meat into the road. In the greatest joy I bounced upon the prize, but not so quickly but that two ragged curs, who were no doubt as hungry as myself, managed to rush to the spot in time to get hold of the other end of it. Then came a struggle for the dainty, and those who do not know how hard dogs will fight for their dinner, when they have had no breakfast, should have been there to learn the lesson. After giving and receiving many severe bites, the two dogs walked off,—perhaps they did not think the meat was worth the trouble of contending for any longer —and I was left to enjoy my meal in peace. I had scarcely, however, squatted down, with the morsel between my paws, than a miserable little puppy, who seemed as if he had had neither dinner nor breakfast for the last week, came and sat himself at a little distance from me, and without saying a word, brushed the pebbles about with his ragged tail, licked his chops, and blinked his little eyes at me so hopefully, that, hungry as I was, I could not begin my meat. As I looked at him, I observed two tears gather at the side of his nose, and grow bigger and bigger until they would no longer stop there, but tumbled on to the ground. I could bear it no longer. I do not know even now what ailed me ; but my own eyes grew so dim, that there seemed a mist before them which prevented my seeing anything plainly. I started up, and, pushing to the poor whelp the piece of meat which had cost me three new rents in my coat and a split ear, I trotted slowly away. I stopped at the corner to see whether he appeared to enjoy it, and partly to watch that no other dog should take it from him. The road was quite clear, and the poor pup quite lost in the unusual treat of a good meal, so I took my way homewards, with an empty stomach but a full heart. I was so pleased to see that little fellow enjoy his dinner so thoroughly.

This sort of life, wherein one was compelled either to fight for every bit one could get to eat or go without food altogether, became at last so tiresome to me that I set about for some other means of providing for my wants. I could not understand how the old doggess used to manage, but though she never had anything to give me, she did not seem to be without food herself. She was getting so much more cross and quarrelsome, perhaps on account of her age and infirmities, that I now saw but little of her, as I often, on a fine night, preferred curling myself up under a doorway or beneath a tree, to returning to the kennel and listening to her feeble growls. She never seemed to want me there, so I had less difficulty in keeping away from her.

Chance assisted me in the choice of my new attempt at getting a living. I was walking along one of the narrow streets of Caneville when I was stopped by an old dog, who was known to be very rich and very miserly. He had lately invented a novel kind of match for lighting pipes and cigars, which he called a "fire-fly," the composition of which was so dangerous that it had already caused a good deal of damage in the town from its exploding ; and he wanted some active young dogs to dispose of his wares to the passers-by according to the custom of Caneville. As he expected a good deal of opposition from the venders of a rival article, it was ne-

cessary to make choice of such agents as would not
be easily turned from their purpose for fear of an
odd bite or two. I suppose he thought I was well
fitted for the object he had in view. I was very
poor—one good reason for his employing me, as I
would be contented with little; I was strong, and
should therefore be able to get through the work;
I was willing, and bore a reputation for honesty—
all sufficient causes for old Fily (that was his name)
to stop me this fine morning and propose my entering his service. Terms are easily arranged where
both parties are willing to come to an agreement.
After being regaled with a mouldy bone, and
dressed out in an old suit of clothes belonging to
my new master, which in spite of a great hole in
one of the knees, I was not a little proud of, with
a bundle of wares under my arm and a box of the
famous "fire-flies" in my paw, I began my com-
mercial career.

But, alas! either the good dogs of Caneville
were little disposed to speculate that day, or I was
very awkward in my occupation, but no one seemed
willing to make a trial of my "fire-flies." In vain
I used the most enticing words to set off my goods,
even going so far as to say that cigars lighted with
these matches would have a very much finer flavour, and could not possibly go out. This I said
on the authority of my employer who assured me
of the fact. It was of no use; not a single "fire-
fly" blazed in consequence, and I began to fear that
I was not destined to make my fortune as a match-
seller.

At length there came sweeping down the street
a party which at once attracted me, and I resolved
to use my best efforts to dispose, at least, of one of
my boxes, if it were only to convince my master
that I had done my best. The principal animal of
the group was a lady doggess, beautifully dressed,
with sufficient stuff in her gown to cover a dozen
ordinary dogs, a large muff to keep her paws from
the cold, and a very open bonnet with a garden-full
of flowers round her face, which, in spite of her rich
clothes, I did not think a very pretty one. A little
behind her was another doggess, not quite so superbly dressed, holding a puppy by the paw. It
was very certain that they were great animals, for
two or three dogs they had just passed had taken
off their hats as they went by, and then put their
noses together as if they were saying something
about them.

I drew near, and for the first time in my life was
timid and abashed. The fine clothes, no doubt, had
something to do with making me feel so, but—I
was still very young. Taking courage, I went on
tiptoe to the great lady, and begged her to buy a
box of "fire-flies" of a poor dog who had no other
means of gaining his bread. Now, you must know
that these matches had not a pleasant smell—few
matches have—but as they were shut up in the box,
the odour could not have been *very* sensible. However, when I held up the article towards her ladyship, she put her paw to her nose,—as though to
shut out the odour,—uttered a low howl, and, though
big enough and strong enough to have sent me head

over heels with a single blow, seemed on the point of falling to the ground. But at the instant, two male servants, whom I had not seen, ran to her assistance, while I, who was the innocent cause of all this commotion, stood like a silly dog that I was, with my box in the air and my mouth wide open, wondering what it all meant. I was not suffered to remain long in ignorance; for the two hounds in livery, turning to me, so belaboured my poor back that I thought at first my bones were broken, while the young puppy, who, it appears, was her ladyship's youngest son, running behind me, whilst I was in this condition, gave my tail such a pull as to cause me the greatest pain. They then left me in the middle of the road, to reflect on my ill success in trade, and gather up my stock as I best could.

I do not know what it was which made me so anxious to learn the name and rank of the lady doggess who had been the cause of my severe punish ment, but I eagerly inquired of a kind mongrel, who stopped to help me collect my scattered goods, if he knew anything about her. He said, she was called Lady Bull; that her husband, Sir John Bull, had made a large fortune somehow, and that they lived in a splendid house, had about thirty puppies little and big, had plenty of servants, and spent a great deal of money. He could hardly imagine he said, that it was the odour of the "fire-flies" which had occasioned me to be knocked down for upsetting her ladyship, as she had been a butcher's daughter, and was used to queer smells unless her nose had perhaps got more delicate with her change of position.

He said much more about her and her peculiarities than I either remember or care to repeat, but, imagining he had some private reasons for saying what he did, I thanked him for his trouble, and bid him good day.

Whatever the cause of my failure, it seemed that I was not fitted for the match-business. At all events, the experience of that morning did not encourage me sufficiently to proceed. So, returning the unsold " fire-flies" to old Fily, I made him a present of the time I had already spent in his service, and, with a thoughtful face and aching bones, took my way towards the kennel by the water-side.

CHANGES.

THE sun was just going down as I came in sight of the river and the row of poor kennels which stood on the bank, many of them like our own, projecting half over the water. I could not help wondering at the pretty effect they made at a distance, with the blue river dancing gaily by their side, the large trees of the wood on the opposite bank waving in beauty, and the brilliant sun changing everything that his rays fell upon into gold. He made the poor kennels look so splendid for the time, that no one would have thought the animals who lived in them could ever be poor or unhappy. But when the rich light was gone,—gone with the sun which made it to some other land,—it seemed as if the whole place was changed. The trees shivered as though a cold wind was stirring them. The river ran dark and sullenly by the poor houses; and the houses themselves looked more wretched, I thought, than they had ever appeared before. Yet, somehow, they were more home-like in their dismal state than when they had a golden roof and purple sides, so, resuming my walk, for I had stopped to admire the pretty picture, I soon came near the door.

It was open, as usual. But what was *not* usual, was to hear other sounds from within than the voice of the old doggess, making ceaseless moans. Now it seemed as if all the doggesses of the neighbourhood had met in the poor hut to pass the evening, for there was such confusion of tongues, and such a rustling sound, as told me, before I peeped inside, that there was a large party got together and that tails were wagging at a fearful rate.

When I stood before the open door, all the scene broke upon me. On her bed of straw, evidently at the point of death, lay my poor doggess. Her eyes had almost lost their fierce expression, and were becoming fixed and glassy—a slight tremor in her legs and movement of her stumpy tail, were all that told she was yet living; not even her breast was seen to heave.

I had not much reason to bear love to the old creature for any kindness she had ever shown me,

14

but this sight overcame me at once. Springing tc
her side, and upsetting half a dozen of the gossips
by the movement, I laid my paws on her; and,
involuntarily raising my head in the air, I sent
forth a howl which shook the rotten timbers of the
old kennel, and so frightened the assembled party
as to make them scamper out of the place like mad
things.   The sound even called back the departing
senses of the dying doggess. She drew me to her
with her paws, and made an effort to lick me. The
action quite melted me. I put down my head to
hers and felt a singular pleasure mixed with grief
whilst I licked and caressed her. I could not help
thinking then, as I have often thought since, of
how much happiness we had lost by not being
more indulgent to each other's faults, forgiving and
loving one another. She also seemed to be of this
opinion, if I might judge by the grateful look and
passive manner in which she received my attentions.
Perhaps the near approach of her end gave a soft
ness to her nature which was unusual to her; it is
not unlikely; but, of a certainty, I never felt before
how much I was losing, as when I saw that poor
doggess's life thus ebbing away.

Night had come on while I sat watching by her
side. Everything about the single room had become more and more indistinct, until all objects
were alike blended in the darkness. I could no
longer distinguish the shape of my companion, and,
but that I *knew* she was there, I could have thought
myself alone. The wind had fallen; the water
seemed to run more gently than it was wont to do:

and the noises which generally make themselves heard in the streets of Caneville appeared to be singularly quieted. But once only, at another period of my life, which I shall speak of in its proper place, do I ever remember to have been so struck by the silence, and to have felt myself so entirely alone.

The moon appeared to rise quicker that night, as though it pitied the poor forlorn dog. It peeped over an opposite house, and directly after, shone coldly but kindly through the open door. At least, its light seemed to come like the visit of a friend, in spite of its showing me what I feared, that I was *indeed* alone in the world. The poor doggess had died in the darkness between the setting of the sun and the moon's rise.

I was sure that she was dead, yet I howled no more. My grief was very great; for it is a sad, sad thing when you are young to find you are without friends; perhaps sadder when you are old; but that, I fortunately do not myself know, for I am old, and have many friends. I recollect putting my nose between my paws, and lying at full length on the floor, waiting till the bright sun should come again, and thinking of my forlorn condition. I must have slept and dreamed—yet I thought I was still in the old kennel with the dead doggess by my side. But everything seemed to have found a voice, and to be saying kind things to me.

The river, as it ran and shook the supports of the old kennel, appeared to cry out in a rough but gay tone: "Job, Job, my dog, cheer up, cheer up;

the world is before you, Job, cheer up, cheer up." The light wind that was coming by that way stopped to speak to me as it passed. It flew round the little room, and whispered as it went: "Poor dog, poor dog, you are very lonely; but the good need not be so; the good may have friends, dear Job, however poor!" The trees, as they waved their heads, sent kindly words across the water, that made their way to my heart right through the chinks of the old cabin; and when morning broke, and a bright sky smiled beautifully upon the streets of Caneville, I woke up, sad indeed, but full of hope.

Some ragged curs arrived, and carried the old doggess away. She was very heavy, and they were forced to use all their strength. I saw her cast into the water, which she disliked so much alive; I watched her floating form until the rapid current bore it into the wood, and I stayed sitting on the brink of the river, wondering where it would reach at last, and what sort of places must lie beyond the trees. I had an idea in my own mind that the sun rested there all night, only I could not imagine how it came up again in the morning in quite an opposite quarter; but then I was such a young and ignorant puppy!

After thinking about this and a good many other matters of no importance to my story, I got upon my legs, and trotted gently along the bank, towards a part of the city which I did not remember to have seen before. The houses were very few, but they were large and handsome, and all had pretty gardens in nice order, with flowers which smelt so sweet, that I thought the dogs who could always enjoy such advantages must be very happy But one of the houses, larger than all the rest, very much struck me, for I had never an idea of such a splendid place being in Caneville. It was upon a little hill that stood at some distance from the river, and the ground which sloped down from the house into the water was covered with such beautiful grass, that it made one long to nibble and roll upon it.

While I was quietly looking at this charming scene, I was startled by a loud noise of barking and howling higher up the river, and a confused sound as if a great many dogs were assembled at one place, all calling out together. I ran at once in the direction of the hubbub, partly out of curiosity and in part from some other motive, perhaps the notion of being able to render some help.

A little before me the river had a sudden bend, and the bank rose high, which prevented me seeing the cause of the noise; but when I reached the top the whole scene was before me. On my side of the river a great crowd had assembled, who were looking intently upon something in the water; and on the opposite bank there was a complete stream of dogs running down to the hill which belonged to the beautiful house I had been admiring. Every dog, as he ran, seemed to be trying to make as much noise as he could; and those I spoke to were barking so loudly, and jumping about in such a way, that I could at first get no explanation of

14*

what was the matter. At last I saw that the struggling object in the water was a young puppy, which
seemed very nicely dressed, and at the same moment the mongrel who had helped me to pick up
my matches the day before, came alongside of me,
and said : " Ah, young firefly, how are you ? Isn't
this a game ? That old Lady Bull who got you
such a drubbing yesterday, is in a pretty mess.
Her thirty-second pup has just tumbled into the
water, and will certainly be drowned. Isn't she
making a fuss ? just look !"

One rapid glance showed me the grand lady he
spoke of, howling most fearfully on the other side
of the stream, while two pups, about the same size
as the one in the water, and a stout dog, who
looked like the papa, were sometimes catching
hold of her and then running about, not knowing
what to do.

I stopped no longer. I threw off my over-coat,
and running to a higher part of the bank, leapt
into the water, the mongrel's voice calling after
me : " What are you going to do ? Don't you
know it's the son of the old doggess who had you
beat so soundly ? Look at your shoulder, where
the hair has been all knocked off with the blows ?"
Without paying the least attention to these words,
which I could not help hearing they were called
out so loudly, I used all my strength to reach the
poor little pup, who, tired with his efforts to help
himself, had already floated on to his back, while
his tiny legs and paws were moving feebly in the
air I reached him after a few more efforts, and,

seizing his clothes with my teeth, I got his head above the water, and swam with my load slowly towards the bank.

As I got nearer, I could see Lady Bull, still superbly dressed, but without her bonnet, throw up her paws and nose towards the sky, and fall back into the arms of her husband; while the two pups by her side expressed their feelings in different ways; for one stuffed his little fists into his eyes, and the other waved his cap in the air, and broke forth into a succession of infantile bow-wows.

On reaching the bank, I placed my load at the feet of his poor mother, who threw herself by his side and hugged him to her breast in a way which proved how much tenderness was under those fine clothes and affected manners. The others stood around her uttering low moans of sympathy, and I, seeing all so engaged and taken up with the recovered dog, quietly, and, as I thought, unseen by all, slid back into the water, and permitted myself to be carried by the current down the river. I crawled out at some short distance from the spot where this scene had taken place, and threw myself on to the grass, in order to rest from my fatigue and allow the warm sun to dry my saturated clothes. What I felt I can scarce describe, although I remember so distinctly everything connected with that morning. My principal sensation was that of savage joy, to think I had saved the son of the doggess who had caused me such unkind treatment. I was cruel enough, I am sorry to say, to figure to myself her pain at receiving such a favour from me—but that idea soon passed away, on reflecting that perhaps she would not even know to whom she owed her son's escape from death.

In the midst of my ruminations, a light step behind me caused me to raise my head. I was positively startled at the beautiful object which I beheld. It was a lady puppy about my own age, but so small in size, and with such an innocent, sweet look, that she seemed much younger. Her dress was of the richest kind, and her bonnet which had fallen back from her head, showed her glossy dark hair and drooping ears that hung gracefully beside her cheeks. Poorly as I was dressed, and wet as I still was from my bath, she sat herself beside me, and putting her little soft paw upon my shoulder, said, with a smile,—

" Ah, Job!—for I know that's your name—did you think you could get off so quietly without any one seeing you, or stopping you, or saying one single 'thank you, Job,' for being such a good, noble dog as you are? Did you think there was not one sharp eye in Caneville to watch the saver, but that all were fixed upon the saved? That every tongue was so engaged in sympathising with the mother, that not one was left to praise the brave? If you thought this, dear Job, you did me and others wrong, great wrong. There are some dogs, at least, who may forget an injury, but who never forget a noble action, and I have too great a love for my species to let you think so. I shall see you again, dear Job, though I must leave you now

I should be blamed if it were known that I had come here to talk to you as I have done; but I could not help it, I could not let you believe that a noble heart was not understood in Caneville. Adieu. Do not forget the name of Fida."

She stooped down, and for a moment her silky hair waved on my rough cheek, while her soft tongue gently licked my face. Before I could open my mouth in reply—before, indeed, I had recovered from my surprise, and the admiration which this beautiful creature caused me, she was gone. I sprang on to my legs to observe which way she went, but not a trace of her could I see, and I thought it would not be proper to follow her. When I felt certain of being alone, I could hardly restrain my feelings. I threw myself on my back, I rolled upon the grass, I turned head over heels in the boisterousness of my spirit, and then gambolled round and round like a mad thing.

Did I believe all the flattering praises which the lovely Fida had bestowed on me? I might perhaps have done so then, and in my inexperience might have fancied that I was quite a hero. Time has taught me another lesson. It has impressed upon me the truth, that when we do our duty we do only what should be expected of every dog; only what every dog ought to do. Of the two, Fida had done the nobler action. She had shown not only a promptness to feel what she considered good, but she had had the courage to say so in private to the doer, although he was of the poorest and she of the richest class of Caneville society

In saving the little pup's life, I had risked nothing;
I knew my strength, and felt certain I could bring
him safely to the shore. If I had *not* tried to save
the poor little fellow I should have been in part
guilty of his death. But she, in bestowing secret
praise and encouragement upon a poor dog who
had no friends to admire her for so doing, while
her action would perhaps bring blame upon her
from her proud friends, did that which was truly
good and noble.

The thought of returning to my solitary home
after the sad scene of the night before, and particularly after the new feelings just excited, was not
a pleasant one. The bright sky and fresh air
seemed to suit me better than black walls and the
smell of damp straw. Resolving in my mind, however, to leave it as soon as possible, I re-crossed the
river, and with a slower step than usual, took the
road which led thither.

———•◆•———

UPS AND DOWNS.

I SHOULD not probably have spoken of these
last incidents in my life, as the relation of them
savours rather too much of vanity, but for certain
results of the highest importance to my future fortunes.

When I reached the old kennel I found, waiting
my return, two terrier dogs in livery, with bulls'

heads grinning from such a quantity of buttons upon their lace coats that it was quite startling. They brought a polite message from Sir John and Lady Bull, begging me to call upon them without delay. As the servants had orders to show me the road, we set off at once.

I was very silent on the journey, for my companions were so splendidly dressed that I could not help thinking they must be very superior dogs indeed; and I was rather surprised, when they spoke to each other, to find that they talked just like any other animals, and a good deal more commonly than many that I knew. But such is the effect of fine clothes upon those who know no better.

We soon reached the grounds of the mansion, having crossed the river in a boat that was waiting for us, and after passing through a garden more beautiful than my poor dog's brain had ever imagined, we at last stood before the house itself. I need not describe to you, who know the place so well, the vastness of the building or the splendour of its appearance. What struck me more even than the palace, was the number of the servants and the richness of their clothes. Each of them seemed fine enough to be the master of the place, and appeared really to think so, if I could judge by the way they strutted about and the look they gave at my poor apparel. I was much abashed at first to find myself in such a company and make so miserable a figure; but I was consoled with the thought that not one of them that morning had ventured, in spite of his eating his master's meat and living in his master's house, to plunge into the water to save his master's son. Silly dog that I was! it did not enter my head at the same time to inquire whether any of them had learnt to swim.

If the outside of the mansion had surprised me by its beauty, the interior appeared of course much more extraordinary to my ignorant mind. Every thing I was unused to looked funny or wonderful, and if I had not been restrained by the presence of such great dogs, I should have-sometimes laughed outright, and at others broken forth into expressions of surprise.

The stout Sir John Bull was standing in the middle of the room when I entered it, while the stouter Lady Bull was lying on a kind of sofa, that seemed quite to sink beneath her weight. I found out afterwards that it was the softness of the sofa which made it appear so; for sitting on it myself, at my Lady's request, I jumped up in the greatest alarm, on finding the heaviest part of my body sink lower and lower down, and my tail come flapping into my face.

Sir John and Lady Bull now thanked me very warmly for what I had done, and said a great many things which it is not worth while to repeat. I remember they were very pleasing to me then, but I am sure cannot be interesting to you now. After their thanks, Sir John began to talk to me about myself—about my parents—my wishes—what I intended to do—and what were my means? To his great surprise he learnt that parents I had none that my only wishes were the desire to do some good for myself and others, and earn my meat; that I had no notion what I intended doing, and had no means whatever to do anything with. It may be believed that I willingly accepted his offer to watch over a portion of his grounds, to save them from the depredations of thieves, on condition of my receiving good clothes, plenty of food, and a comfortable house to live in. It was now my turn to be thankful. But although my heart was full at this piece of good fortune, and I could *think* of a great many things to say to show my gratitude, not a single word could I find to express it in, but stood before them like a dumb dog, with only the wave of my tail to explain my thanks. They seemed, however, to understand it, and I was at once ordered a complete suit of clothes and every thing fitted for my new position. I was also supplied with the most abundant supper I had ever had in my life, and went to rest upon the most delightful bed, so that before I went to sleep, and I do believe afterwards too, I kept saying to myself, " Job, Job, you have surely got some other dog's place; all this good luck can't be meant for you; what have you done, Job, that you should eat such meat, and sleep on so soft a bed, and be spoken to so kindly. Don't forget yourself, Job, there must be some mistake." But when I got up in the morning, and found a breakfast for me as nice as the supper, and looked at my clothes, which if not so smart as some of the others, were better and finer than any I could ever have thought I

15

should have worn, I was at last convinced that although I was poor Job, and although I did not, perhaps, deserve all the happiness I felt, that it was not a dream, but real, plain truth. " As it is so," I said again, " I must do my duty as well as I am able, for that is the only way a poor dog like me can show his gratitude."

After breakfast, I accompanied Sir John to the place of my future home. A quarter of an hour's walk brought us to a gentle hill, which, similar to the one whereon the mansion itself was situated, sloped downwards to the water. One or two trees, like giant sentinels, stood near the top, and behind them waved the branches of scores more, while beyond for many a mile spread the dark mass of the thick forest of which I have more than once made mention. Nearly at the foot of the hill, beneath a spreading oak, was a cottage, a very picture of peace and neatness, and as we paused, Sir John pointed out the peculiarities of the position and explained my duties. It appeared that this part of his grounds was noted for a delicate kind of bird ; much esteemed by himself and his family, and which was induced to flock there by regular feeding and the quiet of the situation. This fact was, however, perfectly well known to others besides Sir John, and as these others were just as fond of the birds as himself, they were accustomed to pay nightly visits to the forbidden ground, and carry off many of the plumpest fowl. The wood was known to shelter many a wandering fox, who, although dwelling so near the city, could not be prevailed on to abandon their roguish habits and live in a civilized manner. These birds were particularly to their taste, and it required the greatest agility to keep off the cunning invaders, for, though they had no great courage, and would not attempt to resist a bold dog, they frequently succeeded in eluding all vigilance and getting off with their booty. Often, too, a stray cur, sometimes two or three together, from the lowest classes of the population would, when moved by hunger, make a descent on the preserves, and battles of a fierce character not seldom occurred, for unlike the foxes, they were never unwilling to fight, but showed the utmost ferocity when attacked, and were often the aggressors. But these were not all. The grounds were exactly opposite that part of the city of Caneville known as the "Mews," and occupied by the cat population, who have a general affection for most birds, and held these preserved ones in particular esteem. Fortunately, the water that interposed was a formidable barrier for the feline visitors, as few pussies like to wet their feet, but, by some means or other they frequently found their way across, and by their dexterity, swiftness, and the quiet of their movements, committed terrible ravages among the birds. When Sir John had told me all this, he led the way down the hill to the small house under the tree. It had two rooms, with a kennel at the back. The front room was the parlour, and I thought few places could have been so neat and pretty. The back was the sleeping-room, and the windows of both looked out upon the soft grass and trees, and showed a fine view of the river.

"This," said Sir John, "is your house, and I hope you will be happy in it yourself and be of service to me. You will not be alone, for there" —pointing to the kennel at the back—"sleeps an old servant of the family, who will assist you in your duties."

He then called out "Nip," when a rumbling noise was heard from the kennel, and directly after a lame hound came hopping round to the door. The sight of this old fellow was not pleasant at first, for his hair was a grizzly brown and his head partly bald; his eyes were sunk, and, indeed, almost hidden beneath his bushy brows, and his cheeks hung down below his mouth and shook with every step he took. I soon found out that he was as singular in his manners as in his looks, and had such a dislike to talking that it was a rare thing for him to say more than two or three words at one time. Sir John told him who I was, and desired him to obey my orders; commanded us both to be good friends and not quarrel, as strange dogs were rather apt to do, and after some more advice left us to ourselves, I in a perfect dream of wonderment, and "Nip" sitting winking at me in a way that I thought more funny than agreeable.

After we had sat looking at one another for some time, I said, just to break the silence, which was becoming tiresome:

"A pretty place this!"

Nip winked.

" Have you been here long?" I asked.

" Think so," said Nip.

" All alone ?" I inquired.

" Almost," Nip replied.

" Much work to do, eh ?" I asked.

The only answer Nip gave to this was by winking first one eye and then the other, and making his cheeks rise and fall in a way so droll that I could not help laughing, at which Nip seemed to take offence, for without waiting for any farther questions he hopped out of the room, and I saw him, soon after, crawling softly up the hill, as if on the look out for some of the thieves Sir John had spoken of.

I, too, went off upon the watch. I took my way along the bank, I glided among the bushes, ran after a young fox whose sharp nose I spied pointed up a tree, but without catching him, and finally returned to my new home by the opposite direction. Nip came in shortly after, and we sat down to our dinner.

Although this portion of my life was, perhaps, the happiest I have ever known, it has few events worth relating. The stormy scenes which are so painful to the dog who suffers them, are those which are most interesting to the hearer, while the quiet days, that glide peacefully away, are so like each other, that an account of one of them is a description of many. A few hours can be so full of action, as to require volumes to describe them properly, and the history of whole years can be written on a single page.

15*

I tried, as I became fixed in my new position, to do what I had resolved when I entered it; namely, my duty. I think I succeeded; I certainly obtained my master's praise, and sometimes my own; for I had a habit of talking to myself as Nip so rarely opened his mouth, and would praise or blame myself just as I thought I deserved it. I am afraid I was not always just, but too often said, " Well done, Job; that's right, Job;" when I ought to have called out, " You're wrong, Job; you ought to feel, Job, that you're wrong;" but it is not so easy a thing to be just, even to ourselves.

One good lesson I learned in that little cottage, which has been of use to me all my life through: And that was, to be very careful about judging dogs by their looks. There was old Nip; when I first saw him, I thought I had never beheld such an ugly fellow in my life, and could not imagine how anything good was to be expected from so cross a looking, ragged old hound. And yet, nothing could be more beautiful, more loveable than dear old Nip, when you came to know him well. All the misfortunes he had suffered, all the knocks he had received in passing through the world, seemed to have made his heart more tender, and he was so entirely good-natured, that in all the time we were together, I never heard him say an unkind thing of living or dead animal. I believe his very silence was caused by the goodness of his disposition; for as he could not help seeing many things he did not like, but could not alter, he preferred holding his tongue to saying what could not

be agreeable. Dear, dear Nip, if ever it should be
resolved to erect a statue of goodness in the public
place of Caneville, they ought to take you for a
model; you would not be so pleasant to look on as
many finer dogs, but when once known, your image
would be loved, dear Nip, as I learned to love the
rugged original.

It can be of no interest to you to hear the many
fights we had in protecting the property of our
master during the first few moons after my arrival.
Almost every night we were put in danger of our
lives, for the curs came in such large numbers that
there was a chance of our being pulled to pieces in
the struggle. Yet we kept steady watch; and,
after a time, finding, I suppose that we were never
sleeping at our post, and that our courage rose with
every fresh attack, the thieves gradually gave up
open war, and only sought to entrap the birds by
artifice; and, like the foxes and cats, came sneak-
ing into the grounds, and trusted to the swiftness
of their legs rather than the sharpness of their teeth
when Nip or I caught sight of them.

And thus, a long, long time passed away. I
had, meanwhile, grown to my full size, and was
very strong and active; not so stout as I have got
in these later years, when my toes sometimes ache
with the weight which rests on them, but robust
and agile, and as comely, I believe, as most dogs
of my age and descent.

The uniformity of my life, which I have spoken
of as making me so happy, was interrupted only
by incidents that did not certainly cause me dis-

pleasure. I renewed my acquaintance with " Fida,"
no longer *little* Fida, for she had grown to be a
beautiful lady-dog. Our second meeting was by
chance, but we talked like old friends, so much
had our first done to remove all strangeness. I
don't think the next time we saw each other was
quite by accident. If I remember rightly, it was
not; and we often met afterwards. We agreed
that we should do all we could to assist one another,
though what *I* could do for so rich and clever a
lady-dog I could not imagine, although I made the
promise very willingly. On her part, she did for
me what I can never sufficiently repay. She taught
me to read, lending me books, containing strange
stories of far off countries, and beautiful poetry,
written by some deep dogs of the city; she taught
me to write; and in order to exercise me, made me
compose letters to herself, which Nip carried to
her, bringing me back such answers as would astonish you; for when you thought you had got to
the end, they began all over again in another direction. Besides these, she taught me to speak and
act properly, in the way that well-behaved dogs
ought to do; for I had been used to the company
of such low and poor animals, that it was not surprising if I should make sad blunders in speech
and manners. I need not say that she taught me
to love herself, for that you will guess I had done
from the first day I saw her, when I was wet from
my jump in the river, and she spoke to me such
flattering words. No; she could not teach me
more love for herself than I already knew. That

lesson had been learnt *by heart*, and at a single sitting.

Our peaceful days were drawing to a close. Sir John died. Lady Bull lived on for a short time longer. Many said, when she followed, that she ate herself to death; but I mention the rumour in order to deny it, for I am sure it was grief that killed her. It is a pity some dogs will repeat everything they hear, without considering the mischief such tittle-tattle may occasion—although it has been asserted by many that in this case the false intelligence came from the Cats, who had no great affection for poor Lady Bull. Whatever the cause, she died, and with her the employment of poor Nip and myself. The young Bulls who came into possession of the estate, sold the preserves to a stranger, and as the new proprietor intended killing off the birds, and did not require keepers, there being no longer anything for them to do, we were turned upon the world.

The news came upon us so suddenly, that we were quite unprepared for it; and we were, besides, so far from being rich, that it was a rather serious matter to find out how we should live until we could get some other occupation. I was not troubled for myself; for, though I had been used to good feeding lately, I did not forget the time when I was often forced to go the whole day with scarce a bit to eat; but the thought of how poor old Nip would manage gave me some pain.

Having bid adieu to the peaceful cottage, where we had spent such happy times, we left the green fields and pleasant trees and proceeded to the town, where, after some difficulty, we found a humble little house which suited our change of fortune. Here we began seriously to muse over what we should do. I proposed making a ferry-boat of my back, and stationing myself at the water-side near the " Mews," swim across the river with such cats as required to go over and did not like to walk as far as where the boat was accustomed to be. By these means I calculated on making enough money to keep us both comfortably. Nip thought not. He said that the cats would not trust me—few cats ever did trust the dogs—and then, though he did not dislike cats, not at all, for he knew a great many very sensible cats, and very good ones too, he did not like the idea of seeing his friend walked over by cats or dogs, or any other animal, stranger or domestic. Besides, there were other objections. Strong as I was, I could not expect, if I made a boat of myself, that I could go on and on without wanting repair any more than a real boat; but where was the carpenter to put *me* to rights, or take out *my* rotten timbers and put in fresh ones. No ; that would not do; we must think of something else.

It must not be imagined that Nip made all this long speech in one breath, or in a dozen breaths. It took him a whole morning to explain himself even as clearly as I have tried to do; and perhaps I may still have written what he did not quite intend, for his words came out with a jump one or two at a time, and often so suddenly that it would have startled a dog who was not used to his manner.

Nip himself made the next proposal, and though I did not exactly like it, there seemed so little choice, that I at once agreed to do my part in the scheme. Nip was the son of a butcher, and though he had followed the trade but a short time himself, he was a very good judge of meat. He, therefore, explained that if I would undertake to become the seller, he would purchase and prepare the meat, and he thought he could make it look nice enough to induce the dogs to come and buy.

Our stock of money being very small, a house-shop was out of the question, so there was no chance of getting customers from the better class,— a thing which I regretted, as I had little taste for the society of the vulgar; but, again, as it could not be helped, the only thing to do was to make the best of it. A wheelbarrow was therefore bought by Nip, with what else was necessary to make me a complete " walking butcher," and having got in a stock of meat the day before, Nip cut, and contrived, and shaped, and skewered, in so quiet and business-like a way as proved he knew perfectly well what he was about. With early morning, after Nip had arranged my dress with the same care as he had bestowed upon the barrow and its contents, I wheeled my shop into the street, and amid a great many winks of satisfaction from my dear old friend, I went trudging along, bringing many a doggess to the windows of the little houses by my loud cry of " Me-eet! Fresh me-eet!"

As I was strange in my new business, and did not feel quite at my ease, I fancied every dog I met, and every eye that peeped from door and casement, stared at me in a particular manner, as if they knew I was playing my part for the first time, and were watching to see how I did it. The looks that were cast at my meat, were all, I thought, intended for me, and when a little puppy leered suspiciously at the barrow as he was crossing the road, no doubt to see that it did not run over him, I could only imagine that he was thinking of the strange figure I made, and my awkward attempt at getting a living. Feelings like these no doubt alarm every new beginner; but time and habit, if they do not reconcile us to our lot, will make it at least easier to perform, and thus, after some two hours' journeying through the narrow lanes of Caneville, I did what my business required of me with more assurance than when I first set out.

One thing, however, was very distasteful to me, and I could so little bear to see it, that I even spoke of it aloud, and ran the risk of offending some of my customers. I mean the *way* in which several of the dogs devoured the meat after they had bought it. You will think that when they had purchased their food and paid for it, they had a right to eat it as they pleased: I confess it; nothing can be more true; but still, my ideas had so changed of late, that it annoyed me very much to see many of these curs, living as they did in the most civilized city in this part of the world, gnawing their meat as they held it on the ground with their paws, and growl ing if any one came near as though there was no such thing as a police in Caneville. I forgot when I was scolding these poor dogs, that perhaps they had never been taught better, and deserved pity rather than blame. I forgot too that I had myself behaved as they did before I had been blessed with happier fortune, and that even then, if I had looked into my own conduct, I should have found many things more worthy of censure than these poor curs' mode of devouring their food.

The lane I was passing along was cut across by a broad and open street, the favourite promenade of the fashionables of Caneville. There might be seen about mid-day, when the sun was shining, troops of well-dressed dogs and a few superior cats, some attended by servants, others walking alone, and many in groups of two or three, the male dogs smoking cigars, the ladies busily talking, while they looked at and admired one another's pretty dresses and bonnets.

By the time I had got thus far, I had become tolerably used to my new work, and could imagine that when the passers by cast their eyes on my barrow, their glances had more to do with the meat than with myself. But I did not like the idea of crossing the road where such grand dogs were showing off their finery. After a little inward conversation with myself, which finished with my muttering between my teeth, "Job, brother Job, I am ashamed of you! where is your courage, brother Job? Go on; go on;" I went on without further delay.

16

I had got half-way across, and was already beginning to praise myself for the ease with which I
turned my barrow in and out of the crowd without
running over the toes of any of the puppies, who
were far too much engaged to look after them themselves, when a dirty little cur stopped me to buy a
penn'orth of meat. I set down my load just in
time to avoid upsetting a very fat and splendidly
dressed doggess, who must, if I had run the wheel
into her back, and it was very near it, have gone
head foremost into the barrow. This little incident
made me very hot, and I did not get cooler when
my customer squatted down in the midst of the
well-dressed crowd, and began tearing his meat in
the way I have before described as being so unpleasant. At the same moment another dog by
his side, with a very ragged coat, and queer little
face, held up his paw to ask for "a little bit," as
he was very hungry, "only a little bit." I should,
probably, have given him a morsel, as I remembered the time when I wanted it as much as he
seemed to do, but for an unexpected meeting.
Turning my head at a rustling just behind me, I
saw a well-dressed dog with a hat of the last fashion placed so nicely on his head that it seemed to
be resting on the bridge of his nose, the smoke
from a cigar issuing gracefully from his mouth,
and his head kept in an upright posture by a very
stiff collar which ran round the back of his neck,
and entirely prevented his turning round his head
without a great deal of care and deliberation, while
a tuft of hair curled nicely from beneath his chin,

and gave a fine finish to the whole dog. But though I have spoken of this Caneville fashiona·ble, it was not he who caused the rustling noise, or who most attracted my attention. Tripping be·side him, with her soft paw beneath his, was a lady-dog whose very dress told her name, at least in my eyes, before I saw her face. I felt sure that it was Fida, and I wished myself anywhere rather than in front of that barrow with an ill-bred cur at my feet gnawing the penn'orth of meat he had just bought of me. Before I had time to catch up my load and depart, a touch on my shoulder, so gentle that it would not have hurt a fly, and yet which made me tremble more than if it had been the grip of a giant animal, forced me again to turn. It *was* Fida; as beautiful and as fresh as ever, who gave me a sweet smile of recognition and encouragement as she passed with her companion, and left me stand-ing there as stupid and uncomfortable as if I had been caught doing something wrong.

You will say that it was very ridiculous in me to feel so ashamed and disconcerted at being seen by her or any other dog or doggess in my common dress, and following an honest occupation. I do not deny it. And in telling you these things I have no wish to spare myself, I have no excuse to offer, but only to relate events and describe feelings precisely as they were.

THE INUNDATION.

THAT evening it seemed as if Nip and I had changed characters. It was he who did all the talking, while I sat in a corner, full of thought, and answered yes or no to everything he said, and sometimes in the wrong place, I am sure; for once or twice he looked at me very attentively, and winked, in a way which proved that he was puzzled by my manner.

The reason of his talkativeness was the success I had attained in my first morning's walk, for I had sold nearly all the meat, and brought home a pocket full of small money. The cause of my silence was the unexpected meeting with Fida, and the annoyance I felt at having been seen by her in such a position. This was the first time I had set eyes on her for several days. When we left our pretty country lodging, I wrote her a letter, which Nip carried as usual to her house, but he was told that she had gone on a visit to some friends at a distance, but that the letter should be given to her on her return. I had not, therefore, been able to inform her of what we had been compelled to do, as I would have wished, but thus, without preparation, quite unexpectedly, I had been met by her in the public street, acting the poor dogs' butcher with the implements of my business before me, and a dirty cur growling and gnawing his dinner at my feet. What made the matter more serious, for serious it seemed to me, though I can but smile *now* to think why such a thing should have made me uncomfortable, was, that the whole scene had taken place in so open a part, with so many grand and gay dogs all round, to be witnesses of my confusion. I did not reflect that of all the puppies who were strutting past, there was probably not one who could have remembered so common an event as the passing of a butcher's barrow; and that if they looked at me at all, it was, doubtless, for no other reason than to avoid running against my greasy coat and spoiling their fine clothes. These confessions will prove to you that I was very far from being a wise dog or even a sensible one; all the books I had read had, as yet, served no other purpose than that of feeding my vanity and making me believe I was a very superior animal; and you may learn from this incident that those who wish to make a proper figure in the world, and play the part they are called on to perform in a decent manner, must study their lesson in the world itself, by mingling with their fellows, for books alone can no more teach such knowledge than it can teach a dog to swim without his going into the water.

Nip and I had our dinner; and, when it was over, my old friend went out to procure a supply of meat for the next day's business. I sat at the window with my nose resting on the ledge, at times watching some heavy clouds which were rolling up the sky, as if to attend a great meeting over-

16*

head ; at another moment, looking at the curs in
the streets, who were playing all sorts of games,
which generally turned into a fight, and often
staring at the house opposite without seeing a single stone in the wall, but in their place, Fidas and
puppies with stiff collars, and barrows with piles
of meat, ready cut and skewered. I was awoke
from this day-dream by the voice of an old, but
very clean Doggess, enquiring if my name was Mr.
Job? I answered that I was so called, when she
drew from her pocket and gave me a pink-coloured
note, which smelt like a nice garden, and even
brought one to my view as plainly as if it had suddenly danced before me, and saying there was no
reply, returned by the way she had come.

I did not require to be told by whom it was
sent. I knew the writing too well. The neat
folding, the small but clean address assured me
that a lady's paw had done it all, and every word
of the direction

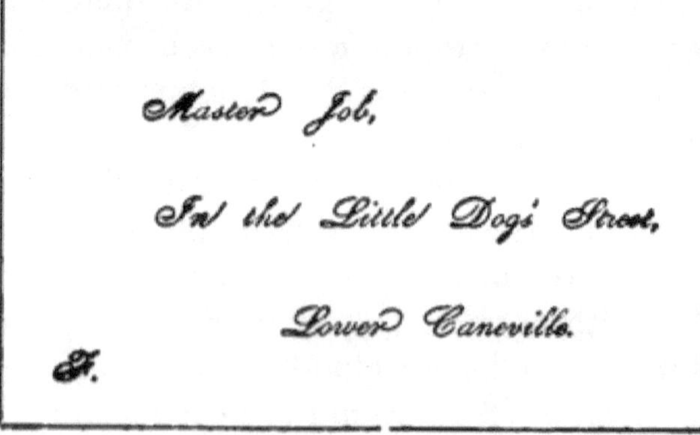

spoke to me of Fida, and did not even need the F. in the corner to convince me of the fact. With her permission I here give you the contents :—

"MY DEAR JOB,

"I am sorry I was away from home when your letter arrived, and would have told you I was going, but that I thought the news might cause you pain, as I by some mischance had got my tail jammed in a door, and was forced to leave home in order to visit a famous doctor who lives at some distance. He fortunately cured me after a few days' illness, and the tail wags now as freely as ever, although it was very annoying, as well as ridiculous, to see me walking up and down the room with that wounded member so wrapped up that it was as thick as my whole body, and was quite a load to drag about.

'But, dear Job, I do not write this to talk about myself, though I am forced to give you this explanation of my silence: what I wish is to say something about *you*. And, to begin, as you have always been a good kind dog, and listened to me patiently when I have praised, you must now be just as kind and good, and even more patient, because I am going to scold.

"Dear Job, when I met you this morning in your new dress and occupation, I had not then read your letter. I had but just returned, and was taking a walk with my brother, who had arrived from abroad during my absence. I knew you at once, in spite of your change of costume, and though I did not particularly like the business you had chosen, I felt certain you had good reasons for having selected it. But when I looked in your face, instead of the smile of welcome which I expected from you, I could read nothing but shame, confusion, and annoyance. Why? dear Job, why? If you were *ashamed* of your occupation, why had you chosen it? I suppose when you took it up, you resolved to do your duty in it properly; then why feel *shame* because *your friend* sees you, as you must have thought she would one day see you, since the nature of your new business carries you into different parts of the city?

"But, dear Job, I feel certain, and I would like you to be equally sure, that there is no need of *shame* in following any business which is *honest*, and which can be carried on without doing injury to others. It is not the business, believe me, dear Job, which lowers a dog; *he himself* is alone capable of *lowering* himself, and one dog may be truly good and noble, though he drive a meat barrow about the streets, while another may be a miserable, mean animal, though living in a palace and never soiling his paws.

"I have a great deal more to say, my dear Job, upon this subject, but I must leave the rest till I see you. I have already crossed and recrossed my note, and may be most difficult to understand where I most want to be clear. Here is a nice open space, however, in the corner, which I seize on with pleasure to write myself most distinctly,

"Your friend,   FIDA."

A variety of feelings passed through my mind as I read these lines. But they were all lost in my wonder at Fida's cleverness in being able to read my face as if it had been a book. I was grateful to her for the good advice she gave me, and now felt ashamed for having been ashamed before. The best way I thought to prove my thankfulness, would be to act openly and naturally as Fida had pointed out, for I could not help confessing, as my eyes looked again and again over her note, that she was quite right, and that I had acted like a very silly animal.

I was interrupted during my reflections by the bursting of rain upon the house-roofs, and the stream which rose from the streets as the large drops came faster and faster down. I went to the door to look for my old friend, but not a dog was to be seen. I was surprised at the sight of the sky, where I had observed the clouds rising a little while before, for now those same clouds looked like big rocks piled one above another, with patches of light shining through great caverns.

As I stared eagerly down the street, torrents of water poured from above, which, instead of diminishing, seemed to be growing more terrible every moment I had never seen so fearful a storm. It did not appear like mere rain which was falling; the water came down in broad sheets, and changed the road into a river. I got more and more anxious about old Nip. It was getting dark, and I knew he was not strong. My hope was that he had taken shelter somewhere; but I could not rest, for I was sure he would try and get home if only to quiet me. While running in and out in my anxiety—the water having meanwhile risen above the sill of the door, and poured into our little house, where it was already above my paws—I spied a dark figure crawling along the street, and with great difficulty making way against the beating of the storm. I at once rushed out, and swimming rather than running towards the object, I found my poor friend almost spent with fatigue and scarcely able to move, having a heavy load to carry besides his own old limbs, which were not fit to battle with such a tempest. I caught up his package, and assisting him as well as I was able, we at length got to our cottage, though we were forced to get upon the bench that stood by the wall to keep our legs out of the water. The rain had now become a perfect deluge. A stream of water went hissing down the street, and rushed in and out of the houses as if they had been baths.

When Nip recovered breath, he told me that terrible things were happening in the parts of the city by the waterside. The river had swollen so much, that some kennels had been carried away by the current, and it was impossible to learn how many poor dogs had been drowned. This news made me jump again from the bench where I had been sitting.

"What is it?" said Nip.

"I am going out, Nip," replied I. "I must not be idle here, when I can, perhaps, be of use somewhere else."

"That is true," said Nip; "but, Job, strong as you are, the storm is stronger."

"Yes, Nip," answered I: "but there are dogs weaker than myself who may require such assistance as I can give them, and it is not a time for a dog to sit with his tail curled round him, when there are fellow-creatures who may want a helping paw. So good bye, old friend; try and go to sleep; you have done your duty as long as your strength let you, it is now for me to do mine." Without waiting for a reply, I rushed out at the door.

It did not need much exertion to get through our street or the next, or the next after that, for as they all sloped downwards, the water more than once took me off my legs and carried me along. Sad as Nip's news had been, I was not prepared for the terrible scene which met my eyes when I got near the river. The houses at the lower part of the street I had reached, had been swept away by the torrent, and a crowd of shivering dogs stood looking at the groaning river as it rolled past in great waves, as white as milk, in which black objects, either portions of some kennel, or articles of furniture, were floating. Every now and then, a howl would break from a doggess in the crowd, as a dead body was seen tossed about by the angry water, and the same dolorous cries might be heard from different quarters mixed up with the roar of the river.

While standing with a group of three or four staring with astonishment at the frightful scene, uncertain what to do, a howl was heard from another direction, so piercing that it made many of us run to learn the cause. The pale light showed us that the torrent had snapped the supports of a house at some distance from the river's bank, but which the swollen stream had now reached, and carried away at least half the building. By some curious chance, the broken timbers had become fixed for the moment in the boiling water, which, angry at the obstruction, was rushing round or flying completely over them, and it was easy to see, that in a very short time the mass would be swept away. Upon the timbers thus exposed, were three little pups scarce two months old, yelping most dismally as they crouched together, or crawled to the edge of their raft, while on the floor of the ruin from which this side had been torn away, was their poor mother, whose fearful howl had attracted us thither, and who was running from side to side of the shattered hut as if she were frantic.

Great as the danger was, I could not bear to think the wretched mother should see her little ones swallowed up by the stormy water, before her very eyes, without a single attempt being made to save them. Although I could scarcely hope even to reach them in safety, and in no case could bring more than one of them to land at once, if I even got so far, I resolved to make the trial. Better save one, I thought, than let all die.

Holding my breath, I launched into the current in the direction of the raft, and soon found that I had not been wrong in calculating the difficulties and dangers of the undertaking. It was not the water alone which made the peril so great, though the eddies seemed at every moment to be pulling me to the bottom, but there were so many things rushing along with the stream as to threaten to crush me as they flew by, and had they struck me, there is no doubt there would have been an end of my adventures. Avoiding them all, though I know not how, I was getting near the spot where the little pups were crying for their mother, when I felt myself caught in an eddy and dragged beneath the water. Without losing courage, but not allowing myself to breathe, I made a strong effort and at last got my head above the surface again, but where was the raft? Where were the helpless puppies? All had gone—not a trace was left to tell where they had been—the river foamed over the spot that had held them for a time, and was now rushing along as if boasting of its strength.

Seeing my intentions thus defeated, I turned my head towards the shore, resolving to swim to land. To my surprise, I found that I made no progress. I put out all my strength—I fought with the water —I threw myself forward—it was in vain—I could not move a paw's breadth against the current. I turned to another point—I again used every exertion—all was useless—I felt my tired limbs sink under me—I felt the stream sweeping me away— my head turned round in the agony of that moment, and I moaned aloud.

My strength was now gone—I could scarce move a paw to keep my head down the river. A dark

17

object came near me—it was a large piece of tim
ber, probably a portion of some ruined building.
Seizing it as well as my weakness would permit
me, I laid my paws over the floating wood, and,
dragging my body a little more out of the water,
got some rest from my terrible labours.

Where was I hurrying to? I knew not. Every
familiar object must have been long passed, but it
was too obscure to make out anything except the
angry torrent. On, on I went, in darkness and in
fear—yes, great fear, not of death, but a fear caused
by the strangeness of my position, and the uncertainty before me—on, on, till the black shores
seemed to fly from each other, and the river to
grow and gro w until all land had disappeared, and
nothing but the water met my aching eyes. I
closed them o shut out the scene, and tried to forget my misery.

Had I slept? And what was the loud noise
which startled me so that I had nearly let go my
hold? I roused myself—I looked around—I was
tossing up and down with a regular motion, but
could see nothing clearly. I was no longer carried
forward so swiftly as before, but the dim light prevented me making out the place I was now in.

Suddenly, a flash broke from the black clouds,
and for a single moment shed a blue light over
everything. What a spectacle! All around, for
miles and miles and miles, was nothing but dancing
water, like shining hills with milky tops, but not
a living creature beside myself to keep me company, or say a kind word, or listen to me, when I

spoke, or pity me when I moaned! Oh! who could tell what I then felt, what I feared, and what I suffered! Alone! alone!

When I think, as I often do now of that terrible scene, and figure to myself my drenched body clinging to that piece of timber, I seem to feel a strange pity for the miserable dog thus left as it seemed to die, away from all his fellows, without a friendly howl raised, to show there was a single being to regret his loss—and I cannot help at such times murmuring to myself as if it were some other animal. " Poor Job! poor dog!"

I remember a dimness coming over my eyes after I had beheld that world of water—I have a faint recollection of thinking of Fida—of poor Nip—of the drowning puppies I had tried in vain to save —of my passing through the streets of Caneville with my meat-barrow, and wondering how I could have been so foolish as to feel ashamed of doing so—and then—and then—I remember nothing more.

———— •♦• ————

PAINS AND PLEASURES.

WHEN I again opened my eyes after the deep sleep which had fallen upon me, morning was just breaking, and a grey light was in the sky and on the clouds which dotted it all over.

As I looked round, you may well think, with hope and anxiety, still nothing met my view but the great world of water, broken up into a multitude of little hills. I now understood that I was on the sea, where I had been borne by the rushing river; that sea of which I had often read, but which I could form no idea about till this moment.

The sad thought struck me that I must stop there, tossed about by the wind and beaten by the waves, until I should die of hunger, or that, spent with fatigue, my limbs would refuse to sustain me longer, and I should be devoured by some of the monsters of the deep, who are always on the watch for prey.

Such reflections did not help to make my position more comfortable, and it was painful enough in itself without them. It was certain, however, that complaint or sorrow could be of no service, and might be just the contrary, as the indulging in either would, probably, prevent my doing what was necessary to try and save myself should an opportunity offer.

The gray light, in the meantime, had become warmer and warmer in its tone, until the face of every cloud towards the east was tinged with gold. While I was admiring the beautiful sight, for it was so beautiful that it made me forget for a time my sad position, my eyes were caught by the shining arch of the rising sun, as it sprang all of a sudden above the surface of the sea. Oh! never shall I forget the view! Between me and the brilliant orb lay a pathway of gold, which rose, and fell, and glittered, and got at last so broad and dazzling, that my eyes could look at it no longer

I knew it was but the sun's light upon the water but it looked so firm, that I could almost fancy I should be able to spring upon it, and run on and on, until I reached some friendly country. But alas! there seemed little chance of such a thing happening as my ever reaching land again.

As the sun got high up, and poured his rays on to the sea, I began to feel a craving for food, and, though surrounded with water, yet the want of some to drink. When the thirst came upon me, I at first lapped up a few drops of the sea-water with avidity, but I soon found that it was not fit to drink, and that the little I had taken only made my thirst the greater. In the midst of my suffering, a poor bird came fluttering heavily along, as if his wings were scarce able to support his weight. Every little object was interesting to me just then, and as I sat upon my piece of timber I looked up at the trembling creature, and began comparing his fate with my own. "Ah, Job," I said, half-aloud, "you thought, perhaps, that you were the only unhappy being in the world. Look at that poor fowl; there he is, far away from land, from his home, from his friends, perhaps his little ones (for many birds have large families), with tired wings, and not a piece of ground as broad as his own tail for him to rest upon. He must go on, fatigued though he may be, for if he fall, nothing can prevent his death; the water will pour among his feathers, clog his wings, and not only prevent him ever rising more into the air, but pull him down until his life is gone. So, Job, badly off as you are just now, there is

17*

another, as you see, whose fate is worse; and who shall say that, in other places, where your eye cannot reach, that there are not others yet so very, very miserable, that they would willingly, oh! how willingly! change places with you, or with that poor fluttering bird!"

This talk with myself quieted me for a time, and I felt a certain joy when I saw the bird slowly descend, and having spied my uncomfortable boat, perch heavily on the other end of it. He did not do so until he had looked at me with evident alarm; and, worn out as he was, and his heart beating as though it would burst through his yellow coat, he still kept his eyes fixed upon me, ready to take wing and resume his journey, wherever he might be going, at the least motion I should make.

Some time passed over in this way; myself in the middle, and Dicky at the end of the beam. We did not say a word to each other; for, as I spoke no other language but my own, and he seemed about as clever as myself, we merely talked with our eyes.

A thought now came into my head. My thirst returned, and I felt very hungry. What if I should suddenly dart on little Dicky, and make a meal of him? I did not consider at the instant that, by so doing, I should be acting a very base part, for Dicky had placed confidence in me, and, killing him for trusting to my honour, and eating him because he was poor and unfortunate, would be neither a good return nor a kind action. Luckily for Dicky, and even for myself, although he was not

able to speak foreign languages, he could read my
meaning in my eyes; for when I turned them
slowly towards him, just to see my distance, he
took alarm, and rose into the air with a swiftness
which I envied. I am sorry to say, my only thought
at first was the having lost my dinner; but as I
watched him through the air flying on and on, until he diminished to a misty speck, and then disappeared, my better feelings came back to me, and
said, "Oh, Job! I would not have believed this of
you!" "But," replied my empty stomach, "I am
so hungry; without food, I shall fall in, and Job
will die." "Let Job die," said my better self again,
in a cold, firm tone; "let Job rather die, than do
what he would live to feel ashamed of."

As the day wore on, I began to think that death
only could relieve me; and the thought was very,
very painful. Nothing before and around but the
salt waves—nothing above but the blue sky and
hot sun—not even a cloud on which to rest my
aching eyes. The want of water which I could
drink was now becoming terrible. When I thought
of it, my head began to turn; my brain seemed to
be on fire; and the public basins of Caneville, where
only the lowest curs use to quench their thirst,
danced before me, to add to my torture;—for I
thought, though I despised them once, how I could
give treasures of gold for one good draught at the
worst of them just then.

There is not a misfortune happens to us from
which we may not derive good if our hearts are
not quite hardened, and our minds not totally im-

penetrable. Great as my sufferings were during this incident of my life, I learnt from it much that has been useful to me in after years. But even if it had taught me no other truth than that we should despise nothing which is good and wholesome, merely because it is ordinary, I should not have passed through those sad hours in vain. We dogs are so apt, when in prosperity, to pamper our appetites, and, commonly speaking, to turn up our noses at simple food, that we require, from time to time, to be reminded on how little canine life can be preserved. All have not had the advantage of the lesson which I was blessed with; for it *was* a blessing; one that has so impressed itself on my memory, that sometimes when I fancy I cannot eat anything that is put before me, because it is too much done, or not done enough, or has some other real or supposed defect, I say to myself, "Job, Job, what would you have given for a tiny bit of the worst part of it when you were at sea?" And then I take it at once, and find it excellent.

As the sun got lower, clouds, the same in shape that had welcomed him in the morning, rose up from the sea as if to show their pleasure at his return. He sunk into the midst of them and disappeared; and then the clouds came up and covered all the sky. I suffered less in the cool evening air, and found with pleasure that it was growing into a breeze. My pleasure soon got greater still, for, with the wind, I felt some drops of rain! The first fell upon my burning nose, but the idea of fresh water was such a piece of good fortune, that I dared

not give loose to my joy until the drops began to
fall thickly on and around me, and there was a
heavy shower. I could scarcely give my rough
coat time to get thoroughly wet before I began
sucking at it. It was not nice at first, being mixed
with the salt spray by which I had been so often
covered; but as the rain still came down, the taste
was fresher every moment, and soon got most delicious. I seemed to recover strength as I licked
my dripping breast and shoulders, and though
evening changed to dark night, and the rain was
followed by a strong wind, which got more and
more fierce, and appeared to drive me and my
friendly log over the waves as if we had been bits
of straw, I felt no fear, but clung to the timber, and
actually gave way to hope.

I must have slept again, for daylight was once
more in the sky when I unclosed my eyes. Where
was I now? My sight was dim, and though I
could see there was no longer darkness, I could
make out nothing else. Was I still on the rolling water? Surely not; for I felt no motion. I
passed my paw quickly across my eyes to brush
away the mist which covered them. I roused myself. The beam of wood was still beneath me, but
my legs surely touched the ground! My sight
came back to me, and showed me, true, the sea
stretching on, on, on, in the distance, but showed
me also that *I*, oh! joy, *I* had reached the shore?

When my mind was able to believe the truth, I
sprang on to the solid land with a cry which rings
in my ears even now. What though my weakness

was so great that I tumbled over on to the beach
and filled my mouth with sand? I could have
licked every blade of grass, every stone in my ec-
stacy, and when forced to lie down from inability
to stand upon my legs, I drove my paws into the
earth, and held up portions to my face, to convince
myself that I was indeed on shore. I did not
trouble myself much with questions as to how I
got there. I did not puzzle my brain to inquire
whether the wind which had risen the evening before, and which I felt driving me on so freely, had
at length chased me to the land. All I seemed to
value was the fact that I was indeed *there*, and all
I could persuade myself to say or think was the
single, blessed word, SAVED!

I must have lain some time upon the sand before
I tried again to move, for when I scrambled on to
my legs the sun was high and hot—so hot, that it
had completely dried my coat, and made me wish
for shelter. Dragging myself with some trouble
to a mound of earth, green and sparkling with
grass and flowers, I managed to get on top of it;
and when I had recovered from the effort, for I was
very weak, looked about me with curiosity to observe the place where I had been thrown.

The ground was level close to where I stood,
but, at a little distance, it rose into gentle grassy
hills, with short bushes here and there; and just
peeping over them, were the tops of trees still
farther off, with mountains beyond, of curious
forms and rich blue colour.

While considering this prospect, I suddenly observed an animal on one of the hills coming towards me, and I lay down at full length on the grass to examine who he might be. As he drew nearer, I was surprised at his form and look (I afterwards learnt that he was called an ape), and thought I had never beheld so queer a being. He had a stick in his right hand, and a bundle in his left, and kept his eyes fixed on the ground as he walked along.

When he was quite close, I rose again, to ask him where I could procure food and water, of which I felt great want. The motion startled him, and stepping back, he took his stick in both hands as if to protect himself. The next moment he put it down, and coming up to me, to my surprise addressed me in my own language, by enquiring how I came there. My astonishment was so great at first, that I could not reply; and when I did speak, it was to ask him how it happened that he used my language. To this he answered, that he had been a great traveller in his day, and among other places, had visited my city, where he had studied and been treated kindly for a long time; that he loved dogs, and should be only too happy now to return some of the favours he had received. This speech opened my heart, but before he would let me say more, he untied his bundle and spread what it contained before me. As there were several savoury morsels you may believe I devoured them with great appetite,—indeed, I hope Master Ximio's opinion of me was not formed from the greediness with which I ate up his provisions.

After I had refreshed myself at a spring of water, we sat down and I told him my story. He heard me patiently to the end, when, after a pause, he exclaimed—

"Come, Job, come with me. A few days' rest will restore your strength, and you can return to your own city. It is not a long journey over land, and with stout limbs like those, you will soon be able to get back and lick old Nip again."

I need not dwell upon this part of my story, although I could fill many pages with the narration of Master Ximio's dwelling, and above all of his kindness: he kept me two or three days at his house, and would have detained me much longer, but, besides that I was anxious to return to Nip, I felt certain pains in my limbs, which made me wish to get back to Caneville, as I did not like the idea of troubling my good friend with the care of a sick dog. He was so kind-hearted, however, and showed me such attention, that I was afraid to say anything about my aches, lest he should insist on keeping me. He seemed to think it was quite natural I should desire to get home, and when he saw my impatience to depart, he assisted to get me ready.

Having supplied me with everything I could want on my journey, and pressed upon me many gifts besides, he led me by a little path through the wood, until we came to the sea. "Along this shore," he said, "your road lies. Follow the winding of the coast until you reach the mouth of a broad river, the waters of which empty them-

lves into the sea. That river is the same which
ins through your city. Keep along its banks and
ou will shortly arrive at Canoville, where I hope
ou may find every thing you wish,—for I am
sure you wish nothing that is unreasonable. If
pleasure awaits you there, do not, in the midst of
it, forget Ximio. If, against my hopes, you should
find yourself unhappy, remember there is a home
always open to you here, and a friend who will do
his best to make you forget sorrow. Farewell!"

I was greatly moved at his words and the memory of his kindness. We licked each other tenderly—murmured something, which meant a great deal more than it expressed—and then we parted. I turned my head often as I went, and each time beheld Ximio waving his hand in the air; at last a dip in the ground hid him from my sight, and I continued my journey alone.

It was fortunate I had been well furnished with provisions by my good friend, for as I proceeded, I found the pains in my limbs so great that I could scarce drag one leg after the other, and should probably have died of hunger, as I had no strength left to procure food, and did not meet with any more Ximios to assist me had I stood in need. With long rests, from which I rose each time with greater difficulty,—with increasing anxiety as I drew near my home, to learn all that had taken place during my absence,—and yet with legs which almost refused to carry me; after many days that seemed to have grown into months,—they were so full of care and suffering,—I toiled up a hill, which

18

had, I thought, the power of getting steeper as I ascended. At length I reached the top, and to my joy discovered the well-known city of Caneville, lying in the plain beneath me. The sight gave me strength again. I at once resumed my journey, and trotted down the hill at a pace which surprised myself. As I got warm with my exertions, the stiffness seemed by degrees to leave my limbs; I ran, I bounded along, over grass and stones, through broad patches of mud which showed too plainly to what height the river had lately risen, out of breath, yet with a spirit which would not let me flag, I still flew on, nor slackened my speed until I had got to the first few houses of the town. There I stopped indeed, and fell; for it then seemed as if my bones were all breaking asunder. My eyes grew dim; strange noises sounded in my ears; and though I fancied I could distinguish voices which I knew, I could neither see nor speak; I thought it was my dying hour.

From the mouths of Nip and others I learnt all which then occurred, and all that had passed after my supposed loss on the night of the inundation. How my noble conduct (for so they were kind enough to call it, though I only tried to do my duty, and failed), had been made known to the great dogs of Caneville, and how they had sought after me to thank me for it;—how they had offered rewards to those who assisted in my recovery;— how, when it was supposed that I was dead, they took Nip from our modest home, and placed him in this present house, fitted with every thing that could make him comfortable for life;—how, when all hope was gone, my unexpected appearance brought a crowd about me, each one anxious to assist me in my distress, though some maliciously said, in order to lay claim to the reward ; and how I was finally brought again to my senses through the care of our clever canine doctors, and the kind nursing of dear old Nip.

It was long, however, before I recovered my legs sufficiently to be able to use them without support. My long exposure at sea; the want of food, and the trouble I had gone through during my involuntary voyage, had all assisted to weaken me. But my anxiety to enjoy the fresh air again, took me out into the streets directly it was thought safe for me to do so, and with a pair of crutches beneath my arms I managed to creep about.

Never shall I forget the first time this pleasure was allowed me. The morning was so fresh and bright; the sun shone so gaily upon the houses; the river, now reduced to its usual size, ran so cheerily along, that I got into my old habit, and began to think they were all talking to me and bidding me welcome after my long illness. Kind words were soon said to me in right earnest, for before I had got half way down the street, with old Nip just behind me,—his hat still adorned with the band which he had unwillingly put on when he thought me dead and gone, and which he had forgotten to take off again,—the puppies ran from different quarters to look up in my face and say, "How do you do, Job? I hope you are better,

Job." Many a polite dog took off his hat to bid me good morrow, and praises more than I deserved, but which I heard with pleasure, came softly to my ear as I hobbled slowly along. Nip told me afterwards, that there had been another in the crowd who kept a little back, and who, though she said nothing, seemed to be more glad to see me than all the rest. I had not seen her, nor did he mention her name, but that was not necessary. My heart seemed to tell me that it could only have been Fida.

------------◆------------

DUTY.

THE idle life which I was compelled to spend gave me time for reflection, and I believe my mind was more active during the few months my body was on crutches than it had been for years previous. My thoughts received little interruption from Nip, who, after having recounted the events which had taken place during my absence, had little more to say. The kindness of the great city dogs having removed all fear of want, or even the necessity of labour from our comfortable home, produced, at first, a pleasing effect upon me; but as my strength returned, and I managed to walk about the room without assistance, a desire for active employment became quite necessary to my happiness.

" What have I done, Nip ?" I would often say

as I took my usual exercise in our modest parlour;
" what have I done, Nip, that I should be clothed,
and fed, and housed, without labouring for such
advantages, like the rest of dog kind? These paws,
large and strong as they are, were never intended
for idleness; this back, broad as it is, was meant
for some other purpose than to show off a fine coat;
this brain, which can reflect and admire, and resolve,
had not such capabilities given to it in order that
they might be wasted in a life of ease. Work, Nip,
work; such work as a dog *can* do should be sought
after and done, for nothing can be more shocking
than to see an animal's powers, either of body or
mind, wasted away in idleness."

Nip replied but little, although he winked his
eyes very vigorously. I was used to his manner
now, and could understand his meaning without
the necessity of words. Both his looks and gestures
told me that he thought as I did, and I only waited
till I could use my own legs freely, to set about a
resolution I had been forming in my mind.

It was a happy day when I could again mix in
the bustle of the streets, and find my strength once
more restored. The first use I made of it was to
go to the great house where the chief dogs of Caneville are accustomed to sit during a certain time of
the day to judge matters relating to the city. When
I arrived, they were almost alone, and I was therefore able to present myself without delay, and explain my business.

I began by thanking them for what they had
done for me and my old friend Nip, in providing
  18*

us with a house and with so many comforts. I told them, although the goodness of Nip rendered him worthy of every attention, as he had grown old in a useful and laborious life, I had no such claims. I was still young—my strength had come back to me—I had no right to eat the food of idleness, where so many dogs, more deserving than I, were often in want of a bone, but whose modesty prevented them making known their necessities. I would still thankfully enjoy the home, which the kindness of the great animals of Caneville had furnished me, but they must permit me to work for it—they must permit me to do something which might be useful to the city in return, for I should devour the fare provided for me with a great deal more appetite, if I could say to myself when I felt hungry, "Job, brother Job, eat your dinner, for you have *earned* it."

The assembly of dogs heard me with great attention to the end; not a bark interrupted my little speech, not a movement disturbed my attention. I was pleased to see that tails wagged with approbation when I had concluded, and was charmed to hear the chief among them, who was white with age, express himself *delighted*, yes, that was the word, delighted with my spirit.

"We are pleased, Job," he said, at the end of his reply, " we are pleased to observe that there are yet *true dogs* in Caneville; there have been animals calling themselves so, whose character was so base, and whose manner was so cringing, that they have brought disrepute upon the name; and we are sorry to say that in many countries the title of a *dog* is given to the vilest and most worthless creatures. All the finer qualities of our race have been lost sight of, because a few among us have been mean or wicked; and a whole nation has been pointed at with scorn, because some of its members have acted badly. We are happy, Job, to find in you a 'worthy subject,' and we shall be glad to give you all assistance in choosing an occupation in which you may employ your time, and be of use to your fellow-creatures."

I should not have repeated this to you, as it is not, perhaps, necessary for my story, but that I wished to correct an error which many have made concerning the character of this very dog. He has been described by several as cold, and proud, and sometimes cruel; and yet to me he was warm, and friendly, and most kind. Do not you think when we hear animals grumbling against their fellows, it would be just as well to think who the grumblers are, before we form our opinions? or, at least, hear the opinions of many before we decide ourselves?

I need not tell you all that passed between us, and what was said by this dog and by that, about the choice of my occupation. It was agreed at last that I should be appointed chief of the Caneville police, as the place had become vacant through the death of a fine old mastiff some days previous. I wonder whether he was a relation of my own, for I have already told you my mother belonged to that great family. He had received some severe wounds when trying to capture a fierce beast of the name of Lupo, the terror of the city, and he had died from the effect of them in spite of all the care of the doctors. What made the matter worse, was the fact that Lupo was yet at liberty, and many dogs were afraid to go out at night for fear of meeting with this terrible animal.

To tell the truth, I was rather pleased than otherwise that Lupo had still to be taken. It was agreeable to me to think that work, difficult work, was to be done, and that *I* was called upon to do it. I felt proud at the idea that the animals of the great city of Caneville would look up to me, *to me*, poor Job, as the dog chosen to relieve them of their fears, and restore security to their streets. "Job," I cried out to myself, in a firm tone, "Job, here is a chance of being useful to your country; let no danger, no fear, even of death, stop you in the good work. Job, you are called upon to perform a duty, and let nothing, mind *nothing*, turn you from it."

After I had become acquainted with all the dogs who were under my command, I spent much time each day in exercising them, and in endeavouring, by kind words, and by my own example, to make them attend strictly to their work. I was pleased to observe that I succeeded. Some, who were pointed out to me as difficult to manage, became my most faithful followers, and I had not been two months in my employment before all were so devoted to me, that I believe they would have died to serve me.

In all this time, nothing had been heard of the

terrible Lupo, and all my enquiries procured no information concerning where he was to be found I learned that he was not a native of Caneville, although his father once belonged to the city. He was born in a country beyond the great wood, and his mother came from a fierce tribe of wolves, who, although they a little resemble dogs in appearance, and speak a very similar language, are much more ferocious, and seem to look upon the whole canine family as natural enemies.

The opinion began to spread in Caneville that Lupo had at length left the city, and the inhabitants, by degrees, recovered their usual quiet; when, suddenly, the alarm spread more widely than before; as, two nights in succession, some rich dogs were robbed and ill-treated, and one of them was lamed by the ferocity of the chief of the terrible band who had attacked them, and whose description convinced me it was Lupo.

These accounts caused me much pain, as I had neither been able to prevent the attacks, nor discover the animals who had made them. In my desire to find out and capture the robbers, I could scarcely take food or rest. I managed to sleep a little in the day-time, and at night, dressed in the simplest manner, so as to excite no attention, I wandered quietly from street to street, stopping to listen to the slightest noise, and going in any direction that I heard a murmur. One or two of my dogs generally followed at a distance, ready to assist me if I called for help.

It was a fine night. The moon and stars were

brilliant in the sky, and made the blue all the deeper from their own bright rays. I had been already two hours crawling through the lower parts of the city, and was mounting the hill which led to a fine building, where my steps often carried me;—sometimes without my intending it;—in order to watch over the safety of those who slept within. It was the house of Fida, that Fida who had been to me so kind, so tender; that Fida who had so patiently softened down my rudeness, and had tried to teach me to know what was good by letting me become her friend.

I had nearly reached the top of the hill, and paused an instant to observe the bright light and dark shadows which the house displayed, as the moon fell upon it, or some portion of the building interposed. Profound sleep had fallen upon the city. The river might be seen from the spot where I was standing, running swiftly along; and so deep was the silence, that you could even hear the gush of the water as it fretted round some large stones in the centre of the stream.

Suddenly, there rose into the air from the ground above me, the sharp, clear howl of a female voice, and at the same instant, the sound of a rattle broke upon my ear as a signal of alarm. I sprang up the few feet which were between me and the house, with the speed of lightning, and turning rapidly the corner of the building, reached the principal entrance. One look told me everything: at an upper window, in a loose dress, was Fida herself, springing the rattle which she held in her paw with a strength that fear alone could have given her; and below, where I myself stood, were four or five dogs differently engaged, but evidently trying to get into the house.

A kick from my right leg sent one of them to the ground, and, with my clenched paw, I struck a blow at the second. Never do I remember feeling such strength within me, such a resolution to attack twenty dogs if it were necessary, although the next minute I might be torn in pieces. I have sometimes asked myself whether the presence of Fida had anything to do with it, or if a sense of duty only inspired me. I have never been able to reply to the question in a satisfactory manner. I only know that the fact was as I say, and that the blow I gave was surprising even to myself; my paw caught the animal precisely under his chin, and sent him flying backwards, with his nose in the air and his hat behind him; and as the moon shone brilliantly upon his upturned face, I recognised the features described to me as those of Lupo. He lay so still upon the ground, that I thought he must be killed; so leaving him for a moment, I pursued some others who were running off in the distance, but did not succeed in catching them. I said a few cheering words to Fida at the window, and returned to the spot of my encounter with Lupo, but instead of that terrible beast, found some of my own followers, the father of Fida, and one or two servants, who had been roused by the tumult, and had come out to learn the cause. Lupo was nowhere to be seen. He had either partly recov

ered from the blow, and had managed to crawl
away, or had been dragged off by some of his
troop.

Nothing could have been more fortunate to me
than this night's adventure. The father of Fida,
who had seen the attack from his window, was the
head of one of the best families of dogs in Caneville, and being, besides, very rich, he enjoyed
great power. He was so pleased with what I had
done, that he not only took a great liking to me
himself, but he spoke of my conduct in the highest
terms to the great assembly. I received public
thanks; I was admitted to the honour which I now
hold, that of forming one of the second assembly
of the city; I was loaded with rich presents, and
equally rich praise; and I may also date from that
night, the obtaining the richest gift of all, the gift
which has made the happiness of my best years; I
mean the possession of my wife, the beautiful Fida.

It is true that I did not procure that felicity at
once. There were many difficulties to be got over
before the noble spaniel would think of allowing
his daughter to become the wife of plain Mr. Job.
His son, also, of whom I have spoken previously,
could not bear, at first, the idea of his sister not
marrying some one as noble as herself, and thought,
very naturally, that she was far too good to have
her fortunes united with mine. Fida herself, how·
ever, was so firm, and yet so tender; so straight-
forward, and yet so modest, that she finally broke
down all opposition. She persuaded her father
that no title could be more noble than the one I

had acquired, that of "Honest Job;" she won
over her brother, by slyly asking him, which
among his grand companions could have met a
whole band of fierce dogs, with Lupo at their
head, and, single-pawed, could have conquered
them all? By degrees, every objection was cleared
away, and Fida became mine.

The chief interest of my life terminates here;
for, although in my position as head of the police,
I had many other adventures, they were too much
alike, and of too common an order, to be worth
relating. Before I close, however, I must mention
a circumstance which occurred shortly after my
battle with the robbers, as it is curious in itself,
and refers to an animal of whom I have before
spoken.

I was quietly walking along a bye-street of
Caneville, when a miserable, thin, little puppy
came behind me, and gently pulled my coat. On
turning round to ask him what he wanted, he
begged me in the most imploring tone to come
and see his father, who was very ill.

"And who is your father, little pup?" I en-
quired.

"His name is Lupo," said the thin dog, in a
trembling voice.

"Lupo!" I cried out in surprise. "But do you
not know who I am, and that I am forced to be
your father's greatest enemy?"

"I know, I know," the pup replied; "but
father told me to come and seek *you*, for that you
were good, and would not harm him, if you knew

19

he was so miserable." And here the little dog began howling in a way which moved me.

"Go on;" I said after a moment; "go on; I will
follow you."

As the little dog ran before, through some of the
low and miserable parts of the city, the idea once
came into my head, that perhaps this was a scheme
of Lupo's to get me into his power. But the pup
py's grief had been too real to allow me to believe,
young as he was, that he could be acting a part; so
with a stout resolution I went forward.

We arrived at a low and dirty kennel, where
only the greatest misery could bear to live. We
passed through a hole, for so it appeared, rather
than a doorway, and I found myself in a little room,
lit by a break in the wall. On the single poor bed
lay a wretched object, gasping for breath, while a
ragged pup, somewhat older than my little guide,
had buried his face in the clothes at the bottom of
the bed. Three other tiny creatures, worn to the
bone with poverty and want of food, came crowding round me, in a way that was piteous to behold,
and with their looks, not words, for they said
nothing, asked me to do something for their miserable parent. I procured from a neighbouring
tavern a bason of broth, with which I succeeded in
reviving the once terrible Lupo, but it was only a
flash before life departed for ever. In broken
words, he recommended to my care the poor little
objects round. Bad as he was, he still had feeling
for them, and it was easy to observe that at this
sad moment his thoughts were more of *them* than

of himself; for when I promised to protect them,
he pressed my paw with his remaining strength to
his hot lips, moaned faintly, and expired.

My tale is over. Would that it had been more
entertaining, more instructive. But the incidents
of my career have been few, and my path, with the
one or two exceptions I have described, has been a
smooth one. I have heard it said that no history
of a life, however simple, is without its lesson. If
it be so, then, perhaps, some good may be derived
from mine. If it teach the way to avoid an error,
or correct a fault; if any portion of it win a smile
from a sad heart, or awake a train of serious thought
in a gay one, my dog's tale will not have been un-
folded in vain.

A CHAPTER ON PETS.

THE love of pets is one of the flowers of civilization, a feeling either openly apparent or lying dormant until warmed into existence by circumstances. Many carry this affection too far, but on the whole there is something humanizing in a pet.

Gratitude sometimes causes the adoption of a pet. A dog that has saved your own or child's life, or, as in the case of Lord Forbes's dog, which discovered that the house was on fire and saved the inmates, has a right to be regarded, during the rest of its life, with care and gratitude. We hear of a Turkish emperor who rewarded a horse which had carried him safely through a great danger, by giving him a marble stable, an ivory manger, a rack of silver, shoeing him with gold, and settling an estate upon him. We hear of prisoners taming the sparrows that perched on the bars of their cells, and making friends of a stray rat or mouse ; we all know the story of the plant Picciola.

Tameness and domesticity produce every imaginable "eccentricity" in animals. There is scarcely a horse without some peculiarity. I knew one whose particular fancy was window-breaking ; if he *could* slip his collar at night he would break every piece of glass he could get at. Another who would stop at certain liquor stores, when he came to them, and nothing could induce him to pass without stopping. A third, whenever he got loose, would, with the greatest assiduity, collect brooms, buckets, curry-combs, everything, in short, portable within reach, and put them all together in his manger.

I have heard of a lady keeping a large green frog as a pet; its leaving or seeking the water was found to beat all the barometers, so true a prophet was it of the coming weather. It knew its mistress, who used to receive by post a pill-box of flies for its support. Monkeys are now quite out of date. I suppose they went out of fashion as china came in. They were, I believe, the earliest species of pets of which we have any record. I heard of a great cultivator of pets taking a monkey with him by railroad in a basket. One of the officials saw something suspicious, as he thought, smuggled into the carriage—

" You must pay for that dog."

“ It is not a dog,” said the traveler.

“ It is a dog,” said the official, poking his finger so near a hole in the basket as almost to feel the wind of a snap made at him.

“ It is not a dog but a monkey, and monkeys don’t pay,” rejoined the owner.

“ I don’t care what it is,” said the other, “ it is a hannimal, and hannimals pays.”

“ I suppose you will make me pay for this, next,” said our friend, pulling from his breast-pocket a tortoise.

“ No,” said the official, “ that’s not a hannimal, that’s a hinsect.”

Few can realize the number of cage-birds sold every year in London. We may divide them into parts: those bought for their song, like the night-ingale, thrush, blackbird and linnet; those for their plumage and song combined, namely the canary, bulfinch and goldfinch, etc.; the imitators of the human voice, as the parrots, magpies, star-ling and raven; and those for their plumage alone, as the lovebirds, humming-bird, etc. I will give you a few statistics to show the amount of busi-ness carried on in these pets, taken from “ May-hew’s London Labour and London Poor.” Six thousand live larks are sold every year in Lon-don. These birds require fresh turf, the cutting of which employs forty men who cut 600,000 turfs about six inches square, weighing nearly

546 tons, which placed side by side would extend fifty-six miles. Perhaps you have heard the tale of the lark taken to Canada by an emigrant; the vessel in which he sailed was wrecked, and the lark (Charley) was all he saved. His owner settled at Toronto, and three separate times he was offered one hundred dollars for Charley; another time a farmer offered one hundred acres of land; and a Sussex carter, hearing him, offered his team and cart, all he possessed, without success. Seven thousand linnets, 3,000 bulfinches, 1,500 chaffinches, 700 greenfinches, 200 nightingales, 600 redbreasts, 3,500 thrushes, 1,400 blackbirds, 1,000 canaries, 1,500 starlings, 500 magpies and jackdaws, and 2,000 *duffed* birds are supposed to be sold yearly in the streets, the value of which, including parrots, would produce a yearly sum of more than twenty-five thousand dollars.

Two thousand four hundred squirrels are required to fill up the vacancies, and bring the sellers about one thousand two hundred dollars a year. There is a curious tale told of a Scotch magistrate who had a case before him of a servant girl who sued her mistress for her wages; the defense being that she had allowed a favorite squirrel to escape. The magistrate, after hearing the parties, said: "That although the girl was to blame for leaving the cage door open, yet the mistress was more to blame than her, for she sud hae clippit

the beast's wings, sae that it cud na flee away!!"
A pet dog is the most extravagant thing to keep
in London, owing to its being so easily stolen.
The sale of dogs in London reaches the sum of
forty-five thousand dollars a year. Pigeons are
another specimen of pets. One of the great uses of
pigeons as messengers is now at an end, owing to
the invention of the electric telegraph. Perhaps
the most remarkable instance of the successful
employment of pigeons was at the time of the
death of the Duke of Orleans, the eldest son of
Louis Philippe. He was killed by jumping out
of his carriage in Paris, which happened after the
publication of the papers in Paris, and an account
of it appeared in the London *Times* next morning
before it was really known in Paris.

I must not forget the cat, which they average
to be about one to every ten inhabitants. Thus in
London there must be an army of over 200,000
cats; and, as dogs and cats must be fed, they employ in London about one thousand men who sell
cat's meat; this is the flesh of dead horses, which is
boiled and peddled through the streets in barrows. It is calculated they boil every year for
this purpose fifty-two thousand horses, and the
people pay for this five hundred thousand dollars.

Many English regiments have their pets, which
always lead the march. The Twenty-third Fusi-
liers, a Welsh regiment, always have a goat;

another will have a sheep ; one, I know of, has an elephant. Scotch regiments like the deer. The Seventh once had a bear. The Sheffield militia, for years, always had a dog. He regularly appeared the first day of training, and disappeared on the last, no one knowing where he came from. A French regiment of Spahis in Algeria had a lion's cub, which was brought in by Jules Gerard, but the attempt to tame him proved futile.

THE MOOSE HUNT.

SOME years ago, being sent into Maine for the benefit of my health, having broken down through over-study at college, I had the good fortune to be present at a moose hunt: a treat worth living a year in the forest to be at.

We started, that is four of us, at daybreak, on snow-shoes. The novelty of thus traveling was great: they take you so rapidly over the ground. They are from three to four feet long, and rather narrow, the frame work is generally of ash wood and woven across with leather or moose-hide thongs, very like basket-work, with straps to hold them on the feet; two or three pairs of stockings and moccasins are generally worn with them; being so light and strong, they bear you on the surface of the snow, while your feet would strike through. The first day we could not find any trace of game. About noon the next, my uncle, with an Indian, appeared on the scene. My uncle and Pete (the Indian) arranged their snow-

shoes and then we started again in quest of
our prey. Before long I felt certain, by watching
Pete's curious ways, that we were on the track of
moose; and when darkness came on, and not any
signs of them, I felt disappointed. "All right,
me get them yet; moose neber go off that way —
throwing his hand forward in a tangent — sure
come again; go round, so," describing a circle.

So we commence to scoop out the snow, and
prepare to make ourselves comfortable for the
night with our buffalo robes over us, with a good
fire to help to keep us warm.

At the earliest dawn we awoke, and having
eaten our breakfast, and fastened on our snow-
shoes, we prepared to start again, and soon found,
to our great joy, that Pete was right: we were in
the center of a moose circle. Pete told me as
well as he could that a few moose congregate
together, and tramp down the snow in a circle,
sometimes of a mile, inside of which they browse
on the young trees. The sun had hardly risen
before we saw one of these splendid fellows loom-
ing up, as he roamed about in search of his breakfast. I was delighted with this opportunity of
watching the native of these forests perfectly at
home, browsing from one tree and another. No
museum or picture can give an adequate description of their movements so well as one glance at
them will do it. Pete said: "He hear 'em soon;

soon smell 'em!" and so he seemed to be scenting
the danger; then the chase began. The sound
of the first shot, it failing to hit him, has started
him into a rapid trot. Away we fly over the
snow, now seeing him, then losing all sight of
him in the forest-aisles.

Toward noon we sighted a pair of these grand
animals, when the greatest excitement prevailed.
I never witnessed such a scene; all shouting like
boys. In less than an hour we had run down
and shot one. The exertion and excitement
began to tell on my weak frame, and my uncle
insisted on my return to the camp, not, however,
before we had skinned the animal, so I could take
some of the meat back with me. Before starting,
we broiled some, and I never enjoyed a steak so
much before; the exercise and pure air made it
taste far superior to a porterhouse steak, which it
much resembled.

Before we left the beat, I stumbled over a protruding moose-horn which we dug up. I intend to
have it dressed for my room, for I feel sure I must
have shot him. A gentleman once succeeded in
partially taming a pair, and drove them in a carriage, but they only lived a short time.

FOUR-FOOTED HUNTERS.

THERE were twelve lions in the troop — old males, females, and whelps of different ages! A terrific spectacle to look upon, in any other way than through the bars of a cage, or out of a third-story window. But we beheld them on an open plain, and at the dangerous proximity of three hundred yards!

It is needless to say that a sudden stop was put to our advance, and that every one of the six was more or less alarmed. Although we knew that, as a general rule, the lion will not attack man without provocation, it might be different where such a number were together. Twelve lions would have made short work of one and all. No wonder we trembled at sight of such a troop, and so near; for the brow of a ridge, running abruptly down to the plain, was all that lay between us and the dreaded assemblage. A few bounds would have brought the lions to the spot on which we stood!

After the first moments of surprise and alarm had passed, we bethought ourselves how to act. Of course, the pallahs were driven completely out of our mind, and all ideas of a hunt given up. To have descended into that valley, would have been to have encountered twice our own number of lions. We did not think for a moment of going farther, nor, indeed, of anything but retreating; and it cannot be said that we *thought* of that, for it was the instinct of the moment.

"Back to our horses!" we whispered, the moment we set eyes on the lions; and in less than two minutes' time, we were seated in our saddles.

Our presence had not been discovered by the lions. Two circumstances had favored us, and prevented this. The ridge over which we were passing was covered with underwood, and the "bosch," reaching as high as our heads, had sheltered us from view. The other circumstance in our favor was that the wind was blowing *down* the valley, and therefore *from* the lions and toward ourselves. Otherwise, we should have been scented, and of course, discovered. Still another circumstance — we had been advancing in silence, on account of the design we had formed of stalking the pallahs. The lions, therefore, still remained ignorant of our proximity. Once on horseback our party felt secure, and soon got over their little "flurry." Each knew that the noble creature that carried him, could show any lion his heels. Once mounted, all felt that the danger was over.

Two of our number were not satisfied to retreat in this way. They were resolved on, at least, having another " peep " at the dangerous game ; and, therefore, prepared to return to their former point of observation, of course this time on horseback.

The antelopes were still feeding quietly near the center of the open ground. The lions were, as yet, on the ground where they had been first observed. That the deer knew nothing of the proximity of their dangerous neighbors was very evident, else they would not have been moving so sedately along the sward. They had no suspicion that an enemy was near. The lions were in the lower end of the valley, and therefore to leeward of them — for the wind was blowing fair down stream, and came right in the faces of the hunters. A thicket, moreover, screened the lions from the eyes of the herd.

It was equally evident that the beasts of prey were well aware of the presence of the antelope. Their actions proved this. At short intervals one trotted to the edge of the "bosch," in crouching attitude, looked out to the open plain, and after a moment or two returned to his companions, just as if he had been sent to " report." The old males and lionesses stood in a thick clump, and seemed to be holding a consultation! We had not a doubt but that they were doing this very thing, and thåt the subject of their deliberation was the herd.

At length the " council " appeared to break up. The troop separated, each taking a different direction. Some went along the bottom of the valley, while several were seen to proceed towards the mountain foot.

When these last had reached the groves before mentioned, they turned upwards ; and, one after another, were seen crouching from clump to clump, crawling along upon their bellies, as they passed through the long grass, and evidently trying to shelter themselves from the view of the deer.

Their object now became clear. They were proceeding to the upper end of the valley, with the design of driving the game upon those that had remained below—in fact, carrying out the identical plan which we had projected but the moment before ! We marveled at this singular coincidence ; and as we sat in our saddles could not help admiring the skill with which our *rivals* were carrying out our own plan.

Those—three there were—that had gone skulking up the edge of the valley, were soon out of sight—hidden under the " bosch " that grew at the opposite end, and which they had been seen to en-

ter.   Meanwhile, the other nine had spread themselves along the bottom of the valley, each taking
station under cover of the bushes and long grass.
The trap was now fairly set.

For a few minutes no movement was observed
on the part either of lions or deer.   The former
lay crouched and stealthily watching the herd—
the latter browsed peacefully along the sward, perfectly unconscious of the plot that was "thicken-
ing" around them.

Something at this moment seemed to render
them suspicious.   They appeared to suspect that
there was danger threatening.   The buck raised
his head; looked around him; uttered a hiss,
somewhat like the whistling of deer; and struck
the ground a smart rap or two with his hoof.   The
others left off browsing, and several of them were
seen to bound up into the air—after the very singular manner of springboks.

No doubt they had scented the lions, now at the
upper end of the valley—as the breeze from that
quarter blew directly towards the herd.

It was surely that; for after repeating his signal, the old buck himself sprang many feet into
the air, and then stretched himself in full flight.
The others of course followed, leaping up at intervals as they ran.

As the lions had well calculated, the antelopes
came directly down the valley, breast forward, upon

their line. Neither the wind nor anything warned them of the dangerous ambuscade ; and in a few short moments they were close to the patches of brushwood. Then the nine huge cats were seen to spring out as if moved by one impulse, and launch themselves into the air. Each had chosen a rooyebok, and nearly every one succeeded in bringing his victim to the earth. A single blow from the paw of their strong assailants was enough to stretch the poor antelopes on the plain, and put an end at once to their running and their lives. So sudden was the attack, and so short-lived the struggle, that in two seconds from the time the lions made their spring, each might be seen crouching over a dead deer, with his paws and teeth buried in its flesh !

Three alone escaped, and ran back up the valley. But a new ambush awaited them there ; and as they followed the path, that led through the thicket at the upper end, each became the prey of a lurking lion.

Not one of the beautiful antelopes, that but the moment before were bounding over the plain in all the pride and confidence of their speed, was able to break through the line of deadly enemies so cunningly drawn around them !

We remained for some minutes gazing upon the singular spectacle and then rode back to the wagons.

Arriving there, a consultation was held how we were to proceed. It would be a dangerous business to trek up the narrow valley guarded by such a troop. For there is no time when these animals are more dangerous to attack than just after they have killed their game and are drinking its blood. At such a moment they are extremely ferocious, and will follow with implacable vengeance any one who may disturb them. It would be more prudent, therefore, not to provoke such a powerful band, but to retire altogether from the spot. A ford was therefore sought for, and found at some distance below; and, having crossed our wagons, we encamped on the opposite side, as it was too late to move farther that night.

We had done well to go across the river, for during the whole night the fierce brutes were heard roaring terrifically upon the side where they had been observed. In fact, the place appeared to be a regular *den of lions*.

STORY OF REYNARD THE FOX.

THE Spring appeared in all its glory, and the husbandman anticipated the coming season with joy; the trees were clothed in verdure, and the fields were enamelled with flowers; the birds saluted the morning sun with hymns of gladness, and poured forth vesper songs, as the glorious luminary descended behind the western mountains. The brilliant loveliness of nature, and the exhilarating influence of the atmosphere, mollified the stern heart of the royal Lion, King of beasts and birds, insomuch that he determined to hold a solemn festival at his imperial palace, and, under the guise of apparent condescension and friendly conviviality, investigate any charges of partiality against his judges, or oppression on the part of his other powerful subjects. Accordingly, he issued a proclamation, commanding all his lieges, both beasts and birds, to attend his court, on pain of his royal displeasure; announcing at the same time, that a sumptuous entertainment would be provided for them. When the important day arrived, birds and quadrupeds from every quarter might be seen thronging the court. The gates of the grand saloon were thrown open, and the great feudatories—such as Bruin the Bear, Isegrim the Wolf, Pard the Leopard, Grevincus the Badger, and Springer the Hound, took their places near the throne, while the herd of the commonalty kept at a respectful distance.

One of the most sagacious barons of the kingdom, however, had absented himself. This was no less a personage than Reynard the Fox. He had formerly held high office under his Majesty; but while he pretended to live only for the good of the commonweal and the honour of his master, self-interest was his ruling passion; moreover, he had such a strong liking for dainties, that he had been known to disguise himself, and purloin the King's poultry on their way to the royal demesne; and yet, next day, with unequalled address and consummate dexterity, he would throw the odium of the theft on some political rival whom it was his interest to keep down; thus making the prostrate body of an innocent competitor a stepping-stone to power, and strengthening the royal partiality by unworthy means. Conscious of guilt, the ex minister pretended to be grievously sick, and could not do himself the honour to wait on his Majesty; while the fact was, that he was afraid to trust the royal amnesty, as he well knew he should be accused by certain of his political or personal enemies when they became exhilarated by the influence of

the delicious wine which was sure to circulate with
regal hospitality. After an interchange of friendly
greetings and salutary conversation, the august
party descended to the banqueting hall, where they
found the table furnished with regal magnificence.
Each took his place with decorum, while his Majesty addressed his guests with dignified familiarity
and amicable courtesy. The viands disappeared
with great rapidity from the well-replenished board;
the goblet circulated right royally; the company,
who were at first awe-struck by the imperial glance,
were now at their ease; political disquisitions became loud and fiery; and atrocious stories were
told off, and heavy accusations made against Reynard the Fox.

Up rose Isegrim the wolf; and having made
his *congé* to the throne, bellowed forth his complaint against Reynard until the gilded cornices
rung again. "I beseech you, dread Sovereign, take
pity on me and my wife for the injuries we have
suffered by that false craven Reynard. He intruded
himself into my house, insulted my dear partner,
did violence to my helpless children, whereby some
of them lost their precious eye-sight, and then, like
a coward, slunk to his hole without giving me the
satisfaction of a gentleman. Were I to record his
crimes, it would be a black indictment, and would
fill many volumes. By setting the laws at defiance,
Sire, he slights you, while he injures the public
with impunity." Isegrim having caught the eye of
the Monarch, again made his obeisance, and resumed
his seat. Whereupon Springer started to his legs,

and, having crouched before the throne, accused the
unhappy culprit Reynard of robbing him of his per-
quisites of office, namely, the skeletons of geese and
other fowls, beef and mutton bones, together with
rancid sausages and decayed bacon.   He averred
that such proceedings were intolerable, and ought
to be punished by the laws of this and every well-
regulated kingdom; and this failing, such vaga-
bonds should be proceeded against by fire and
sword.   Upon which, Malkin the Cat, with a fiery
countenance and bristling whiskers, mewed forth a
speech in the ears of Majesty which plainly showed
that self-interest had blinded her judgment.   So
making a semicircle of her back, and stretching out
her tail, she said—"My lord, I confess that Reynard the Fox is an atrocious villain, fraudulent,
and a thief; but there are certain others who may
be proved as bad as he.   Springer the Hound has
all the will to be a thief without the ability.   The
bacon which he alleges to have been stolen from
him by Reynard, he meanly stole from me—although he knew very well I risked life and limb
in taking it out of the mill by night when the miller
lay asleep."

Bruin the Bear, who thought himself the hand-
somest person in the assembly, and anxious to display his elocution before royalty, got upon his hind
legs, and, leaning on a pole to which he had been
accustomed in a caravan, he hoarsely complained
of grievances and losses.   He gazed in the Monarch's
face, and, unabashed, told his Sovereign that he had
more important information to lay before his ma-

jesty than any that had yet been tendered ;--"They are worthy of the care of a prince and the anger of a king.   Although your Majesty has thought the Fox a saint heretofore, I will prove him a fiend. His father was hanged, his mother was burned for sorcery, he was inured to thieving from infancy, which malady can only be cured by a rope. Often has he wished you laid with your fathers, and made vows to the evil spirits for your destruction, in the vain hope of cajoling the giddy crowd and ascend·ing your royal throne.   On the faith of treaties, a harmless Rabbit came to sojourn in your imperial city ; Reynard, the villain, sneaked up to the sim·pleton, and smilingly asked him if he would learn a song.   The knave made him believe that he would not only teach him music, but that he had interest enough to introduce him to court, and pro·cure him the privilege of singing before royalty— when, if successful, his fortune was made.   The fool believed him, and elevated his head and ex·panded his chest, as ordered by the singing master. While in this attitude, he seized his victim by the throat, just as he was warbling and quavering the first or second bars of an Italian air; and would have doubtless murdered the innocent but for me, who happily interfered at the critical moment. The gash on his throat may yet be seen; and the silly wretch is now here to prove my accusation. There are none secure from his treasons.   He de· ceives the rich, robs the poor, murders the weak, and betrays the strong.   Your Majesty's crown is in danger if he is suffered to prowl longer through

your dominions; and with one voice we cry for
justice." The crowd rent the sky with their plau-
dits, and all repeated, "Let the traitor perish!"

Grevincus the Badger, who was Reynard's
nephew, being moved with high wrath and indignation on hearing his kinsman thus impeached, and
on the brink of condemnation, manfully stood up,
and told the revellers in plain terms, that "If
Reynard were here, they durst not abuse the ear of
their Sovereign with falsehoods, nor give prominence to the faults of others to hide their own.
Thou, Isegrim, now so loud and clamorous, hast
found him friendly, and publicly bepraised his high
mental qualities. The cunning which thou up-
braidest has often saved thee from starvation.
Well dost thou remember when the fishmonger's
cart was driven through the village, how he stif-
fened his limbs, drooped his head, and glazed his
eyes. The hind, thinking he had been dead, threw
him into the cart, and, being snugly ensconced
there, threw thee out as many fish as served thy
famishing family for a fortnight. At the peril of
life and limb, my sagacious kinsman procured a fine
sucking Pig, and while it was becoming beautifully
brown on the spit over a pool of rich gravy, thou
ingrate, didst thou not meanly and feloniously tear
it thence, and, like a craven as thou art, slink away
to the forest with it? thus doing treason to thy
hospitable entertainer, and giving a proof of thy
worthlessness.

" As to the charge against my traduced relative,
made by Bruin, the Rabbit was his scholar, and

bound by oath to be his servant also.   Had not the master a right to chastise his servant, the teacher to correct his pupil?   Besides, the lad was both coxcomb and dullard at the same time.   It would have been the simpleton's ruin if my friend had acted otherwise.   Springer the Hound pretends that he has been robbed!   What exclusive right he had to goods which he himself had stolen, I own passes my comprehension.   Fair plunder ir. righteous wars is approved of by our greatest generals; but envy follows merit, as surely as the shadow follows the substance.   The humble, I should say the lowly, condition in which my relation lives, should move your pity rather than your hatred.   Austere in his dress, severe in his morals, frugal in everything except charity, coarse his fare, and rigorous in his fasting and penances, he lives an inflexible recluse, and only thinks of his latter end.   Besides, he is often insulted by the application of opprobrious epithets, and assaulted by the meanest of your Majesty's subjects; his reformation is termed hypocrisy, and the humility of his bearing cowardice.

"It was only the other day, when meditating in the fields, and arrayed in full canonical costume, he chanced unwittingly to pass a poultry yard; and although he was armed with your Majesty's decree, commanding peace and amity among the various tribes of your kingdom, the whole colony rushed out on the harmless recluse with bludgeons, brooms, pitchforks, and other deadly weapons, and but that he was 'cunning of fence,' they would have taken

his life; and, to crown the indignity, a contempti-
ble Peacock, tricked out in gaudy frippery, but a
coward at heart withal, soared to a place of safety,
and screamed forth such a torrent of vile language
as was never heard in any of your Majesty's fish-
markets. If during the fray some of the family
of Gallus suffered in either life or limb, I know
not, but one thing I am certain of, that the *intentions* of my much abused relative were in strict accordance with your Majesty's decree."

While Grevincus was labouring towards his
climax, he was stopt short by seeing a sad procession approach the court.   Gallus the Cock, together
with a long train of sons and neighbours, advanced
lamenting, and crying for justice; and, to enhance
the melancholy scene, the body of Gallena, his
daughter, was laid on a bier, who had been lately
murdered by Reynard.

Gallas the Cock stood before the King's tri-
bunal, impatient to avenge the blood of his
beloved daughter.   Her brothers bemoan their
father's bereaved condition, and bewail the untimely fate of their sister.   When the first paroxysm of grief subsided a little, Gallus addressed
himself to the Monarch:—"Behold, Sire, a loyal
subject wretched and old; robbed of his children
who were dearer than life. I was the happy father
of twelve stately sons, and twenty fair daughters.
They had board and education in an abbot's yard,
where their physical and moral health were well
looked after. They were guarded by six friendly
mastiffs day and night. This circumstance that

culprit Reynard knew full well, and despaired of
ever catching them by surprise. He accordingly
resorted to stratagem, dressed himself like a monk,
covered his villain's head with a cowl, and produced your royal mandate that feuds and fear, and
hostile acts should forever cease and determine. I
saw the imperial seal on the document, and bent
my head in token of reverence and obedience.
The wily thief spoke demurely and penitentially
of his former immoral courses; told me that pen-
ance should be his daily task hereafter; that he
should endeavour to divest himself of all earthly
cares, all worldly passions; that cooling herbs
should be his food, and these only to be used in
sparing quantities. He, moreover, produced a
forged certificate to prove himself a member of the
brotherhood; and when the vesper bell rung, he
counted his beads, and went through certain devo-
tional mummeries with the dexterity of an adept.
I heard, saw, and believed. The tidings flew over
the whole yard. The gates were opened; and the
good mastiffs, who had watched my children with
so much fidelity, were thrown off their guard. The
hypocrite took advantage of the negligence which
his falsehood had produced. He rushed in and
devoured my daughters, and destroyed my sons.
I have only been able to save the relics of Gallena,
which I lay before your Majesty as a proof of the
desolation which has overwhelmed my house."

Maugre the imperial diadem and mantle, the
golden sceptre, and the jewelled throne, the Sovereign wept! and, frowning sternly on Grevincus

the Badger, exclaimed, "Ha! is this the way the new monastic spends his time? He seems to defy Jove's thunder and his Sovereign's mandates. We can bear this insolence no longer. He dies! Inter the dead decently, and proceed instanter with the vile assassin!" The funeral rites being performed, the feudatories assembled, and debated the matter amicably, how the murderer might be brought to justice with the greatest speed and security. All seemed repugnant to the task, and many were the excuses offered. At length Bruin the Bear, animated more by personal hatred than duty to his King, undertook the task; and with an oath—such as none but bears use—promised to bring him up to justice, dead or alive.

The Monarch held out the golden sceptre to Bruin the Bear, previous to his commencing his dangerous mission—"Go, Bruin, I command, but take care that thou art not baffled by the strategy of the rebel; give no heed to his smiles; trust not his flattery; it is unworthy of a great statesman to be circumvented."

Impatient of advice, Bruin felt a little hurt, and growled forth a gasconade. "Hear me, O Cæsar! If Reynard proves too cunning for me, let the darksome womb of the earth engulf a wretch unworthy of the light." And bowing towards the throne, took leave. He traversed many wilds, passed rapid floods, descended into caves, and searched the forests all round, but saw nothing of the outlaw, and consequently had to put up with "traveller's lodgings" for the night.

Reynard had built an impregnable fort, where guilt and infamy might find a retreat. He dug it deep, and compassed it with walls, hedges, and a deep trench. He also contrived a sallyport, known only to himself. This stronghold Bruin at length found out, and knowing it sheltered the rebel, he thundered at the door, and in tones of authority accosted Reynard, who gave him a salute from the walls. "See," says Bruin, "the King's august command; here is his signature, and this is the impression of the royal signet; unbar your gates, and allow the representative of majesty to enter." Reynard answered the ambassador in the most polite manner,—"Read the King's commission, if you please. Ancient feuds, you know, have passed between us; but when we are both safe, we may be free."

The Bear replied that his Majesty was highly exasperated against him. "If you dare refuse to obey his summons, he vows by his throne that he will put your person to the rack, and raze your house to the ground."

When Reynard became assured that our egotistical envoy was alone, he thought all was as it should be, so went down and opened the narrowest wicket. "Your pardon, noble Bruin. I have kept you waiting by far too long, but I hope you will excuse my fright. My matin service is now over, and I hasten to pay my duty. I am astonished to see such an august guest within these poor walls as yourself. You renew your former favours in this visit. Great was your journey! Ah; 'tis very rare to see lords of your rank visit such humble individuals as myself. Homely fare and a hearty welcome is all your excellency must look for from me."

The insolence of office is sometimes laconic. "Come, Sir! my time is short; pack up your baggage and march, or I shall find a method to quicken your movements."

"If health permit, I shall follow your excellency to-morrow; they can never restrict a person of your high rank to a day. I am brought low by pain and sickness. Alas! I have scarcely strength to walk. My stomach is weak, and I am prescribed to eat gruels and salads, and to abstain from flesh altogether. I have as fine a chicken as ever was turned on a spit, but Dr. Owl prohibits me from touching it." The ambassador, after his long and devious journey, being somewhat sharp set, was already in fancy picking the bone.

"You are well provided, Reynard," said his excellency, in a softened tone. "Time was, my lord, when I had enough and to spare, but I cannot forage now as formerly; I find myself at once sick and poor. I have, however, plenty of *honey*, but eating much of that brought on the colic. 'Tis rich and pleasant, but far too luscious and sweet for me and my ailments."

"Ha! you astonish me; is honey really so plentiful here? I prefer it to flesh, or fish, or venison, or lobsters, sturgeon, jellies, or soups. I shall never forget your favour, Sir, if you oblige me with a pot, and the larger the better."

Reynard was delighted to find that Bruin **had** swallowed the bait so greedily, and, bowing and smiling, he said, "Since your lordship is such a lover of honey, my neighbour the husbandman, I have to inform your lordship, has such a large stock of bees, that their hives will furnish you with as much honey as you can consume in a month If your excellency will be pleased to walk, I will exert all my remaining strength to accompany you; 'tis only a short league."

To the husbandman's orchard, accordingly, they trudged on in the most friendly manner; the en-voy bent on delicacies, the rebel on revenge.

The orchard having been reached under cloud of night, the invaders surveyed the ground for a breach or opening whereby they might enter.   At length they found a great oak tree with two wedges in it, and the cleft open.   "I humbly beg your excellency," said the Fox, "be careful, for within this tree is much honey; eat moderately, for a sur-feit is dangerous."

"Leave that to my prudence," says Bruin.   So he entered the cleft with eagerness, which his wily antagonist perceiving, pulled out the wedges, and caught Bruin in so sharp a trap, that the poor en-voy howled with pain, while the Fox at a distance jibed and jeered the crest-fallen statesman.

"How does your excellency like the honey?   As you value your duty to the King, do not surfeit yourself, seeing ye are on an important mission."

The noise alarmed the whole village, the in-habitants of which came and belaboured the Bear's sides with clubs, and hoes, and pitchforks, until, mad with rage, he tore his bleeding face and paws from the tree, and rushed blindly into a river that ran close by, knocking into the water many of the boors, and among the rest the husbandman's wife, for whose sake every one bestirred himself. Amidst the confusion the Bear limped away, and was no more seen in that quarter.

Meanwhile, the slippery politician Reynard having stolen a plump cockerel from the husbandman's roost, carried it to his stronghold, and having made a banquet thereon that might have served a cardinal, he sallied out by his secret postern to procure drink, and sauntering along the margin of the brook, he came upon the unfortunate Bear, growling in an under tone, and licking his lacerated paws. Adding insult to injury, he sneeringly observed,

"Ha! by your looks you have fed upon delicious honey to repletion, but I fear you have paid too great a price for your luxuries. Your coat, too, has also changed colour. If I mistake not, it was formerly sable, now I perceive it is crimson. Perhaps you mean to leave the cares of statesmanship, and retire into the bosom of mother-church. Ah! my dear friend, when you receive a cardinal's hat, I hope your eminence will remember me, as my inclinations run in the same direction.—Why do you employ such a clumsy barber? He has scraped your chin too close, and scarified your jaw! Your tusk—your very bones, appear; nay, as I live an honest life, he hath denuded you of half of one of your ears!"

The discomfited Bear, writhing with mental and physical anguish, replied not a word, but limped away to the grand assembly, where, in dismal accents, he recounted the sad trick that Reynard had played him. The mighty autocrat of birds and beasts was never known to be in such a towering passion on any former occasion. He started from his throne—his mane bristled, his eyes flashed fire, and his tail swung from side to side like a pendulum; so, elevating his right paw, he exclaimed—

> "Now, by this earth and yon empyreal sky!
> The traitor shall with ignominy die;
> The forms of law from which we never swerve,
> Our judges must advise, and we observe."

The senate, *nem. con.*, thanked him for his speech; and an impeachment was moved by the Bruin party. Grumble the Ass was the foremost spokesman; he was an advocate by profession, but was poor, proud, formal, obstinate, and dull. Nevertheless, he stood up before the august assembly—for ignorance is always impudent, and constantly self-possessed. He brayed a long invective against the panel, exhibiting his crimes in the blackest hues his ingenuity, such at it was, could suggest; and urging conviction, " for the honour of the Sovereign and the laws, the safety of the weak, and the terror of the wicked."

A bill was drawn, read, and unanimously approved of, and Reynard was condemned to capital punishment. It were wise, however, for people to catch their fish before they count them.

It became necessary that a new commissioner be chosen in order to bring the arch offender to justice, and the choice of the house unanimously fell on Malkin the Cat, who, conscious of the extreme hazard of the mission imposed on him, and fearing disgrace and discomfiture, urged a thousand reasons not to be employed on this piece of state service, seeing how stronger beasts than he had been hood-winked and circumvented.

"It is your wisdom, Sir Malkin, I employ," said the great King, "and not your strength; many prevail with art, when violence returns with lost labour; we brook not reply."

With a heavy heart Malkin made ready for his journey, and being well acquainted with the intricacies and sinuosities of the road, arrived at Reynard's fortalice about eventide. He found the object of his search sitting comfortably with Dame Emelin, his wife, their children sporting around them.

After a slight but kindly greeting, the new envoy produced the King's summons, and assured the recusant that, if the tenor of the document was not instantly complied with, "there is nothing more assured unto you than a cruel and sudden death."

"Welcome, welcome, to my poor habitation," said Reynard; "in you I behold the representative of my master, whom I revere. We have a gracious King, and a just senate. My life and lands are at his pleasure whom you serve; but you see it is late—so, walk in and spend the night in my humble domicile. I shall carefully peruse the royal letters, while my wife makes ready a cleanly, though, I fear, a coarse supper. But pardon me, my dear cousin, what food do you fancy best; we have delicious honey."

"You will pardon me for making so free; but I prefer a delicate mouse to all the honey and nectar in the world."

"Now, dear friend," says the Fox, "I can suit your appetite better than the royal purveyor can do even to our imperial master. My neighbour the parson has yards full of tithes, dairies full of cheese, vaults full of corn, so that the mice there are not only plentiful, but excel the finest venison in flavour."

"Ah!" says Malkin, "the sooner you lead me there the better. You know the old adage, 'A parson's mouse is most delicious fare.'"

Then away they went to the parson's barn, which was well walled about with a mud wall, where but the preceding night the Fox had broken in and stolen a fat hen, at which the worthy parson was so justly incensed, that he had set a snare before the hole to catch him at his next coming, which the false Fox knew of, and therefore said to the Cat, "Sir Malkin, creep in at this hole, and you shall not tarry a minute's space before you have more mice of the first quality than you are able to discuss; hark! how they squeak! When you are satiated, come to me again, for I will wait for you at this hole. To-morrow we shall go together to court, but stay not too long, for I know my wife will hourly expect us."

Malkin sprang quickly in at the hole, but in a moment was caught by the neck in the snare, by which he was half strangled—the more so, indeed, as he struggled for life, and mewed most piteously.

"You sing most sweetly, dear cousin," says the betrayer, "and I make no doubt but you could dance equally well, were it not for that confounded trap, which spoils the gracefulness of your movements. As you are a cat of quality, you should have had your mice cooked according to the canons of Soyer, and not rushed on the harmless creatures, like a rapacious courtier as you are."

The servants were all alarmed, and the cry was set up, "The Fox is taken!" and away they all ran to where poor Malkin was caught in the snare, and without finding out their mistake, they beat him unmercifully, and wounded one of his eyes. Mad with pain, the Cat suddenly gnawed the cord, sprang on one of the head servants, and scratched him so severely that he fainted; and when every one ran to afford his mite of assistance, Malkin leaped out of the hole, and limped as fast as his wounded legs would carry him to court, where the King was extremely angry at the treatment he had received, and in rage commanded his council to nominate yet another messenger to bring that audacious rebel Reynard to justice, when Grevincus the Badger, Reynard's sister's son, fearing it would likely go hard with his uncle, volunteered to carry his Majesty's message to his most subtile kinsman, to which the king graciously consented; so Grevincus set forth, and ere long arrived at the castle of his relatives.

Having saluted the Fox, he said, "Take heed, uncle, that your refusal to come to court may not do you more harm than you are aware of; for the complaints against you are many and grievous. This is the third summons, and if you delay coming, you and yours will find no mercy, for in three days your castle will be demolished, all your kindred made slaves, and you yourself a public example, unless indeed you can make your innocence appear, which I doubt not, but by discretion and ingenuity you can; false pleading, you well know, is often as fortunate as true. How many capital suits has Grumble the Ass gained, who seldom speaks sense, and never speaks truth?"

Whereupon Reynard put on a show of candour, and said, "Why should I distrust the court, or fear my judges? My cause is just, my innocence is injured; but that I hope soon to clear up. If the Monarch and his ministers encourage slander and slanderers, the demand will aways bring a supply; but who in such a state of things can be safe. I grant that I have failings, but who are without them? In trifles I may now and then transgress, but nothing serious can be proved against me. I'll go to Cæsar. My honour has been injured, and my name made a byeword. I shall obliterate all this, or bravely fall."

While wending his way to the royal presence his sincerity was put to a severe test, having been required to pass a wellknown poultry yard, which

had often contributed to his larder. He triumphed,
however, and on consideration, thought it would
not be altogether out of place to enumerate a few
of his *crimes*, which he had heretofore denominated
failings, by way of confession, to his nephew Grevincus, who had always led an hermit's life. The
catalogue is by far too long for a place here, but it
consists of thefts, robberies, and murders—lambs,
hares, rabbits, geese, ducks, cocks, hens, pigs, all
perished beneath the voracious fangs of this irre-
claimable freebooter. In one word, he was a terror
to the whole district where he lived; and although
he had address enough to elude his pursuers, he
was well known by every farmer, cottager, and
gamekeeper in the country-side. He even had the
hardihood to glory in his misdeeds, and set some
of them to measure and music. Take the following
as a specimen :—

> " Eh," quo' the Tod, " it's a braw light night,
>   The win's i' the wast, an' the mune shines bright,
>   The win's i' the wast, an' the mune shines bright,
>   An' I'll awa' to the toun, O !

> " I was down amang yon shepherd's scroggs,
>   I had like to been worried by his dogs,
>   But, by my sooth ! I minded his dogs,
>   That night I cam' to the toun, O !"

> He's ta'en the grey goose by the green sleeve,
>   Eh, ye auld witch ! nae langer shall ye leeve ;
>   Your flesh it is tender, your banes I maun preeve,
>   For that I cam' to the toun, O !"

> Up gat the auld wife out o' her bed,
>   An' out o' the window she shot her auld head—
> "Eh, gudeman! the grey goose is dead,
>   An' the Tod has been i' the toun, O!"

The news of Reynard's arrival spread like wild-fire through the assembly. When he took his place near the throne, every member of that august house stood up in order to catch a glance of one so celebrated. Some feared him—some pitied him—others despised him—and many hated him.

With the withering glance of injured innocence, he indignantly scowled on the junto, and, falling on his knees before the throne, he called loudly for justice. "Lowly, O Cæsar! like my altered fortunes, I sue at your feet for law and justice! My greatest crime has been my inflexible attachment to your person and government. Had I, like some pretended loyalists, sold your subject's charters and their lives, to enrich myself—had I sent your favourite heroes to their certain fate—had I betrayed your fleets and armies by secret correspondence to your Majesty's enemies, I had not this day been encompassed with such impending dangers. Like certain others, I might have purchased large estates, erected lordly mansions, and fostered my family on the lap of wealth at the expense of my country; but my patriotic principles were too strong, and my duty to your Majesty paramount to my very existence. Believing your Majesty to be wise and just, I troubled you with no petitions, knowing well that rounded periods and florid eloquence, where truth is lacking, would have been as smoke

in your nostrils. Conscious that my services were
sincere, both in word and action, and secure in rectitude, I considered myself above the reach of
malice. They have traduced me, but how can
they prove their allegations? they have impeached
me, but how can they bring home guilt to me?
They have charged me with disloyalty and malver-
sation—let them prove it." Here, folding his arms
across his breast, he made a profound obeisance,
and retired backward.

"Peace, recreant," exclaimed the King, "I loathe
to hear thy vile defence and thy wicked plea. Thy
crimes are enormous, so shall be thy punishment.
A more wretched cause than thine was never vin-
dicated—a more atrocious villain never stood up in
a court of justice, urging laws and citing precedents.
Thy treason is already proved; behold Bruin's
wounds and Malkin's lacerations! Were such
felons as thee allowed to go at large, our very
slaves would insult us!"

With more than Oriental humility in his demeanour, Reynard ventured to ask, "Why should
Bruin's folly be charged on me? Like a plunderer
as he was and is, and while holding your Majesty's
seal of office, he went forth under cloud of night to
rob an honest man's bee-hives, and if he was caught
in a cleft oak, was that any fault of mine? I
humbly submit that he has disgraced himself for
ever—brought obloquy on the commission he bears
—and that his evidence is inadmissable. The case
of Malkin is equally atrocious. In place of following up the letter of his instructions, and making

every thing give way, in order that your Majesty's behests might be obeyed with promptitude, the brainless coxcomb, giving way to his gluttonous propensities, neglected or despised the high commission with which he was charged; and, like a common burglar, feloniously broke into the parson's enclosures, to the disgrace of himself and the dishonour of your majesty; and if he was caught in a gin, and half strangled, lacerated, and buffeted, he really deserved it, but I humbly submit that I could neither foresee nor prevent what took place. If it is your Majesty's high pleasure to put me to the rack, devour me by fire, or suspend me from a gibbet, I shall gladly die a martyr to the state; but historians hereafter will arise, who, I hope, shall do justice to my memory; the example will not be lost, and I shall not have died in vain!"

Hot was the debate, and learned were the argu ments which pervaded the assembly; much eloquence and more verbiage were displayed for and against the accused. Some attempted to vindicate Bruin; others stood up in favour of Malkin; a small knot of third-rate orators spoke in favour of Reynard; but it was evident from the beginning that the great majority would vote for the death of the culprit at the bar. The bill was read thrice, and ultimately it was touched by the golden sceptre, which was decisive of the fate of the criminal.

"Our very enemies," says the Monarch, "will confess that lenity has been often fatal to the throne and the laws. Traitors abuse the royal clemency. A base impostor, intoxicated with the hopes of
27*

empire, which hopes have been fed by the factious, has had his crimes laid bare before us, and no doubt remains on our mind that he has been bribed thereunto by foreign powers."

Whereupon the Senate arose simultaneously, and yelled forth, " Long live the King, and down with the rebel."

The attainted baron was stript of his cognisance, and fettered ; and the Sheriffs with their officials brought out the doomed from the presence to be consigned into the hands of the finisher. Reynard ever had few friends, but now, when fortune had seemed to have forsaken him, these diminished to half a dozen of his blood relations ; who wept and lamented, not so much, perhaps, for the impending fate of their kinsman as for the disgrace which his ignominious exit would bring on themselves.

" What a pity," cried they, " that his untimely end should stain the ancient honours of our race ! Why should we witness it?—let us turn to Cæsar and crave leave to return to our homes, that we may mourn in secret and in silence "

" Peers, powers, and sages," replies the King, " I know you to be loyal and just, nevertheless, I cannot trifle with justice. Faction is in favour of Bruin, who has been anything but prudent, and no doubt deserves to be executed; of that hereafter. But your cousin *must* be hanged ; there is no mercy in store for such a flagrant rebel, but that circumstance shall never make me part with you, nor lose the benefit of your counsel."

Accordingly Bruin and Malkin pinioned Rey

nard's hands behind his back; and Isegrim the
Wolf, although imbrued with innocent blood, was
as noisy and as eager to have Reynard brought to
the gallows, as if he had been as pure and as honest
as Keyward the Hare, or any other harmless beast,
Shoving and pressing through the gaping crowd,
he cried,—"Come on, bring the thief along; let
some fetch the halter, and let others bring the ladder; I'll guard him safe, and see him fairly swung.
Haste! if the rascal escapes, we shall have to pay
dearly for our negligence. Look sharp, the knave
is as slippery as an eel; perhaps he may yet wrig
gle through our fingers. Lord Bruin, I entreat you,
have a care of him." "My life for his," says the
Bear, "until you are entirely ready, leave the vagabond with me; fix you all the tackling securely,
and see that the gibbet be well driven into the
ground.

Meanwhile the Queen, radiant in beauty, and
glowing with gold and jewels, appeared on the
ground to behold the death-scene of such a notable
public offender as Reynard. Immediately all eyes
were turned on her Majesty; when Isegrim the
Wolf cried out with vehemence, "Are you mad to
loose this rogue? I know his malice, as well as
his cunning; if he get away from us, your necks
will be in danger!"

Reynard, as a kind of forlorn hope, appeals to
the Wolf. "If, noble Isegrim, you despise justice,
friendship, or gratitude, never forget that my blood
circulates in your veins; this should move your
pity—your care is needless. I am, alas! too weak;

a silken thread or a spider's filament would secure me; for what, then, are you so barbarous? and why will you reward my good with evil?"

"I'll dash my halbert in your teeth," replies Bruin. "Come, noose him quickly; we'll teach him, brother Isegrim, how to plot against the state."

All Reynard's arts of persuasion having failed, he was at length pinioned, and carted to the foot of the gibbet. Stung by terror and remorse, he begged leave, as a final favour, to make a speech before the fatal noose was applied to his neck. This piece of formality was reluctantly granted; and protruding his snout over the cart, he said,—"Good people, my destruction has been long threatened, and death has come at last; my crimes sit heavy on me, in pity let me ease my mind. If you will petition your gracious Sovereign, he may yet prolong my days. I have much to confess, and, believe me, it is of great importance to the state, but this I can only relate to the King. It is for my Sovereign's interest and that of the whole empire. Small venial trespasses I will own here, such as robbing orchards, slaying geese, chickens, turkeys, and all sort of fowl, young kids, pigs, lambs and various small quadrupeds. But, Sir Isegrim, who is so wondrous busy here to-day, shared the plunder, and should also share the shame. We roamed together, and, in a friendly manner, I invited him to my house. The winter stores which I had provided, he stole again and again; and my family would have starved but for the golden treasure which I discovered in a ruin. I never revealed this piece of good fortune although the hoard was worth the ransom of ten kings. Some foreign enemy, I suppose, had sent this great mass of golden ore to purchase votes against the Government."

As the sound of "gold" fell on the tympanum of royalty, he cried loudly from a scaffold—"Carman, hold! Inform us, Reynard, where this treasure is hidden. Speak out, man, and despise the fury of thy enemies!"

"For what," says Reynard, "can such a heap of gold be hid but for mischief to your Majesty? My enemies, if I were dead, believe that their treasonable plot would prosper; and I would have divulged this important state secret sooner, but your Majesty was wroth, and would not grant me a hearing. I know, of a truth, that the money is still in the same place where I found it; and, if your highness will condescend, I will show your Majesty the secret passage." The King drank in the story greedily, and longed vehemently to touch the precious metal.

Her Majesty the Queen sat and listened to the story of this new Eldorado with more than ordinary attention and solicitude; and, smiling graciously on the Fox, replied—"you must not think to impose on us with your ingenious falsehoods; but if you really speak the truth, I shall use my feeble interest with his Majesty to disengage you from the noose, and procure you a reprieve, perhaps a pardon."

"Alas! madam," says Reynard, "this is neither the time nor place to utter falsehoods My friends

and brethren, I fear, will be found not wholly guilt
less, as I wish they were, but I durst not at this
hour presume by lies to avert a righteous sentence.
His Majesty would soon discover the deceit, and I
should be more wretched than ever, to be repinioned
and sent back.   I defy the most implacable of my
enemies to urge I ever would impose on wisdom
and sagacity, such as all the world knows his gracious Majesty eminently possesses. If so, the world
might well believe me to be as great a fool as Isegrim, and as stupid as Bruin."

Since the moment her Majesty heard of the golden
tidings, her bowels yearned for the treasure; so,
leaning fondly on the Monarch's shoulder, she pat-
ted his cheek and said—" It grieves my heart to
the core, my lord, this cruel piece of business.   Indeed, you must not hang poor Reynard. You will
be the cause of my death if you proceed any farther,
especially when you know that my whole heart is
bent upon saving him."

His Majesty, with a combination of love and
benevolence in his looks, gazed on the Queen and
said—" We desire him to reveal all he knows, and
as we like his story, so shall it be done unto him;
the noose may be relaxed, and the condemned
permitted to speak." Whereupon Reynard, with
trembling lip and faltering accent, made the following disclosure:—" My liege, the treasure which
I have alluded to, I willingly confess was stolen;
and had it not been stolen in that manner in which
it was, it might have cost your Majesty your life.
Long may that inestimable life be extended."

When the Queen heard of her lord's life being
in hazard, she started up and said—"I command
you, as you value your own life, unfold all those
doubtful speeches, and keep nothing secret that
concerns the life of my royal husband."

"Know then," says the doomed one, "my dread
Sovereign, that my father, by a strange accident,
digging in the ground, found a great mass of treasure, jewels innumerable, and gold beyond calcu-
lation, of which being possessed, he grew so proud
and haughty, that he held all the beasts of the
forest in scorn and derision. At last he despatched
Malkin the Cat to the forest of Arden, where Bruin
the Bear sojourned for the time being, and tendered
him fealty and homage, and offered to place the
imperial crown on his head—desiring him to come
into Flanders, where he would find ways and means
to accomplish his traitorous purpose. Bruin being
excessively ambitious, and having long thirsted for
sovereignty, thereupon came to the place of rendezvous, where my father received him with regal
magnificence. They were joined by Isegrim the
Wolf, Malkin the Cat, and my nephew Grevincus
the Badger. These five held solemn council for
the space of a whole night; and being intoxicated
by my father's inexhaustible wealth, it was agreed
that your Majesty should be forthwith murdered,
and Bruin crowned king, with immediate possession of all the rights, privileges, and immunities
which you or your royal predecessors ever enjoyed,
together with a complete monopoly of all the honey
found in the various bee-hives in the kingdom;

and if any of your blood or kin gainsayed them, that assassins should be hired with a portion of my father's treasure, who should exterminate them— root and branch—from the forest. To these hor- rid and treasonable measures each and all of them took the big oath, with all its formalities, to make it feel the more solemn and binding. Under the influence of rich old champagne—a wine which he had never been accustomed to—my nephew Gre- vincus blabbed the secret to his wife, who, in great secrecy told the matter to my wife, and she discov- ered it to me. It grieved me to the heart to think that they should depose my own rightful Sover- eign, to whom I had sworn allegiance, and elevate a vulgar clumsy vulgarian like Bruin to the impe- rial purple; and knowing that money is the sinews of treason as well as of war, I became desirous of finding out my father's treasure, and by constant watching, both by night and day, I at length, to my infinite joy, discovered his hoard, and with the assistance of my wife, removed it to a place more convenient for us, where we laid it safe from the search of all and sundry.

"When my unhappy father went to view his treasures, and found them all taken away, he rent the air with his howlings, and wandered from place to place, but could find no rest. He at last grew gloomy and morose, and, finding his misery beyond endurance, he hanged himself. It is meet that I take this opportunity to remind your Majesty of my father's services as court-physician ; and that, soon after your Majesty's ascension to the throne, having been struck down by a grievous malady, you were restored to health, strength, and the functions of royalty, by the medical skill and perseverance of him who is now no more. Thus have I defeated Bruin's treason—thus have I circumvented the deep-dyed traitor Isegrim—and hence all my misfortunes have accumulated on my devoted head. These foul conspirators being of your Majesty's privy council, and having your royal name constantly in their mouths, they traduce me, tread on me, and work my disgrace. But although I have lost my natural father for your sake, I would gladly lay down my own life also for you; but I detest the idea of dying under the false accusations of my political enemies. 'Tis that, and that alone, which embitters the cup."

Now their Majesties felt an ardent desire to possess the treasure; and the Queen stepped forward, and whispered—"Discover where this immense wealth is concealed ere it be too late; I shall intercede for you; his Majesty is not of an implacable nature; he is as generous as he is brave. Disclose the secret, and trust to the King's clemency."

"Why, Madam," replied Reynard, "should I give this enormous treasure to one who has condemned me? Your Majesties put implicit faith in the asseverations of my enemies, who are thieves and murderers, while you disbelieve every word I say in defence."

"Courage, Reynard. my lord shall not only forget the past, but sign your pardon also; nay, more, a portion of the riches shall be reserved for

your especial use and benefit, while a small sum
shall be scattered among the rabble, in order to
gain you popularity; and, no doubt, I will retain
somewhat for my own private use, as a remuneration for my intercession."

"My most gracious princess," says the accused,
"if the King will vow in your presence that I have
his pardon, he shall be the most wealthy sovereign
of the age in which he lives!"

"Believe not the arch deceiver," said the King,
"except when he confesses to robbery, murder,
and falsehood."

The Queen put on one of her most fascinating
smiles, and said,—"No doubt Reynard's past life
has not earned for him either our regard or confidence; but think only how he has accused his own
father—to me that sounds very like sincerity of
purpose; and therefore I implore your Majesty to
extend your clemency to him this once."

"Well, on the faith of your sagacity," said the
King, "I'll pardon him; but it is the last time, so
let him be cautious for the future."

Kneeling down, his eyes glistening with pretended gratitude, the Fox looked upwards to their
Majesties and exclaimed—"Imperishable honour
and enduring renown be yours! your goodness I
shall ever confess. Sooner shall envy cease to
traduce merit, or modesty prevail over impudence
—sooner shall sectaries forget their hatred, or
misers their hoarded treasure, than I shall forget
your Majesty's royal clemency—this is, indeed, the
brightest jewel in your imperial crown. Now I

will tell you where the treasure is hid, and shall tell nothing but the truth:—

"There is a forest in Flanders which has as yet escaped the ravages of war. Some give it one name, some another—the neighbours call it Hustelo. A rapid river runs through it, which, from its springs to where it debouches into the sea, glides past a hundred towns. Here the larks warble matins, and the nightingales sing their vesper songs. An enormous oak, which has stood the shock of tempests for many ages, is conspicuous above all the trees of the forest; at its root flows a fountain, and hard by is a deep cavern. That no one may reveal the secret, you must descend yourself and explore it in person. You will find an imperial crown, worn formerly by Emmeric. The rebels, who so successfully abused your Majesty's ear, had purchased it for the head of Bruin, when you should either be decapitated or abdicate. There are also hid precious pearls, and valuable jewels for his dowdy queen. And I humbly trust that when your Majesty is in undisputed possession of this great treasure, you will not forget your loyal slave, who has impoverished himself and brought his father's memory to infamy, that your Majesty might be great, glorious, and free."

Whereunto the King replied,—"Reynard! If thou art sincere, what need have we to go so far ourselves? 'Tis below our state to travel; and moreover, I have heard of Flerus and the Meuse, of Arden and Enghien, of Cologne, Antwerp, Brussels, Namur, and Mons, but never of Hustelo.

In whose dominions does this forest grow? In what map will we find it?   Is it in Eutopia or the country of Prester-John?   Ah, Reynard, I know thou lovest a lie! and I fear this is one."

" It grieves me to the heart's core," says Reynard, " that I should be thought capable of deceiving my own Sovereign.   Hustelo is in Flanders, which I shall prove by the testimony of travellers who have been in the locality.   With your Majesty's gracious permission I shall cite the Hare as an unimpeachable witness."

The heralds call on Keyward the Hare, who, at the summons, trembled in every limb; the fear of Reynard fell on him, and he confirmed the statement by affirmation.   " When hinds and hounds pursued me, I have often retreated to the forest of Hustelo, I think they call it ; and there is a tradition that a profane prince, called Sylvio, hid money there ; and the story goes that the place has been haunted ever since.   This is vouched for by the wicked ; as for me, I dare attest no more than that the forest is there."

" Enough," replied the Sovereign.   " We shall depart on the important mission to-morrow, and you, Reynard, shall point out the spot; so make preparation."

" I know of no higher honour, no greater distinction, than the privilege of accompanying you, my beloved Sovereign, on this or any other enterprise. No higher fortune could have fallen on me; but, alas ! Fortune has never been a friend to me.   If I had been in a condition to have attended on your

Majesty, then poets would have celebrated my name
in immortal verse. I should have been recorded
in history as the companion of a king, and unborn
generations would have sounded my praise. But
my company and companionship would scandalize
your Majesty. I am under the ban of Rome, and
lie under the sentence of the greater excommuni-
cation. I am ashamed of the fact, but I must confess it. It will, I trust, be another link in the
chain of evidence, that my whole testimony is
honest and candid. Isegrim took it into his silly
head to become a friar; he sported the cowl, tied
a cord around his waist, went through all the stages
of discipline, fed on monastic fare, such as herbs
and roots, begged from door to door even for that.
I became vexed to see his bones protruding through
his hide, and aided and assisted him to desert the
church and take refuge in my poor domicile. The
rage of the bishop knew no bounds. He declared
me a reprobate, cursed me from the altar, and accused me of heresy. What would your subjects
say if they saw your Majesty holding intercourse
with a spiritual outlaw. Besides, is it decent to
have intimate communication with a newly pardoned felon ? By waiting on your Majesty on the
present occasion, I should rather disgrace you than
be of service to you. My name would reflect on
yours, and the Flemings would make a jest of
yourself, your mission, and your train. No, no;
I must cross the Alps, make my appearance before
the sovereign pontiff, propitiate him by gold and
penitence, purchase large quantities of indulgences,

kiss the toe of St. Peter's successor, and obtain absolution; and when I return with a newly scoured conscience, with your Majesty's pardon in one pocket and the Pope's in the other, my fame shall have been recovered and my mind at peace, and *then* shall I follow you to Flanders, or where you please."

The King approved of his reasons, and ordered him to proceed on his pilgrimage forthwith; enjoining him to procure the counsel of some pious and discreet friend, and to observe fasting, and let his future life atone for the past. A throne was erected on the green, to which the King and his royal consort mounted. Silence was declared, on pain of forfeiture. Not the least murmur was heard through the crowd. The nobles lay dejected on the sward, while Reynard is preferred to a distinguished place. Though all envy the distinction, none dare condemn the favour that advanced him there. His Majesty told them that he preferred lenity to severity. "If the laws are cruel I am not so. We cherish the great and we maintain the poor. All have relief and succour in this court. Your just rights shall be supported, and we desire only to reign in your hearts. I have state reasons for striking the chains off Reynard. Whom I bound I can loose; and throughout my wide empire I declare him free, and whoever wrongs him injures me."

The tidings of Reynard's pardon ran through the woods with great rapidity; having so suddenly grown great in his master's favour, indicated

danger to the persons or offices of certain states-
men, who had recently hoped to feast their eyes,
and glut their vengeance on their implacable foe.
A general discontent crept over the multitude;
many grew jealous at his rapid elevation in court
favour, while Isegrim and Bruin were almost reduced to despair.

Strapping his budget on his back, and grasping
his pilgrim's staff, Reynard, at the proper time,
commenced his journey, making pious genuflexions,
and appearing as simple as a new made novice.
Many were the farewells he uttered, rendered half
inarticulate by sighs and sobbing. He was attended
in his pilgrimage by Bellin the Ram as domestic
chaplain, and the Rabbit, who had pitied him very
much when fortune had apparently forsaken him;
and having gathered a basket of delicious fruit, he
brought it along with him, to be presented to the
pilgrim at their first halting-place; for the Rabbit
being rather a simple youth, and well disposed,
was highly gratified at the apparent piety of Reynard, and considered it his duty to encourage reformation, not only in his sagacious neighbour, but
also in all carnivorous animals—for the poor Rabbit
was a strict vegetarian, and often attempted to in-
fuse a taste for vegetables among his associates.
On the party journeyed, but in place of proceeding
to the city of the seven hills, the leader made the
best of his way to his fortalice of Malepartus.

"Bellin, my reverend friend," says the pilgrim,
"remain outside and enjoy the sweet grass; I will
take my young companion in with me to console

my poor wife, for the tones of his voice are much softer than mine, and fitter for a lady's ear."

So the poor Rabbit went in with Reynard, where he found Dame Ermelin sorrowing in a dark chamber, for she had despaired of ever beholding her husband again. Seeing him enter with staff, scrip, and scallop shell, she burst into a frenzy of joy, and said, " Reynard, my love, how has it gone with you?"

" Ah !" he said, " I was condemned upon false evidence, but the King extended his pardon. I left him as a pilgrim, and Isegrim and Bruin have become bail for me. His Majesty bestowed the Rabbit on me as a peace-offering ; we may do with him as best suits us, for the King told me at parting that it was he who betrayed me."

The fear of death descended on the Rabbit, and he sought to escape ; but Reynard stood in the doorway, and seized him by the neck. Loud were his cries for help from Bellin : " I am undone ! The pilgrim murders me." But he did not cry long, for the Fox soon bit his throat asunder. " Come now, and let us dine on him,—'t is the first time the simpleton has been good for anything."

It was thus he received his too trusting friend and visitor.

During the repast, Dame Ermelin was very inquisitive as to how he acquired his freedom ; but Reynard told her the story was too long and intricate for recital on the present occasion. " This much I will say, however, that the friendship between me and his Majesty will be of short duration.

When he discovers the truth, I have no more mercy to expect."

Meanwhile Bellin cried impatiently on the Rabbit to come forth, whereupon Reynard went out and said, " My dear sir, my young friend entreats that you will pardon him ; he is enjoying the society of my wife, who is his near relation, and he begs that you will amuse yourself for a few minutes longer." Then, said Bellin, " I heard what appeared to me to be cries of murder. Have you done any mischief to him?" The Fox replied, " I was talking of the perils of my pilgrimage, at which my wife became so alarmed that she fainted. This frightened the innocent Rabbit, and he screamed for help!" " I know," said the Ram, " that he cried as in agony." " Not a hair of him has been hurt," swore the Fox. " Now I beg you will lull your suspicions asleep, and listen to me! I have matters of grave importance which the King begged me to write down for him. I have just finished them, and I wish to entrust you with these letters. They contain prudent counsel, which is only meant to meet the royal eye."

" Have a care then," says Bellin, " that you close them well, because I forgot my pocket-book, and were the seals to break it might get me into trouble."

" Leave that to me. There is a scrip made out of Bruin's hide, it is thick and strong, and will just hold the packet. You will be honourably rewarded, and who knows what you may yet obtain?"

The Fox hastened back into the house, and

stuffed the poor Rabbit's head into the scrip. "Hang the scrip round your neck, and be careful not to pry into the missives. I have tied it with a secret knot, known only to the King and myself, so that if you open it you will be assuredly found out. If you wish to secure the King's especial favour, you may tell him, when you come into the presence, with a joyful air, that you have brought a valuable packet, and that you helped to make it up. This, I think, will secure you the favour of our gracious master."

The Ram was overjoyed, and hastened to court at the top of his speed. When the King saw him enter with the satchel, he exclaimed, "What does all this mean? Where is your friend the Rabbit? Speak, man!"

"Gracious King," replied Bellin, "Reynard bade me carry those letters; you will find them contain important matters. What they enclose has been put in by my advice; here they are; Reynard tied the knot. It was not for me to pry into your Majesty's affairs."

When the head of the Rabbit was drawn forth the King stood aghast, and several members of government fainted. Such an atrocity was unprecedented, and such an insult was not to be borne. The Monarch was convulsed with rage; he made his throne to tremble under him, and in the whirlwind of his passion he doomed the reverend chaplain to the rack and the gibbet; and, moreover, reflected severely on his own conduct in being swayed by the advice of the Queen. None durst attempt to calm him but the Pard, who had a double right, being president of the council, and also the Sovereign's near kinsman.

"If passion is vile in a slave, consider how it becomes a King; to rave and threaten is beneath your Majesty; you know the murderer, and you bear the sword of justice. Order Bruin and Isegrim to be liberated from prison, restore order, punish Bellin according to his deserts, for he openly and impudently confessed that he advised the death of the Rabbit. We will then march forth against Reynard, investigate his conduct, probe his crimes, and let the irresistible arm of the law do what is fitting and proper on so momentous an occasion. The goods and chattels of Bellin the Ram may be confiscated, and gifted over to the widowed Rabbit, while Bruin and Isegrim may be pensioned as a solatium to their wounded feelings, and harmony restored."

"Cousin," says the King, "I like your counsel. Fetch the two barons; they shall sit in the highest place next ourselves; all shall do homage to them; and as an atonement to those gentlemen, I will give up Bellin to them and their heirs for ever."

The Ram was executed; and all his relations, and all his posterity are hunted by the race of Isegrim to this day.

High wassail and rich banqueting were held at court for the space of eight days, in honour of the liberation of the two great barons Bruin and Isegrim, while Reynard kept within his stronghold. The King sat at the table beside the Queen,

"And all went merry as a marriage bell,"

When the Hare came before them bleeding, and exclaiming—

"Sire, have pity on me. In obedience to your Majesty's proclamation, I hastened to court, and, taking the nearest way, I unhappily came near the gate of Reynard's castle. There he sat in a pilgrim's habit, reading what appeared to me to be some breviary or missal. He advanced towards me and saluted me politely; but, when opportunity served, he seized me by the ears with such violence, that I thought my head was off. Fortunately I made a sudden spring, and, being swift of foot, escaped the fangs of the felon, but left one of my ears behind me. See how I bleed! Look on these four holes in my neck. Sire, who can travel to your court, if robbers are thus suffered to waylay your subjects?"

Before he had finished his complaint, in hopped Merkenau the Crow, and related a piteous story, how Reynard shammed dead on the heath one morning. "His eyes were twisted in his head, and his tongue hung out of his open mouth. I screamed again and again in order to ascertain if he was really dead; my wife screamed also, but nothing seemed to move him; I tapped on his breast and his head, my wife approached near to his chin, to hear if he breathed; but no. We both were persuaded that he was quite dead. In her sorrow, my poor thoughtless wife put her bill into the rascal's mouth, and in one moment he snapped her head off. He made a dart at me also, but I flew up and sat on a tree. I saw the miscreant devour the dear creature; and when he was gone, I looked, and found a little blood and feathers only. Have compassion on your loyal subjects, Sire; for if the traitor escapes, the world will say that there are neither law nor justice within your realm."

No sooner had the two complainants laid their grievances before the throne, than the Monarch took an oath in the presence of his two nobles, Bruin and Isegrim, that he would destroy Reynard's family, root and branch. "My wife persuaded me, but I am not the first who has followed a woman's counsel and repented of it afterwards. Decide now, my loyal barons, how this culprit may be brought to judgment."

The two barons liked the tenor of the royal speech, but dared not deliver their opinion, because the royal temper was a good deal ruffled; but her Majesty, knowing her influence over her lord, said,—"Make no rash promise, especially when your Majesty is a little chafed. Reynard has not been heard. His accusers would perhaps be silent were he here to explain matters. I thought Reynard prudent and sensible, but he certainly gives his enemies occasion to scandalize his name. I may have been in error about him, but he undoubtedly is clever as a councillor, and his connections are influential. You will not make things better by too much precipitation; and moreover, you are master here—with a code of just laws before you, which should be administered with impartiality and due deliberation."

"With all respect and affection," replied his Majesty, "I might command, but I entreat you, our Queen, to be silent. War is determined on. His house shall be utterly laid waste, and his name blotted out. So let our nobles and their retainers get ready, with harness on their backs, together with bows, spears, and other weapons. We will lay siege to his castle of Malepartus, and take a survey of the inside thereof."

"Whereupon the assembly, with a great shout, agreed to his Majesty's proposal. When Grevincus, his cousin, heard that evil was determined against Reynard, he hastened to his castle to communicate the fatal information, and put him on his guard. When he nearly reached it, he found the proscribed retreating homeward with two unfledged doves which had fallen to the ground, and which the gourmand had snapped up, for he was remarkably fond of fowl. Having seen Grevincus at a distance, he ran to meet him, and tendered a kindly welcome, paying him all manner of compliments. But the Badger, with unwonted haughtiness, desired him to desist from such fulsome and unmeaning stuff.

"Sir, you are in peril! You have brought ruin on yourself and your house by your fraudulent actions; you have provoked the king beyond all endurance; he vows to extirpate you and yours. In six days you will behold his army under your walls, led by Field-Marshal Isegrim; while Bruin,

who is again taken into favour, will collect such a
mass of evidence against you as will quite over-
whelm you."

"If that be all," says the Fox, "I care not a
rush. Though they have sworn to execute me
over and over again, you see I have still escaped;
aye, and still shall. They may debate, and do debate; but it all ends in smoke. Come in, cousin,
and sup with me. These doves are young and
tender—they require little mastication—their bones
are sweet—they melt in the mouth—they are half
blood, half milk. Light diet suits me, and my wife
is of the same opinion. Come in then. She will
be delighted to see you, only do not tell her what
you came here for. The merest trifle makes her
nervous. To-morrow I shall go to court with you,
and face those mighty chiefs whose rage I shall
laugh at, knowing that I am always safe in their
folly. I trust, nevertheless, that you will give me
all the assistance in your power, like a good kinsman."

" All that a friend or brother should hazard for
you will I do; and if I have any little influence in
high places, it is very much at your service."

The Fox conducted the Badger into his house
with great ceremony, and presented him to Dame
Ermelin and her young family as a near relation.

The lady of the mansion spread the board with
good things; the two tender doves were not forgotten; each partook of the dainty with zest; and
Grevincus was in ecstasies with the flavour of
everything. When the cloth had been removed,

and familiar chit-chat had taken place, Reynard said to his cousin the Badger,—

"How do you like my family? Do you not admire my children? My eldest son, for instance, is he not like me every inch? My second son, too, a strapping little fellow. He has his mother's leer, and he'll be the wag of the family. The rogues are both ripe already. They'll *filch* a pullet or *nim* a goose with the most practised of our sept · in truth they are fit for anything, and they will get on in the world, or they are no sons of mine. I would send them oftener out to hunt, but I must not neglect their education. They have to be taught prudence and foresight, and how to escape the snare, the huntsman, and the hound. When they have finished their education, they shall go out into the world and labour on their own accounts. Already they bite like a vice, and their leap is as certain as the return of an unpaid creditor."

Grevincus, like a sage, laid his paws upon their noddles, and tendered a long catalogue of good advices, much easier given than acted up to. The night waned apace, and the friends retired to their respective places of repose; but in place of sleeping, Reynard fell into a train of thinking, and slept none.

Conscious guilt is a bad soporific, especially on the eve of appearing before one's accusers and judges; so he arose from his uneasy couch, and said to his wife—"I am invited to court by our cousin Grevincus, which invitation I mean to comply with. Do not make yourself uneasy. Stop quietly at home. If anybody asks for me, you know what to say, and you know full well how to take care of the castle." Dame Ermelin used all her eloquence, and practised all her blandishments, to dissuade her lord from going to court. Every argument she could think of was used to induce him to stay at home; but all to no purpose.

"Be calm, I entreat you; there is nothing to distress yourself about. I have business of importance; and in five or six days you will see me here again."

So he set out for the court, together with Grevincus the Badger. The two friends scampered to court by paths only known to themselves, and, to a casual observer, they seemed to be in high glee. Guilt, nevertheless, was pressing on the mind of the Fox; and he could not help feeling misgivings as to his ultimate acquittal.

" I have abused his majesty's ear; I have slain his faithful servant; I have falsely entrapped Bellin, and had him unjustly executed; I wounded the Hare; I put the Crow to death; and what I believe will tell against me worst of all, is a trick I played on Isegrim. One day, as we travelled over a flowery meadow, we saw a beautiful Colt sporting by the side of its dam, and, being somewhat anxious for a *tit-bit* for dinner, I offered to buy the Colt of its mother, and asked the price The Mare replied that the price was written on her hoof, and that it was ready cash. I pretended that I was no great scholar; and Isegrim wishing to display his abilities, put his spectacles on his nose, and pored over her hoof, as if he had been employed to cut her corns. Taking advantage of the precise moment, the lady salutes him with a tremendous kick, which sent him spinning breathless. His snout was battered, and his face was besmeared and clotted with gore—in one word, he cut a pitiable figure, while I sat on the park wall, and jeered him with all the ironical questions which occurred to me. He raved, and roared, and threatened; while I was thrilled by the very acme of enjoyment. There now, nephew, I have made confession; teach me how to obtain pardon."

"Ah!" says Grevincus, "you are laden with fresh sins. They follow at your heels, and you have no time to escape them, for I fear you are near your end. You can never think to be forgiven for the death of the Rabbit and the Crow; and the affront you have put on the noble baron Isegrim can neither be forgotten nor forgiven. How could you behave so rashly?"

"Pooh," said Reynard, "one has to make one's way in the world. One can't behave as if he were in a monastery. He who sells honey, licks his fingers now and then. The Rabbit's fat little body tickled me, and I forgot both love and prudence. As for Bellin, his stupidity gave me a great deal of trouble; but we will change the subject. Were I to speak my mind I could tell you who are robbers and manslayers of the first order; but I know full well my want of privilege, and therefore shall be silent."

"I am astonished, uncle," said the Badger, "that you should confess the sins of other people, when you have so many of your own to think of."

So they came near the court, and met Martin the Ape travelling out as a pilgrim. They stopped by the way, and Reynard had some confidential conversation with him. Reynard told how he was persecuted by his enemies, and, being under ban, was yet afraid to go to Rome, and leave his family in the vicinity of Bruin, one of his most deadly foes. The Ape enlightened his friend Reynard upon the practice of the Church of Rome; and having himself great interest with the Pope, promised to get the Fox his absolution,—for what says the couplet made by his Holiness' laureate?

> "Pardons, indulgences, I buy and sell,
> They're good commodities, and answer well.
> With money, you your agent must supply,
> To bribe the Court, and what you want to buy
> The Pope will favour, and defend you here,
> Let heretics and unbelievers sneer."

Reynard thanked his friend Martin the Ape for his kindness, and proceeded to court without farther delay with his kinsman the Badger. Having again arrived at court, Reynard knelt before his Sovereign; and ascribing honour to his master in the most courtly style of language; nor did he forget to pay those compliments to the Queen which was most agreeable to her royal husband's ear, and secretly pleasing to herself. The courtiers pressed round, astonished at his audacity; but the King appeared fierce and implacable.

"Renowned Monarch," said Reynard, "you are crowned—not with the imperial diadem only—but with Valour, Victory, and Justice. Rewards and punishments are alike yours. The world expects that you should reward virtue and punish vice. All pretend to truth and honesty, but were our crimes written on our foreheads, Bruin and Isegrim would not sit so near your royal person, nor loll upon the bench while I am trembling at the bar. I should then need no witnesses to prove my zeal and devotion to the person and government of my master. But I must check myself; I can have no reason to fear when you judge my cause."

With an ingenious eloquence, he explained away the non performance of his pilgrimage; rebutted with great tact and talent the accusation of the Hare; proved to the secret conviction of every one that the Crow had made a false accusation against him, and not only so, he proved that the Crow had committed the murder himself. Keyward, the Hare, and the Crow, then left the court; all shunned a war of words with such an accomplished orator; and Reynard was apparently on the eve of triumph, when the King arose in royal ire, terrific in his gestures and terrible in untamed majesty— reminding the horror-struck spectators of the sub- lime quatrain of the poet:—

> " He waved his sceptre north away,
>   The Arctic ring was rift asunder;
> And through the sky the startling bray
>   Burst louder than the loudest thunder."—Hogg.

Here the favourite nurse, whose untiring atten-
ticn to the wants and weaknesses of majesty, had
entitled her to the high privilege of being seated in
the royal presence, became hysterical with sheer
terror, and the page upon her lap was by no means
insensible to the probable consequences of such a
paroxysm; and having rolled himself into as small
a space as possible, laid his head meekly on his
paws, like an Oriental slave previous to decapitation; while the moles penetrated into their deep
est fastnesses; and the crawling worms, with all
the rapidity of which they were capable, trans-
formed themselves into little red globules, so as to
be mistaken for damaged berries.

Reynard alone retained his equanimity in the
midst of the hurricane, trusting to his unrivalled
powers of persuasion. The Monarch babbled in-
cessantly of the Rabbit's Murder, and the execution
of Bellin; but extreme passion diverted the cur
rent of his thoughts from their right channel, and
choked his utterance; whereupon Reynard interposed in the blandest of his tones, but somewhat
tremulous for the sake of effect, asked,—

" What do I hear? Is the Rabbit dead, and is
Bellin no more? Alas! I have lost a treasure
with them, such as the most wealthy Jews have
never been in possession of. They were the bear-
ers to you of gold and gems, such as the world has
seldom seen. Who could have believed that Bellin
would have murdered the Rabbit, in order to rob
his most gracious master the King? Alas! this
world is full of danger and deceit."

The King did not listen to Reynard, but retired
to his private chamber in very bad humour, where
the Chamberlain was closeted with the Ape's wife,
who pleaded hard for Reynard, and reminded his
Majesty of his ability, and of his wise decision in a
certain contest between a countryman and a ser-
pent.   The King, a little soothed, returned into the
judgment hall, still, however, threatening the Fox
with death ; while Reynard eloquently regretted
the lost gifts, which, if he were free, he would live
only to recover.   He proceeded to describe the
treasures with a minuteness that had all the appearance of truth, and with an air of sincerity and
candour :

"I sent your Majesty a ring, on which were in-
scribed mystic letters, which only Abryon, the
Jew of Treves, could read.   He who wore it could
not suffer from cold or hunger; could not be defeated in a contest; could not be hated by a be-
holder; knew no darkness; and could not suffer
by water or fire.   There was a comb also, with a
mirror, intended for the Queen, the wonders of
which yet surpassed the wonders of the ring.   Pictures were engraved on each." Reynard explained
the fables appertaining to them.   He reminded the
King of the services performed by his father as
court physician; and who unhappily committed
suicide from the pangs of fell remorse, for having
for a moment swerved from his loyalty to his
Majesty through weakness and evil companionship.

"The benefits which I received from your father

are of such an ancient date that I forget them; bu
what good did I ever receive from you?"

"I dare not bandy words with my royal master,"
said Reynard, "but I refer your Majesty to the testimony of your own heralds, who have publicly
recorded many things honourable to my loyalty,
and the reverse to my enemies. It would look like
self-glorification were I to remind your Majesty of
what I have done for you, and which I cannot help
believing you remember full well."

Reynard again accused Isegrim of dastardly conduct, and, in an indignant style of eloquence, denounced him as a coward and a swindler, who was
utterly incapable of practising honesty; and that
he was a disgrace to the assembly in which he sat,
and to the court to which he was attached. The
Bear was also characterised as a devourer of the
weak, an insulter of the people, and an abuser of
the royal power; and lastly, with a loud voice and
lofty bearing, he defied his accusers to mortal combat,—casting such a look on the Wolf as could
neither be mistaken by the court or the challenged.

The King was secretly overjoyed with Reynard's
proposal, and instantly secured bail for the appearance of the combatants; and ordered the lists to be
prepared for the judicial duel. During the night,
Reynard's friends did all in their power to prepare
him for the combat. Dame Ruckenan the Ape,
who had considerable experience in such matters,
exhorted him to go fasting to the field, and to use
the utmost strategy when engaged with his antagonist.

" 'Tis not always strength that either obtains or
secures victory, and therefore you should lose no ad·
vantage.   Let Grevincus, your relative, shave your
body all over, except the continuation of the spine;
then have yourself anointed with a quantity of
palm oil which I shall send you.   Run round and
round the lists until your enemy's heart palpitates,
and his breathing grows difficult.   You will see a
small pool of water on the east side of the lists
oozing from a brooklet, and thickened with dust.
Immerse your brush there as you pass, and dash
it in the eyes of your opponent.   Do this several
times ere you come to close quarters with him;
then, when he is endeavouring to clear his optics;
seize him by the throat, and, if possible, throw him
to the ground.   The ladies are wholly on your
side, and when you have the semblance of an ad·
vantage, we will wave our handkerchiefs and cheer.
This will not only encourage you, but it will de·
press the spirits of your adversary."

The sinking hopes of the champion now revived;
and he attended minutely to the good counsel he
had received, except in the matter of going to the
field "fasting;" for an unfortunate goose, happening to cross his path that eventful morning, never
returned to the pond of her nativity; and Reynard,
having wiped his lips, wended his way to the lists,
surrounded by his kinsmen and allies.

Not only was he shaved and annointed agreea·
bly to instruction, but his joints were lubricated
with a peculiar kind of ointment; he was, moreover perfumed with balm and other essences.   His

Majesty was highly delighted to see him so spruce, and laughed immoderately when he inspected his smooth well-oiled body.

"Go, Reynard; glory or justice, or both, call thee to the lists. It is meet that thou shouldst defend thy fair fame at the hazard of thy life; for to be infamous is not to live, but to drag out a miserable existence."

Lowly bowed the champion to his master, and eloquent were the thanks which he tendered him, and, looking up with one of his blandest smiles, he bowed to the ground before her Majesty, and entered within the enclosed ground, declaring, that if he should prove dastardly enough to fly from his antagonist in her royal presence, that he deserved to be hanged, drawn, and quartered. While the whole assembly anxiously and painfully awaited the onset, the trumpet sounded, and the Wolf came roaring on the Fox, fierce as the angry Caspian when agitated by mountain blast; but Reynard, in place of grappling with his mortal enemy, ran against the wind and scraped up dust into his pursuer's eyes. Occasionally he dipped his brush into the small pool of water, which had been secretly deepened a little, and dashed it with unerring aim full in the two glaring orbs of his foe. Again and again, like a skilful tactician, he practised this mode of desultory warfare, until Isegrim became almost blinded; and, to add to his disasters, one of his eyes was almost torn from the socket by a random blow from the fore-foot of Reynard as he whisked round him. Long and arduous was the conflict; and the Fox, believing he would soon be master of the field, began to shout after the man-ner of ancient heroes, to shame his adversary, and to exult in anticipated victory. But Isegrim, in a state of mind bordering on despair, and regardless of laceration and pain, put forth all his strength, and by one fortunate effort laid his foe prostrate, and caught one of his fore-feet between his teeth, which he held with all the tenacity of a double screw.

"Yield thee, thou dastard!" muttered the Wolf through his throat.

Reynard became completely paralysed with ter-ror; his last shadow of hope had evaporated like mist before the noonday sun. Like a craven he begged for his worthless life. He shed a flood of tears; he implored pity; he confessed himself an unhappy wretch; promised to proclaim Isegrim the victor wherever he went; that he would be his slave for ever; and that he would fetch his family to kneel before him, in token of the most abject submission. Moreover, he promised to become the Wolf's purveyor. All ducks, geese, hens, or fishes, which he might hereafter catch, should be placed at the victor's disposal; and his chivalrous bearing should ever thereafter be the theme of songs, more during than brass or adamant.

"No!" says Sir Isegrim; "thou shalt cheat no more! I'll rid the world of a flatterer and a thief. The ravens and the crows shall behold thy bones whitening the common, or thrown into the river."

Whereupon Reynard, thinking it was all over

with him, renewed the attack, struggled desperately
and, by a lucky movement, clenched his fangs in
the Wolf's throat. Isegrim shrieked with open
mouth, and Reynard drew out his foot, and with
his two paws he nearly deprived him of his skin.
They rolled together in a pool of blood, into which,
ever and anon, the Fox saturated his brush, and
did tremendous havoc thereby on the enemy. Lacerated, crippled, and blind, Sir Isegrim's friends
implored the Monarch to put an end to the combat.

The heralds accordingly received the royal mandate; the conflict was ended, and Reynard proclaimed victorious; whereupon the whole assembly
rent the air with shouts of acclamation. The entire
monarchy was agitated, from its depth to its surface,
by a turbulent concurrence with the royal decision;
and golden opinions were uttered relative to the
dignity and urbanity, as well as the justice, of the
Sovereign.

Grumble the Ass, although bred to the bar, had,
like many of his relations, a strong propensity for
verse-making; and accordingly he struck off an
extemporaneous ode for the occasion, which was
set to music with equal rapidity by no less a personage than Gallus the Cock, doctor of music, and
sung by all and sundry who hoped for court
favour.

Once more the Monarch of the Woods commanded silence, and selected the Leopard as his representative, who uttered his royal master's will in
some such terms as follow:—

"Victorious Reynard! I bring a laurel wreath

from my august Sovereign, to be placed upon your brow as a symbol of conquest. He decrees a triumph in your honour."

"I have compelled the foe to yield," said Reynard; "the disputed field is mine. I have added VICTOR to my family name; I have earned undying glory to myself by clearing my injured fame; therefore, in accordance with the wishes of my gracious and redoubted Sovereign, let what is past be forgotten; let none hereafter insultingly name him who was overcome; let Sir Isegrim be restored to the favour of his Sovereign. Generous victors do not conquer to insult the proud, but to tame them."

A thousand friends, whose names he had never heard of before, now thronged round him with fulsome congratulations. Even those who voted for his condemnation offered him a largess of plate, and tendered their political support. But neither beast of the field nor fowl of the air was half so obsequious as Grumble the Ass, and poet; who, kneeling at Reynard's feet, supplicated the high honour of carrying him to court on his back, which humble request being complied with, the bard pricked up his ears to an unusual length, looked with contempt on the undistinguished mob around him, and laboured under the hallucination that he possessed more wisdom than Rajah the Elephant, and was a greater proficient in music than Cloudlet the Lark or Amoret the Nightingale.

Preliminaries being adjusted, a regular procession was formed, and to court they marched, through lanes of troops in new uniforms, passing occasion ally beneath triumphal arches, adorned by wreaths and chaplets; while the joyous inmates of the public seminaries strewed the path with flowers, and repeated quatrains from Grumble's ode. Nor were the fascinations of music forgotten. Rajah the Elephant, as bandmaster, struck up a Hindoo air, which had originally been composed in honour of Bramah, and had been a "march" in the Rajah's family for many hundred years; and he had judi ciously selected Trickster the Monkey, a country man of his own, and placed him on his shoulders, because he was conversant both with the instrument and the music. Poodle, a third cousin of Springer the Hound, thundered on the big drum, which happily drowned the discord elicited by Jackoo the Baboon from an old cracked banjee or violin with his *sinister* arm, while the tambourine passed from hand to hand as an instrument which required little previous practice.

One ludicrous incident occurred however, which it may be as well to explain. Grunter the Hog had been appointed standard-bearer, but he became so bewildered with the magnificence of the solemn train, and the elevated part therein assigned him, that he stupidly attached the wrong end of his broad pennant to the staff. His enemies, however, scruple not to say, that he had been indulging in strong grains that morning. This piece of court scandal, however, may or may not be true; certain it is, that the mistake was committed.

On rolled the excited throng toward the royal residence, accumulating in its progress like some mighty river in its transition to the ocean. The hills and valleys rung with Io Pæans, and the streets of the metropolis echoed to the exhilarating notes of the music, and the lusty cheers of the crowd. On approaching the royal presence, the observed of all observers bowed to his peers, but knelt to the Monarch, who graciously raised him from the ground, and after a brief speech, which monarchs sometimes find it necessary to make for the sake of being thought courteous, he concluded by quoting a piece of Grumble's doggerel, who was already smacking his lips in anticipation of the butt of sack—

Your woes are righted, give the Wolf your hand,
I bade the war and now the peace command.

"Your Majesty's will," said Reynard, "has ever been the rule of my life. To accomplish your desires I have struggled through good and bad report. Your royal ear has often been poisoned, but your princely discrimination has as frequently repelled its virulence. I know of no greater luxury than to live and die in your Majesty's service. I appeal to my honourable antagonist if I did aught to heighten his despair during the conflict; and now that it is over, I deeply grieve to see his pretended friends basely desert their patron; but it will ever be thus. When wealth, or royal favour —which is better—set in on you, like the fertilizing waters of the Nile, friends will accumulate, and flattery resound through your hall; let riches and influence depart, and your fawning wheedlers will follow."

Seated on his throne, in the midst of his senate, the Monarch of Beasts and Birds addressed him thus:

"My lords and gentlemen, we have listened to all your complaints—have taken them into our serious consideration. We shall grant remedy to those who may have been injured, and dismiss those statements that appear frivolous. Meanwhile, it is our will and pleasure to redress the wrongs of our faithful liegeman Reynard, and reward his worth. His wisdom, experience, and zeal, deserve our favour, and we have determined to strengthen our government by his vast political knowledge, his high legal experience, and that personal influence which genius alone can exercise over the masses. We commission him to perform the onerous duties of Lord High Chancellor, to be the keeper of our royal conscience, and to utter those decisions in equity, from which there is no appeal. As our highest legal functionary, we will hear no murmuring at the conclusions he arrives at, and wherever he sits, you are to believe the King is there. He shall receive embassies in our name, with power to treat and to conclude, and we command all our loving subjects to obey him, as they hope for our favour. He is no bigot, no lazy thoughtless drone —a burthen to himself and his colleagues in the cabinet; he is active and eloquent, ever on the alert; his judgment is not to be biassed, even by our own royal will; neither power nor party interest will tempt him from the path of rectitude; he'll fear no faction, and he'll accept no bribes. Such is the person which we have elevated to the highest post in our realm—'tis yours to obey."

The members of senate were struck dumb with astonishment; they glared upon each other with amazement; but opposition to the royal will would have brought on confiscation, banishment, or even death, to any daring individual possessed of the temerity; so all were silent, which his Majesty construed into loyalty and acquiescence. Painfully anxious to return to his castle of Malepartus, where Dame Ermelin was suffering the sorrow of uncertainty in a darkened chamber, Reynard humbly solicited the royal permission to revisit his desponding spouse for a short space. The request was granted on condition that he should return to court with all convenient speed; for his presence and oracular wisdom had become almost necessary to the royal pair. Being so overwhelmed by regal grace, he scarcely wist what to say; but kneeling to the throne, and kissing the feet of the beauteous Queen, he said—

" I bend with awe before your imperial Majesty, and also before you, the fairest Queen the sun ever shone upon. Long may you reign in the hearts of your subjects. Under your beneficent auspices may the age of iron depart, and the age of gold return. May you live, not only in plenty, but in peace; and may you not only prove a blessing to your own subjects, but to the era in which you flourish."

So, laden with royal presents, he departed for

Malepartus, accompanied by a numerous train of friends, suitors, and time-servers, who, from motives of self-interest, fluttered round the new made Chancellor, as winged moths do round a lighted candle.

Beguiling the way with "diverting talk," Reynard remarked—"You see our mighty foes, although impelled by envy and malice, could not prevail against me; we must forget past peril and past disgraces; the times are changing for the better. Our royal master is bountiful, generous and good: he prefers blunt, unassuming honesty, to clever chicanery; and, what is more uncommon still, he prefers wisdom to gold."

When the towers of his residence burst on his view, he halted for a little, and flattered his satellites, buoyed up their hopes as to their future fortunes through his patronage, retained a chosen few as his companions, to swell his triumph when he should appear in the presence of his wife and family, and bowed an obsequious farewell to the residue, although he despised them in his heart. Rumour, with her thousand tongues, had already proclaimed to the world the altered circumstances of him who was recently arraigned in the high court of justice, as a felon, for great crimes and treasonable practices.

His trembling consort could hardly trust the testimony of her eyes, when he sprung to her embrace. Her articulation was restored after she had shed a flood of tears, and she welcomed him joyfully. His sons were transported with happiness, and his very servants exulted with pride to see their venerated master once more. After mutual felicitations, he gave a modest narrative of the challenge, the duel, the victory, and the favourable change in the royal mind regarding him.

"I am now honoured with the highest position which a subject may hold; my friends are in ecstacies at my elevation; my enemies depressed and despondent. But albeit I have them in my power, I shall not blight the verdure of my laurels by crushing them precipitantly, nor provide for my friends too hastily; my opinions, nevertheless, are beyond control, and my power absolute. Moreover, the King, my master, as the climax of his powers, tendered me the Great Seal with his own hand;

> Bade me enjoy it with the place and honours,
> During my life, and to confirm his goodness,
> Tied it by letters patent;

so that I may truly say in the language of another great personage, 'I am the state.'"

After having recruited his health, feasted his retainers, and gleaned golden opinions from his neighbours and dependants, he repaired to the metropolis, entered his court, mounted the bench, and awarded such decisions as if he had been an embodiment of Truth, with Justice and Equity for his assessors.

But the novelty of acting justly and honourably wore off—the glare of popularity ceased to dazzle him. A compound of avarice, fraud, and cunning, his judicial conduct had been a piece of acting; and his determinations gave him pain in proportion as these approximated to truth and righteousness.

" Why should I injure my health, and waste my intellect, like a small pettifogger in the courts below, for a poor limited remuneration? If my position is lofty, my expenses correspond therewith; and if I am the second in the monarchy, why should not my revenue be second only to that of the monarch himself? Besides, I am ambitious of becoming the founder of a family, and of transmitting, not only my name and honours, but also something of a more tangible nature to my descendants; and I must make hay while the sun shines."

Such were the cogitations of the rapacious Chancellor as he twirled his paws or stroked his beard in his own court, while he pretended to give his most attentive consideration to the pleadings of the barristers in Chancery, and endeavoured to pass for an oracle of wisdom, and a prodigy of legal integrity. It is said, that " a crafty knave needs no broker:" it may be true in ordinary cases, but such was the depravity of this mushroom Chancellor's nature—such was his vehement desire for the accumulation of filthy lucre—such his insatiable craving for the mammon of unrighteousness, that, like the horse-leech, he sucked the blood alike of pursuer and defendant, rich and poor, as opportunities presented themselves. Nay, not content with this abominable procedure, his hired emissaries beset those who resorted to his court, together with their kith, kin, and allies. Throughout the various provinces of the kingdom, fraud and extortion were the order of the day. Decisions in Chancery were known to be marketable commodities, and the whole department voted a delusion and a snare.

Sir Isegrim the Wolf drew up a memorial on the subject, largely and influentially subscribed, and presented it to the King, entreating his Majesty to remove the arch-offender from his high office.

Grumble the Ass—who had failed in obtaining the laurel—fired off paper pellets at the head of the wicked and fraudulent official, in shape of dull pasquinades and pointless epigrams, together with a satirical lyric, which obtained some popularity, not from its own merits, but from the beautiful air to which it was set by Dr. Gallus.

Rajah the Elephant amused the lieges by playing the significant air, entitled "The Highway to Newgate," and Poodle, the third cousin of Springer the Hound, beat the "Rogue's March" every evening at sunset—the import of which was well known to all within hearing. Grunter the Hog, who had previously acted as standard-bearer, defaced the hated name from his pennon, and bartered it—staff and all—with Jackoo the Baboon, who conducted a brewery, for a bushel of his strongest grains. Even Malkin the Cat, who never either forgot or forgave her laceration, bequeathed her skin to the author of the best essay on "Tyranny under colour of Equity."

Society was fast verging towards anarchy, and various constitution-makers had begun to labour in their vocation, when happily the King took the alarm, and made minute and laborious investigation into the alleged malversations of his Chancellor. The result was, that he revoked his letters patent, deprived him of the Great Seal, and determined once more to have him impeached and tried before his peers as a great state criminal—

> ————————————"He is attack'd,
> Call him to present trial. If he may
> Find mercy in the law, 'tis his; if none,
> Let him not seek't of us."

Meanwhile the sleepless vigilance which had hitherto characterised the degraded ex-official had not diminished. His eyes were open to every movement, his ears to every whisper. His emissaries were to be found everywhere; but the more information which they collected the darker grew the page on which it was written, while his un-rivalled sagacity assured him that he could hope for no clemency, except the axe and the block, as substitutes for the more vulgar halter and gibbet.

"His high-blown pride at length broke under him,"

and, accordingly, he concerted secret measures with his cousin Grevincus the Badger, for depriv-ing an ungrateful community of his eminent ser-vices, or, in other words, for absconding like a felon from the scorn and contempt of an insulted and injured people. Well did the arch-peculator know that eloquence would prove ineffectual and inge-nuity powerless; that the prejudice of the multitude would be confirmed by irrefragable facts; and that acquittal was hopeless—condemnation certain. Whereupon the wily politician was reduced to the bitter alternative of choosing between ignominy and exile, or certain death. After some hours of agony spent in deliberation, he preferred the former; and calling up all his sagacity, he started an hour before dawn.

This movement, however, was anticipated by the police authorities. Scouts had been stationed in the various localities through which it was likely the fugitive would pass, and sentinels placed on the heights. The alarm was at length given, and the whole posse, under the guidance of Springer the Hound, gave chase to the hated delinquent, who exerted himself with all the energy arising from the impulsive powers of despair, and love of life. With masterly dexterity he evaded the fury of Sir Isegrim the Wolf, and the fleetness and fangs of Springer the Hound, who hung upon his haunches for several hours; but torn, bleeding, and breath-less, he was at last obliged to give up the chase, and call off his broken-down followers.

Thus Reynard escaped decapitation; but history and tradition are silent as to the country of his adoption, his future career, or the termination of his existence. This much may be affirmed, that remorse, with her cat-o'-nine tails, would haunt his meditations by day and his dreams by night, and he himself would exclaim in the language of the poet—

> " My conscience hath a thousand several tongues,
> And every tongue brings in a several tale."

Agreeably to the juridical canons of the monarchy a writ, bearing the signature of the Sovereign,
was issued from the Council Office, summoning
" Reynard the Fox to appear at the bar of the Privy
Council, to answer to the charge of having committed high crimes against the state." The members of that august body met, and citation made,
but no answer was returned either by principal or
attorney. Upon which, sentence of outlawry was
passed against the fugitive; his real and moveable
possessions escheated to the crown, and his family,
with whose concurrence and assistance he had
acted, attainted, declared incapable of serving the
state from henceforth, and rendered infamous for
ever.

It is admitted on all hands, that the expatriated
ex-chancellor possessed all the requisites which
form a great character. He was sagacious and
penetrating, acute and observant, an orator of the
first order, and one whose ingenuity was seldom
or never at fault. His legal knowledge was above
and beyond that of all his compeers; and his urbanity and courtesy, especially when they suited
his own purposes, were fascinating. His business
habits were exact and methodical, and his wisdom
proverbial; but that wisdom was alloyed by low
cunning, that sagacity and penetration by extreme
selfishness, that legal knowledge by a morbid avarice which he sometimes could ill conceal, and

that inflexible justice which he was elevated by his Sovereign to dispense to all the lieges, was perverted by the lust of procuring wealth, and an insatiable covetousness which he neither could, nor sought to repress. Hence, with all his transcendant talents, and the favour of an indulgent Sovereign, he was precipitated from his place of pride and power, and became an outlaw, an exile, and a vagabond; proving the truth of the proposition promulgated by the illustrious fictionist, that "guilt, though it may attain temporal splendour, can never confer real happiness. The evil consequences of our crimes long survive their commission; and, like the ghosts of the murdered, forever haunt the steps of the malefactor. The paths of virtue, though seldom those of worldly greatness, are always those of PLEASANTNESS AND PEACE."